5

COOPER'S C[O...]

Local H[...]

Who can ever forget the [...] of seeing Wendy Monroe set off on her quest for gold at the Winter Olympics in Lillehammer, Norway, nine years ago this month? According to her father, Howard Monroe, Wendy practically grew up on skis, and as a child soon mastered the local runs at Brodie and Jiminy Peak. Competitive downhill skiing was in her blood, and local residents were devastated when news came that our hometown hero had been seriously injured in a practice run in Norway.

Wendy has lived in France since leaving Cooper's Corner, so townsfolk were delighted to spot her back home on Main Street last week. Her mother, Gina, insists that Wendy is here

and family will be very happy if she decides to stay.

At first glance, Cooper's Corner may not seem to boast the romance of France, but perhaps a special something—or someone—will convince Wendy that her heart belongs here!

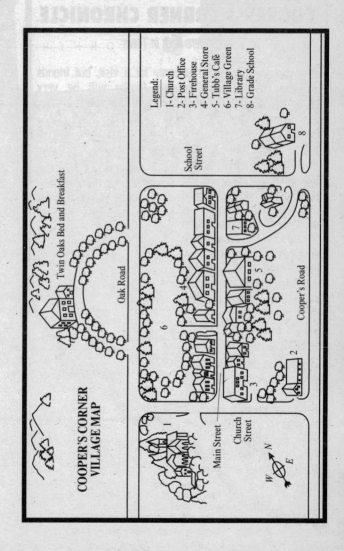

COOPER'S CORNER
VILLAGE MAP

Twin Oaks Bed and Breakfast

Oak Road

Main Street

Church
Street

School
Street

Cooper's Road

Legend:
1- Church
2- Post Office
3- Firehouse
4- General Store
5- Tubb's Café
6- Village Green
7- Library
8- Grade School

COOPER'S CORNER

SANDRA MARTON

Dancing in the Dark

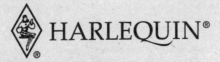

HARLEQUIN®

TORONTO • NEW YORK • LONDON
AMSTERDAM • PARIS • SYDNEY • HAMBURG
STOCKHOLM • ATHENS • TOKYO • MILAN • MADRID
PRAGUE • WARSAW • BUDAPEST • AUCKLAND

HARLEQUIN BOOKS
225 Duncan Mill Road, Don Mills,
Ontario, Canada M3B 3K9

ISBN-13: 978-0-373-61256-7
ISBN-10:   0-373-61256-7

DANCING IN THE DARK

Sandra Marton is acknowledged as the author of this work.

Copyright © 2002 by Harlequin Books S.A.

This edition published by arrangement with Harlequin Books S.A.

® and TM are trademarks of the publisher. Trademarks indicated with ® are registered in the United States Patent and Trademark Office, the Canadian Trade Marks Office and in other countries.

Visit us at www.eHarlequin.com

Printed in U.S.A.

Dear Reader,

I had a wonderful time writing *Dancing in the Dark*. It's always fun to be invited to write a book that's part of a special series, but this was a very personal project for me. I live in New England, in a small town that's only an hour or two from the imaginary village of Cooper's Corner. My husband and I moved here twelve years ago. We gave up the bustle of New York City for the quiet beauty of rolling hills, deep forests and narrow country roads. Like Seth, whom you're about to meet in *Dancing in the Dark*, we felt instantly at home; like Wendy, we discovered that no matter how far we may travel, our hearts will always belong to New England.

Welcome to Seth and Wendy's story of love lost and rediscovered. There were times I smiled as I wrote it, and times I found myself weeping. I hope those same emotions fill you as you read their story.

With love,

Sandra

THE COOPERS OF COOPER'S CORNER

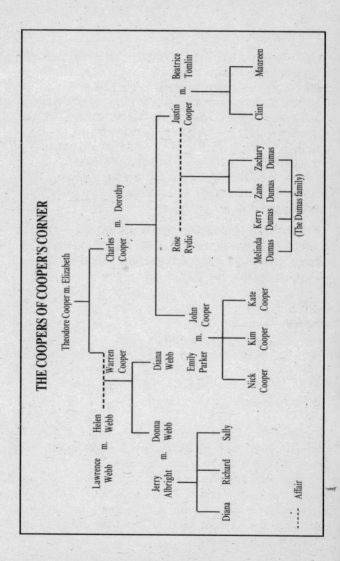

Theodore Cooper m. Elizabeth

Warren Cooper / Charles Cooper m. Dorothy

Lawrence Webb m. Helen Webb

Donna Webb / Diana Webb

Emily Parker m. John Cooper

Rose Rydic ---- Justin Cooper m. Beatrice Tomlin

Jerry Albright m. Sally

Diana Richard

Nick Cooper Kim Cooper Kate Cooper

Melinda Dumas Kerry Dumas Zane Dumas Zachary Dumas
(The Dumas family)

Clint Maureen

---- Affair

CHAPTER ONE

IT WAS COLD THAT DAY, colder than usual, even for Norway. The sky was bright blue, the sun golden, the wind a gentle sigh.

Wendy stood poised in the chute at the top of the ski run. Excitement flowed through her blood like a river of quicksilver. She had never felt more alive.

"Empty your mind of everything but the mountain," her coach said, and then the horn sounded. She dug her poles into the snow and began her run down the slope. Through the first gate. Through the second, and the third, and...

Too fast. Too wide on the turn. Recover, damn it! She'd made worse mistakes. Surely this wasn't enough to make her lose control....

She flew through the air, bindings never releasing. Somebody screamed as she hit the netting and bounced over it.

This wasn't supposed to happen, she thought with great clarity—and then she saw the trees...and the rocks.

After that, there was only blackness.

"LADIES AND GENTLEMEN, welcome to John F. Kennedy International Airport. Please keep your seats until the captain brings the plane to a complete stop."

Wendy jerked awake. A dream. That's all it was, just a dream. She hadn't had it in a long time. Now she was returning to Cooper's Corner for the first time in the nine years since the accident, and she'd had the dream again.

Welcome home, Wendy.

Whoever it was who'd said you couldn't go home again had been right.

You can still change your mind, a little voice whispered. All she had to do was turn around and head back to Paris, where she'd been living for the past seven years. Yes, she'd given up her tiny flat in the Marais because she didn't know how long she'd be gone, but she'd made friends. Gabrielle or Celeste would be happy to let her sleep on the sofa until...

Until what?

Wendy wasn't about to regain the life she'd loved by teaching English to a bunch of French kids all day. One of the supporters of the American team had gotten her the job when she moved to Paris to continue therapy on her leg, but sitting in a stuffy classroom quickly lost its appeal even if your window looked out over a sea of chimney pots. She'd been born to schuss down a snow-covered mountain with the wind in her face, and if she was going to do that again—ski and race and feel as if she were truly alive— she had to go home. For a little while, anyway.

The 747 lurched to a stop. People unbuckled their seat belts, stood up, sought their carry-on luggage. Wendy clutched the handle of her duffel bag and followed the other passengers from the plane, through the terminal and to the line snaking toward Customs.

Even if she'd wanted to change her plans, it was too late. What excuse could she give? Her parents were expecting her, and her mother was ecstatic that she was coming home. Only her father knew the real reason for her visit, and she'd asked him not to say anything to her mother. Wendy would have to tell her the truth, but she'd do it face-to-face. Gina would take it better that way.

That's what Wendy hoped, anyway.

And then there was Alison, driving the fifty or so miles from Cooper's Corner to Albany Airport to meet the connecting flight from Kennedy. Wendy's folks had offered to pick her up but she'd refused.

"You guys don't have to take the day off," she'd said when they'd phoned the last time. "I know how crazy things get at school. Besides, I haven't seen Allie in years. This way, we'll have time for girl talk."

It was another half-truth. Gina and Howard had visited her every six months, but she hadn't seen Alison in nine years. So, yes, it would be nice to spend some time with her—and if it also gave Wendy a little longer to adjust, out from under her mother's watchful eye, so much the better.

Wendy reached the Customs counter and handed over her passport and declarations form.

"Nothing of value to declare?" the Customs officer said.

"Nothing," Wendy replied briskly.

Nothing the government would want to hear about, anyway. Only Oprah or Ricki would lift an interested eyebrow if she said, "Well, actually, there's a swarm of butterflies in my stomach right now because I'm coming home so I can convince a doctor to perform an operation my own physicians call insane."

That kind of thinking wasn't good. This was her life. She had to do what she thought best, and why have second thoughts now? The thing to do was concentrate on how great it would be to see Allie. They hadn't done anything except talk on the phone since the night before the ski team left for France…

The same night Seth made love to her for the very last time.

The thought was so sudden, so unexpected that it almost stole her breath away. She must have made a sound because the Customs guy, who was holding out her passport, raised his bushy eyebrows.

"Miss? You okay?"

"Yes. I'm fine." Wendy smiled brightly, took back her

passport and walked to the exit doors that led into the terminal.

There was a sign just ahead. She paused to check the directions for the connecting flight to Albany. People brushed past her, everyone in a hurry to get somewhere. She was in a hurry, too. The sooner she got to Cooper's Corner, the sooner she could get started on the future.

Once she'd reached the right terminal, she limped to the waiting area at the gate. Her leg ached something fierce. The doctors had warned her that it would, after all the hours in the air. Inactivity wasn't good for bones that were held together with screws and steel plates. Muscles didn't like stretching themselves for the benefit of all that hardware, either.

Not that she'd never had cramped muscles until the accident. A weekend of hard, competitive skiing had often left her feeling as if a sadist had tied her in knots. Seth would see her wince as she rubbed her calf or ankle, and he'd know she was hurting.

"Here," he'd say, "let me help."

She'd smile and put her foot in his lap—not easy to do in the confines of the cab of his old truck—and he'd knead her flesh gently, stroke her gently, and after a while a sensation that had nothing to do with pain would turn her bones to liquid.

"Miss?"

Wendy blinked. A middle-aged man had risen from his seat.

"Would you like to sit down?"

She wanted to. Lord, yes, she wanted to. Instead, she gave a thin smile. "Thank you, no."

"I noticed…" He cleared his throat. "I, uh, noticed that your duffel looks heavy."

"It isn't," she said, trying to sound polite.

Who was he kidding? What he'd noticed was the way she limped. She walked away as quickly as she could, never looking back, tired of people's good intentions, tired of wanting to scream and tell them that trapped inside the woman with the limp was a girl who'd once been graceful, who'd flown down snow-covered slopes and through the gates like a hawk after a dove.

A sign blinked on. The commuter flight to Albany was boarding.

Not a moment too soon, Wendy thought, and didn't slow her pace until she was on the plane and in her seat.

IT WAS THIRTY DEGREES in Albany, with a windchill that made it feel more like eighteen, according to the pilot's cheerful landing announcement.

Wendy looked out the windows of the terminal as she made her way to the exit. Snow was piled in gigantic mounds. Fresh snow, from the pristine look of it. There'd been a time when she could tell how long snow had been on the ground just by the way the crystals reflected the light, especially on Jiminy Peak. Jiminy didn't have the highest slopes in the area; compared with the mountains she'd skied in Colorado and Utah, Jiminy was hardly worthy of being called a mountain at all. But she'd skied there as a little girl, discovered her passion for speed on its trails, and it would always hold a special place in...

In what? Those days were gone. Damn it. Was a quick visit home turning her into a bundle of sloppy sentimentality?

An icy wind bit through her as she exited the terminal. She shivered, put down her duffel and zipped her anorak all the way to her chin. Her long, auburn hair was whipping around her face and she put up her hood and tucked the unruly curls inside while she looked around in search of Alison.

"I'll meet you right outside the door," Allie had said when they'd touched base a couple of days ago. And then she'd laughed and said how wonderful it was going to be to see each other again. "I can't believe you're coming home!"

"It's just a visit," Wendy had answered, correcting her oldest friend the same way she'd corrected her mother. Allie had said yes, sure, she understood that, but in a way that made it clear she didn't believe it any more than Gina.

Snow began to fall, big, fat flakes. Wendy tugged a pair of gloves from her pockets and put them on.

That was all it was. A visit. She was here for a purpose, and if she was successful, she'd be ready to begin life again in a place that was free of memories. Not France, where she'd lived in a kind of twilight world these last years. Not Cooper's Corner, where everything would only be a reminder of what had once been. She'd find a place where there were no ghosts, no shadows from the life she and Seth had once planned....

"Wendy?"

The snow was falling faster, tumbling down like feathers from a torn pillow in a heavily overcast sky. Someone was rushing toward her. A woman, bundled in a tweed coat.

"Wendy, oh my God, it's really you!"

"Allie?" Wendy laughed and felt tears burn her eyes. "Allie," she said, and she grabbed Alison Fairchild in a loving hug. "Oh, it's been so long!"

The women held each other for long moments. Then they clasped hands, stepped back and grinned.

"I don't believe it! Allie, you cut your hair!"

"Uh-huh." Alison bit her lip. "Cut it and colored it, too. What do you think? Too big a change or what?"

"I think it's wonderful! You look gorgeous!"

"Well, not gorgeous, but I finally figured that it couldn't hurt to try and improve on Mother Nature. And talk about gorgeous..." Alison cocked her head and her gaze swept Wendy from head to toe. "You look terrific!"

Wendy's smile tilted. "Yeah. Right."

"I mean it. You haven't gained an ounce, for which I

just might not forgive you. No gray hairs in those red curls—and please, do not, I repeat, do *not* bother telling me women don't get gray hairs at our age. Two years ago, and wham, there they were, silver threads among the gold. Not that the rest was gold then, but you know what I mean.''

"You used to talk about going blond when we were in our junior year, remember?"

Alison rolled her eyes. "Do I remember? How could I forget? There I was, everybody telling me I looked like Barbra Streisand—"

"A compliment," Wendy said, falling into the old dialogue as if they were still in high school.

"Yes, if you're la Streisand," Allie said, picking up her end of the conversation with the same ease. "I may have her nose, but it doesn't work on my face."

"You don't still believe that."

"What I believe is that we're going to turn into instant snowmen if we stand here much longer. Let me grab that duffel. My car's in the first lot. Want to wait for the bus or—I mean, the bus stop is right—"

"I can walk."

"Well, sure, but—"

"And I can carry my own bag."

"I know, but—"

"Allie, listen. Let's get this out of the way right now, okay?"

"Oh, hell. Wendy, I didn't mean—"

"I know you didn't. I just want to set the record straight. I'm strong as a horse. Honestly, I am. I spent years in rehab. I still do hours of exercise each day. I can walk. I can carry stuff. I can do anything I want...." Her mouth twisted. "Anything but ski."

Her voice broke on the last word. Horrified, she covered it with a cough. She'd only meant to let Alison know that she could handle the truth, but her emotions were right there on the surface. Well, why wouldn't they be? The long flight, too much sitting still, and under it all, the persistent worry that the surgeon she'd come so far to see wouldn't help her....

Alison was looking at her as if she didn't know what to expect next.

Wendy smiled. "You know what?"

"What?" Allie asked cautiously.

"How about we get out of the snow? That terrific haircut's getting plastered to your head."

"Yeah. Good idea." Alison cleared her throat. "So," she said briskly, "you up for a stop at the Barn?"

"The…?" Wendy looped her free arm through Alison's. Dipping their heads against the wind, they crossed the roadway and headed for the parking lot. "You mean the Burger Barn? Is it still there?"

Alison clucked in dismay. "Is it still there, she asks. Certainly, it's still there, only a ten-minute detour on our way to town. Of course, you're probably not into juicy, charcoal-broiled hamburgers and hot, crisp, salty fries after all these years of gourmet dining in gay Paree, but I thought, if there was the teeniest possibility that you *were* interested…"

"Gourmet dining?" Wendy laughed. "Not on a teacher's salary. If I never see another hunk of cheese or sausage, it'll be too soon."

"You mean Mademoiselle DuBois was wrong?" Alison unlocked the car door and Wendy tossed her things into the back seat. "I thought it was supposed to be *fromage* and *saucisson*—much more exotic sounding."

"Cheese and sausage are cheese and sausage, whether it's French or English," Wendy said. "Trust me." She shut her door and looked at Alison, who was buckling her seat belt. "The Burger Barn would be paradise. Just tell me that the fries are still greasy."

"Cholesterol City," Alison said cheerfully.

"Does a straw still stand up in a chocolate shake?"

"Scout's honor, nothing's changed."

"Great," Wendy said, but in her heart, she knew that everything had.

ALISON TOOK THE LONG WAY home.

It was a pretty road that wound into the Taconic Mountains before they fell away into the more subdued contours of the Berkshires. The scenery, at least, was still the same. Cozy old houses, rolling pastures, deep forests mantled with white, and everywhere the sense that time had reached this place and decided to pause for a while before moving on.

Wendy sighed and laid her head back. "I'd forgotten how peaceful it is here."

"Peaceful's the word, all right." Alison raised an eyebrow. "On the other hand…"

"What?" Wendy looked at her friend. "Something exciting happened in Cooper's Corner?"

"Well…yeah, you could say exciting."

"Don't tell me. Let me figure it out." Wendy put on an innocent look. "Philo and Phyllis Cooper decided to give up gossip."

Alison laughed. "I said 'exciting,' not 'unbelievable.'"

"Well then, you'll have to tell me. What new and exciting stuff happened?"

"Well, Bonnie Cooper—remember her? Bonnie was on a date with a guy in New York and they witnessed a mob hit."

Wendy sat up straight. "You're kidding!"

"Cross my heart, it's the truth. Oh, and we had a visitor go missing, too."

"Somebody hiking in the fall?"

"No, it wasn't like that. This was a guest at the B and B, and he—"

"What B and B?"

"Remember the old Cooper place? Twin Oaks?"

"Sure. Big house, up on the hill across from the green."

"Uh-huh." Alison glanced in the mirror, signaled a turn. The sound of the engine deepened as they started up a hill. Ahead, the red taillights of a snowplow blinked hypnotically in the haze of the falling snow. "Old man Cooper died and left the place to his niece and nephew. A sister and brother from New York. Well, originally they were from around here."

"From Cooper's Corner?"

"Yeah. They moved away when they were kids. Anyway, they came up to see the house, and the next thing anybody knew, they'd kicked out of their old lives and moved here. Caught most people by surprise, especially when they turned Twin Oaks into a B and B."

"I can't believe my parents haven't mentioned any of this. But wasn't the house in bad shape?"

"Not anymore. Clint and Maureen have done wonders. New paint, new wallpaper, and they found a load of old furniture in the attic that just needed cleaning and polishing."

"And that did it? Fresh paint, old furniture and a good cleaning?"

"Well, no. There was more. Bonnie did the plumbing."

"Good for her."

"Yeah, I said that, too. She put in new bathrooms, did some stuff in the kitchen...."

Wendy tried to concentrate, but it was hard. They were approaching a traffic light that marked an intersection whose claim to fame was two mini-malls, one on either side of the road. The Burger Barn was a couple of miles past them.

Minutes after that, they would reach Cooper's Corner.

Her heart gave a little lurch. She was almost home, and nothing that really mattered had changed. The roads were the same, and when they got to town, it would be the same, too. The village green, with its bronze Minuteman standing eternal guard; Main Street and its bundled-up tourists, eager to soak up what they saw as an authentic bit of New England. The windows of the little antique and crafts shops would still be bright with Christmas displays, even though the holiday was over.

The traffic light went from green to amber. The car slowed to a stop and a small knot of people crossed to the mall on the opposite side of the road. Wendy stared out the window. It was hard to identify anyone. People were hunched into their coats, ducking their heads against the snow. Not that she was searching for anyone in particular. Not that she was looking for—

"...Seth," Alison said.

"What about him?"

She thought she'd spoken calmly, but from the way Alison looked at her, she knew she hadn't quite pulled it off.

"Oh, honey, I'm sorry. I was so busy trying to bring you up to date on what's been happening that I... Just forget I mentioned him, okay?"

"Allie, there's no problem. Come on. What were you going to say?"

"Just that Seth did the carpentry at Twin Oaks."

"Seth is a carpenter?"

"A really good one. And it turns out he's got a talent for building fine furniture, too. From the looks of things, he's doing..." She hesitated. "Wendy? You sure you want to hear all this?"

"Why wouldn't I? The past is the past." Wendy cleared her throat. "It's just a surprise, that's all. When he and I... When I left town, Seth was taking business courses at the Massachusetts College of Liberal Arts."

"Yeah. I remember. He quit MCLA after your, uh, your accident. He went to work for somebody in Stockbridge, and a couple of years ago he opened his own shop here." Alison hesitated. "He still doesn't know you're coming home?"

"No." Wendy looked at Alison. "Not unless you told him. You didn't, did you? Allie?"

"Of course not," Alison said, a little stiffly. "You asked me not to."

"Sorry."

"That's all right."

It wasn't, and Wendy knew it. She reached across the console and touched the other woman's hand.

"Allie," she said in a low voice, "it's…it's harder than I figured, you know? Coming home, I mean. So much time's gone by…" She swallowed hard. "Maybe I'm more tired than I realized."

"I'm sorry, too. I didn't mean to jump on you." The light changed to green and Alison stepped on the gas. "I just don't understand why you wouldn't want to see him. I mean, it's been a long time, but you and Seth—"

"There is no 'me and Seth.' There hasn't been for years."

"Yeah. That's the point. When you left for Norway, you two were crazy about each other. The next thing we knew, it was all over. Seth wouldn't talk about you, wouldn't even say your name. And then you didn't come back, and we all wondered—"

"There's nothing to wonder." Wendy's voice turned cool. "I'd think people would have better things to do with their time than gossip."

"It wasn't gossip." Alison slowed the car again, signaled a right and turned into the Burger Barn parking lot. She pulled into a space, shut off the engine and looked at Wendy. "We all cared about you. The whole town turned out to see you off. Remember? There were signs in the windows on Main Street, everything from Good Luck to Our Wendy to Bring Back the Gold. When you got hurt—"

"Allie." Wendy put her hand over Alison's. "That's history. The Olympics, the accident, Seth…it's all in the past. I have a new life now."

"So does he."

The simple words fell between them, as heavy as stones. Wendy looked at Alison. "You mean, that he's become a carpenter?"

"Well, sure." Alison fell silent, averted her gaze. "And—and other things."

"Other things?" Wendy moistened her lips with the tip of her tongue. "Ah. I see." Could she sound casual about this? Yes. Of course she could. Funny that she'd never thought to ask before. "You mean, he's married?"

"No. But he's seeing someone. Her name's—"

"I don't need to know her name. Who Seth dates is none of my business."

"It's more than dating. They've been going together for a couple of months." Alison shot a glance in Wendy's direction. "I guess I shouldn't have dumped the news on you like that, huh?"

"Don't be silly." Wendy stretched her lips in what she hoped was a semblance of a smile. "You know, if we sit here much longer, we'll freeze."

"Meaning, 'Alison, that's enough of that.'"

Wendy tried another smile. "Meaning, did you or didn't you promise me a hamburger at the Barn?"

"Yeah, sure," Alison said, but she didn't move. "There's one other thing. I know you said this was just a visit, but I hoped... You really aren't staying, are you."

Wendy shook her head. "No," she said quietly, "I'm not." She looked at Alison. "Does the name Rod Pommier mean anything to you?"

"Should it?"

"He's a surgeon. From New York."

"What kind?" Alison gave a quick laugh. "If he's a plastic surgeon, maybe my nose and I will go to see him."

Wendy knew it was a desperate attempt to lighten the situation, but nothing could do that. First all the talk about Seth, and now this. Well, telling Allie would be a dress rehearsal for telling her mother. *Go for it,* she thought, and took a steadying breath.

"He's an orthopedic surgeon. They wrote him up in a zillion papers and magazines a few months ago." Wendy lifted her hands and stretched out an imaginary banner. "'Rod Pommier,'" she said in solemn tones, "'the brilliant young surgeon who's developed a break-through bonding technique for healing shattered bones....'"

"Yeah? So what about..." Alison blinked. "Shattered bones?"

"Uh-huh. When the doctors pieced my leg together, they used pins and plates. That's what they've done for decades. But Pommier's found a new technique that allows joints to regenerate normally."

"Interesting, I guess, except you just said your leg is already fixed."

"Pommier's method would make it as good as new. The thing is, he's not taking on new patients. He's booked for the next umpteen years, and besides, the procedure can be dangerous."

"Dangerous how?"

"I don't know. It has something to do with whether your bones are right for the technique or not." Wendy gave a brittle laugh. "Of course, the real question is, if your bones don't work right in the first place, how can they be wrong for it? Anyhow, I phoned Pommier. His receptionist wouldn't put me through. I called the hospital where he's on staff. They wouldn't put me through, either. So I wrote him a letter, gave him a rough rundown on my accident..."

"And?"

"And," Wendy said with a defeated sigh, "I got a letter back. He was very polite. He said he was sympathetic to my situation, yadda-yadda yadda, but—"

"But he wasn't interested." Alison smiled sadly. "Sounds like a message on my answering machine after a blind date with some guy who's a jerk."

"That's just the thing, though. I don't think he's a jerk. I think he's just wrong about not wanting to take me on. If I can talk to him, face-to-face, I can change his mind."

"Are you so sure this new thing he's invented can help you? You had your accident years ago. The surgery—"

"The surgery," Wendy said with a dismissive wave of her hand, "was a disaster. It wasn't the doctor's fault. He did everything he could, but pins and plates can't make up for missing bone. This technique of Pommier's can."

"You think?"

"I *know*." She tapped her fist lightly against her breastbone. "I can feel it. Maybe that's not the most scientific appraisal, but it's what I feel. I just need to talk to him, but he's wary. And I understand why. Pommier's being hounded to death by the media, by desperate patients...." Alison raised a brow, and Wendy colored. "Right," she said, with something close to defiance, "desperate patients like me. That's why he's coming to Cooper's Corner."

Alison's jaw dropped. "Huh? Wendy, honey, you're losing me here."

"Pommier wants to get away from everything for a few days. He's coming to the Berkshires to ski. My dad's a member of the ski club, remember? Well, so's an orthopedist from Pittsfield who's a friend of my father's. It turns out he and Pommier did their residencies together, and Pommier wrote to him, asked him about the town, whether it was as off the track as it seems, and if he could recommend a place to stay." Wendy caught her breath. "Hey. I bet he's going to stay at the old Cooper place. Twin Oaks."

"If he's this big-deal celebrity, wouldn't he stay in Lenox? Or in Stockbridge? I mean, I love Cooper's Corner, but you have to admit it's not big on glitzy amenities."

"That's the point, Allie. The man wants to be just another face in the crowd. No reporters. No microphones and cameras."

"I see." Alison let out a breath. It had grown chilly

inside the car, and her exhalation puffed out like steam. She turned on the engine and gave a little shiver as heat began to seep from the vents. "So, that's why you came back. To corner this guy."

"Yes."

"And convince him to operate on you."

"Exactly."

"Do your folks know? 'Cause when I spoke to your mom the other day, all she could talk about was how thrilled she was that you were coming home."

"My dad knows. My mother doesn't. Don't look at me that way. Don't you think I feel guilty enough? I just think it's best to tell her with my father there as backup." Wendy sighed. "You have a face like an open book, Alison. You think this is a bad idea, don't you?"

"I sure do. You said yourself the surgery's risky. Well, why subject yourself to it?"

"Because I want a life, that's why!"

"You have one. You lived when they thought you wouldn't. Isn't that enough?"

"No, damn it, it isn't. Look, it's hard to explain, but I'm not who I used to be. Can't you see that?"

"Yes," Alison said after a minute, "I can. So, you're home just to get to this doctor. Not because of your mom or your dad or Seth—"

"Seth again!" Wendy flushed. "What does he have to do with this? I was eighteen. He was nineteen. Whatever we had was kid stuff."

"That's not how I remember it. You guys were always together. You had plans."

"I just told you, it was—"

"Kid stuff. I heard you. But I was here when we all got word of the accident. How you'd fallen on that practice run—"

"I don't want to talk about it," Wendy said sharply.

"Seth was like a crazy man. He flew to Norway on the first flight out—"

"Stop it! That was a thousand years ago."

"It was nine years ago, and I've never forgotten how he looked, like somebody whose world had been destroyed."

"It was my world that was destroyed," Wendy cried, "and I did whatever I had to do to survive." The friends stared at each other, each breathing hard. Then Wendy turned away and grabbed the door handle. A frosty breath of snow blew into the car. "I can walk home from here."

"Don't be a fool." Alison reached past Wendy, caught the handle and slammed the door shut. The women glared at each other for a couple of minutes and then Alison sighed. "Can we continue this conversation inside?"

No. They couldn't, Wendy realized. All the talk about Seth and old times…the look on Alison's face when she'd tried to explain that she couldn't accept the path her life had taken… It had been confirmation that her original plan was the wisest one. Lie low, stay away from the old hang-outs, and avoid going through this horrible little scene and the pity of old friends who couldn't understand why she wasn't grateful just to have survived.

"Wendy? Are we going for that burger or not?"

"I think I'll pass," Wendy said quietly. "My folks are expecting me."

Alison nodded. "Of course." She put the car in gear, backed out of the parking space, then put on the brakes and glared at Wendy again. "I'm your oldest friend! If I can't tell you the truth, who can?"

"You don't know the truth," Wendy said, the words tumbling out in a desperate rush. "I'm the one this happened to. Me, not you, or the doctors, or the nurses, or the therapists with their sympathetic looks and endless exercises." She pushed down her hood and dragged her hands through her tumbled auburn curls. "Sometimes I wish I'd died that day, instead of waking up in a hospital bed and finding out that—that…''

"What? That you were alive? That you still had both your legs? I don't understand you. Don't you ever stop to think how lucky you were?''

"I'm trying to move on, Allie. Don't *you* understand that?''

"By pretending Seth doesn't exist? By trying to force a doctor into surgery that might do more harm than good?''

"Seth's got somebody. You just told me that. And the doctor will want to do this operation once he talks to me." Wendy shook her head. "You're right. I lived. I got out of a wheelchair I was never supposed to get out of. But this woman, the one who can't do the things she once did—this woman is a stranger. I can't help it if that sounds selfish. It's the way I feel."

"You're right," Alison said quietly. "I don't understand." She looked at Wendy and smiled, though her eyes glittered with tears. "But I don't have to. I'm your friend. I'll stand by you, no matter what. Okay?''

Wendy nodded, even though it was more than okay. The pledge, the compassion in Alison's eyes… Wendy felt her own eyes fill. For one improbable moment, she thought of letting all the pain inside her spill out. The truth was so much more complex than anyone knew. Maybe if she shared her awful secret…

She knew better. It wouldn't change a thing.

Her heart, not just her body, had been broken in pieces on a winter's day nine years ago. Looking in the mirror, seeing her scarred, twisted flesh was a constant reminder of what she'd almost had, what she'd lost, what she'd never have again. Now she could only pin her hopes on a time when she could stare at her reflection and see a whole Wendy instead of a shattered one. Then, perhaps, the agony would turn into a pain she could live with.

"Wendy?" Alison said softly.

She looked up, saw the confusion in her friend's eyes. "Yes. I heard what you said. Thank you. You're the best friend in the world."

The women gave each other wobbly smiles, then Alison scraped her hand across her eyes. "If you make me cry," she said gruffly, "and my mascara runs, I'm never going to forgive you."

"Too late. It's already running."

"Yeah?"

"Yeah."

"Yours, too, so don't look so smug."

They gave each other sharp looks. Then they laughed, reached out and hugged.

"It's good to have you home," Alison said, "even if it's just for a little while."

"And it's good to be here." Wendy pulled a couple of tissues from her pocket and handed one to Alison. "Even if it's just for a little while."

Alison wiped her eyes and blew her nose. She started the car again and they drove to Cooper's Corner, turned down a familiar old street and stopped in front of a handsome house with bay windows and flower boxes that Wendy knew would overflow with pink and lavender impatiens all summer.

She stepped from the car just as the front door opened. Her mother and father stood poised in the doorway. Then Gina laughed and ran down the steps, with Howard right behind her, and just for a moment, as Wendy went into their sheltering arms, she had to admit that home was the best place in the world.

CHAPTER TWO

IT WAS, Seth Castleman thought, the worst possible kind of day to be wrestling with Santa Claus on a sloped, snow-covered roof.

Almost six inches of snow had been predicted overnight, and that was exactly what had fallen. Those six inches, coming hot on the heels of an earlier storm, had been enough to make taking down the ten-foot Santa figure a nasty, fairly dangerous job.

"I hate to ask you," Philo Cooper had told Seth when he phoned at nine that morning, "but I can't reach the guy who rented it to me up in Pittsfield and it's due back to-morrow. His answering machine's on but maybe he's away."

"In Florida, if he's got half a brain," Seth had said dryly. "I'll stop by later this afternoon."

"Thanks, Seth."

"No problem," Seth had replied, which wasn't really true. It *was* a problem to move around on the pitched roof with ice under your boots. But the job was simple, and he was almost finished. The Santa was now in the back of Philo's truck and Seth had just one more brace to remove.

Actually, the view from here, twelve feet above Main Street, was pretty interesting. The town looked like a Currier and Ives Christmas card. Spruce boughs, accented with big silver balls that dangled and swayed in the wind, were wired to a cable that stretched from one side of the street to the other, and holly wreaths hung on the old-fashioned lampposts. It wouldn't be long before all those decorations were taken down, too.

Seth pulled out another nail from the brace.

Cooper's Corner was beautiful all year, but winter was special. He'd first seen the town in December a long, long time ago. He'd been eighteen then, a sullen kid who'd bounced from one New York City foster home to another, with no bigger plan than to find a job at one of the ski resorts, make a few bucks and then move on. But he'd found something here, not just a job but a way of life that had turned *his* life around.

Even at eighteen—hell, especially at eighteen—he'd been a cynic, world weary and hard-shelled. At first, he'd scoffed at the town's old-fashioned setting. Surely it was phony, something carefully constructed for the tourist trade.

After a couple of months, he'd been surprised to learn that the town was what it seemed, a village whose residents cared about each other and even about him, tough guy that he tried to be.

Gradually, without him even realizing it, his carefully constructed walls of cynicism started to crumble. Tough guys weren't supposed to fall in love, but Seth had, with the pretty little town that time seemed to have bypassed. He'd fallen in love with its solid, old-fashioned houses and quiet roads, with its friendly people…

…with a girl whose hair was the fire of maple leaves in autumn, whose eyes were the blue of a mountain lake in midsummer.

"Damn it!"

Seth mouthed a string of four-letter words as the brace broke free and clipped the side of his hand. Well, that was what you got for daydreaming. You worked with tools, you worked on a slippery roof, you had to pay attention. A mistake could be a lot worse than a bruised hand, and what in hell was wrong with him, anyway, thinking about what used to be? Wendy was history. Ancient history. It made more sense to think about the people who'd left the giant stone heads on Easter Island than it did to waste time thinking about the year Wendy had been his girl.

The giant stone heads, at least, were still around. Wendy sure as hell wasn't.

Seth shoved the hammer back into his leather tool belt. He had no idea why she'd been on his mind so much lately. Maybe it was because he'd met her this time of year, and lost her the same time, too. No, he thought as he gathered up his tools, no, that couldn't be it. Nine Januarys had come and gone since then, and except for the first two—okay, the first two or three, or maybe even four—except for them, the pages of the calendar hadn't triggered memories of Wendy.

Not like this.

He woke up thinking about her, fell asleep the same way. Just last night he'd shot up in bed, yanked from sleep by a dream of her in his arms, her mouth on his, so real that, just for a second, he'd believed she was there.

"Wendy?" he'd said, and Joanne, curled beside him, had sat up, too, and put her hand on his arm.

"What's wrong?" she'd murmured sleepily. "Seth? What is it?"

The image of Wendy had faded. Joanne's perfume, a scent still not as familiar to him as the scent that had clung lightly to Wendy's skin so long ago, filled his nostrils. He'd thrust his hands into his hair, shoving it back from his forehead.

"Nothing's wrong. I was dreaming, that's all."

Jo started to put her arms around him, looking to soothe him, he knew, but he'd drawn away, as riddled with guilt as if he'd actually been about to go from holding Wendy to holding another woman.

"It's late," he'd said. "I have an early start in the morning. I might as well get going."

He'd felt Jo's disappointment and couldn't blame her. He

never stayed with her through the night, and even though she hadn't commented on it, he knew damned well she was aware of it, just as she was surely aware that he'd never asked her to spend the night at his house, never made love to her there.

"The roads will be bad," she'd said softly as he dressed in the dark. He'd kissed her temple and assured her that the roads would probably be clear.

He'd been half-right. The roads were awful, but halfway to the home he'd built for himself on Sawtooth Mountain, he'd lucked out and fallen in behind a state plow going straight up Route 7 to where he made the turnoff onto the long driveway to his house. His truck's four-wheel drive had seen him safely through those last couple hundred feet.

Once inside, he'd built a fire in the living-room hearth, poured himself a brandy and sat in the flame-lit darkness, staring out the wall of glass that overlooked the valley until the first, faint light of dawn, telling himself there was no reason in the world he should be thinking about Wendy....

And thinking about her all the same, just the way he was right now.

Enough.

Carefully, Seth made his way across the icy roof, then down the ladder he'd left propped against it. He dumped his toolbox in the truck and headed into the store.

The bell over the door jingled merrily and Philo came out from the back room, wiping his hands on his denim apron.

"All finished?"

Seth handed him the braces and nodded. "That's it until next Christmas." He smiled. "Still planning to put up George and Abe for Presidents' Day, same as always?"

"Absolutely." Philo tapped a key on the old-fashioned cash register. "How much do I owe you?"

"I'll send you a bill."

"You sure? If you want me to pay you now—"

"No need." Seth rubbed his hands together. "But I'll hang around a few minutes and warm up by the stove, if you don't mind."

"Sure. One minute, and I'll join you."

Philo disappeared behind the curtain. Seth tucked his hands into the back pockets of his jeans, whistled softly between his teeth and strolled over to the cast-iron, pot-bellied stove that radiated heat throughout the store.

It was a cozy setting. Half a dozen chairs were drawn around the old stove; prints hung on the nearby walls. Seth recognized some—there were lots of Norman Rockwells. No surprise there, he thought, smiling as he rocked back a little on his heels. Rockwell had lived in these parts and his paintings and illustrations had immortalized the hardworking people of the area. One print in particular, of a boy warily dropping his trousers for a physician holding a hypodermic syringe, made him smile.

"That's always been one of my favorites."

Seth turned. Philo grinned and eased into one of the chairs.

"Same here." Seth sat down, too, and extended his hands toward the stove. "That's a good fire you have going."

"Pretty cold work up on that roof, huh?"

"Sure was."

The men sat in companionable silence. That was another thing Seth liked about Cooper's Corner. Nobody ever felt the need to fill the air with chatter. If you had something to say, fine. If you didn't, it was perfectly okay to keep still.

"So," Philo said after a minute, "how're things going?"

"Fine. Just fine. I'm keeping busy."

"Guess that house of yours is almost finished, huh? How long have you been at it, now? Two years?"

"Three," Seth said. "I should be done this spring." He shrugged. "Or this summer, for sure."

"Well, it can't be easy, puttin' up a place all by yourself, workin' only weekends."

"It's the only way I could manage to do it."

"Uh-huh. Nothing like free labor. Heard tell you got a good price when you bought that land, too."

Seth bit back a smile. Philo heard everything sooner or later. "Yeah, I did. I guess I could have hired somebody to help me out, but I enjoy the work."

"Figured that." Philo opened the stove's fire door and added another maple split. "It's none of my business, I know...." He cleared his throat. "It's just, well, the wife and I were talkin' at breakfast this mornin' and we were wonderin'... Are things okay between you and the lady?"

Seth raised one dark eyebrow. This was a small town. What passed for gossip elsewhere was neighborly concern here, but asking him such a personal question about his love life—or what passed for his love life—was, well, unusual.

"Sure," he said carefully. "Things are fine."

"Ah." Philo nodded as if a burden had been lifted from his shoulders. "Well, the wife'll be happy to hear it. Phyllis always liked her. Me, too, for that matter, though I never knew her very well."

Seth looked at Philo with curiosity. There was an off-kilter feel to this conversation, not just the sudden interest in his private life and his relationship with Joanne, but the way Philo was talking about it. Jo had only moved into the area a couple of years back. She lived in New Ashford. As far as Seth knew, she'd never even been into the Coopers' store.

"Well," he said, even more cautiously, "she's a private sort of person."

"Uh-huh. We figured that. Especially now with, you know, all the stuff that went on...." Philo's Adam's apple slid up and down. "So," he said briskly, "is she back for good? Or is it true, like some folks say, that she's only here to visit?''

Seth felt his heart give an unsteady thump. They definitely weren't talking about Joanne. He searched his mind for a "she" who might fit the conversation, a woman he'd know well enough for Philo to ask him such intimate questions. Then he realized from the look in Philo's eyes, from last night's dream, from the memories that had been tormenting him...

He knew who they were discussing, and what it meant.

Wendy was home.

Except he didn't believe that you dreamed about what was going to happen. The images in his head were there because of the time of year, and all this proved was that he'd never quite gotten past thinking about her.

''Is who back for good?'' he said, as if Philo's question might simply be about one of the winter visitors who'd asked him to do some repairs on her cabin.

He thought he'd spoken with casual ease. One look at Philo and he knew he hadn't pulled it off. The other man's plump cheeks reddened. Even his ears seemed to burn with embarrassment.

''Damn it,'' he mumbled, ''I'm sorry, Seth. I told Phyllis this wouldn't be a good idea. 'Phyl,' I said, 'honey, did it ever occur to you that the man might not want to talk about this? That he just plain might want to avoid—'''

''I'm not trying to avoid anything. I just don't understand the question. Who are we talking about, Philo?''

Philo looked as if he wanted the floor to open up and swallow him. He lifted the poker, reached into the fire, made a show of rearranging the burning wood, then stared at the dancing flames as if they held the answer to Seth's question.

Finally, he looked up.

''Wendy Monroe,'' he said with a swift exhalation of breath. ''And if you want to tell me to mind my own business about why she's come back to Cooper's Corner, or how long she's goin' to stay, that's okay with me.''

THE SUN WAS LOW in the sky, the wind had picked up and it had begun to snow again. Main Street was one long sheet of ice. The sanding trucks hadn't come through yet.

Seth drove carefully and fought to keep his mind on what he was doing. It wasn't easy. All he could think about was Wendy. She was back. She was in Cooper's Corner. The whole town probably knew it.

Now he knew it, too.

A car pulled out from the curb, skidded delicately to the left before its tires gained purchase. Seth braked gently, then fell in behind the slow-moving automobile.

Philo had all the details, though he'd been uncomfortable providing them. She'd flown in yesterday. Alison Fairchild had picked her up at the airport in Albany and driven her to town.

Seth's jaw knotted. He'd seen Alison just a couple of days ago, at Twin Oaks, when he'd stopped by to double-check the dimensions of the corner where Clint and Maureen wanted to put the china cabinet he was making for the dining room. On the way out, he'd bumped into Alison. Literally. He'd been trotting down the porch steps, his head full of measurements; she'd been coming up, on her way to visit Maureen, and they'd collided.

''Whoops,'' she'd said with a quick smile, then apologized for having her head in the clouds. They'd had a perfectly normal conversation about how well the B and B was coming along, about the weather and the season and every damned thing in the world except the one that would have mattered to him—that Wendy was returning to Cooper's Corner. There was no way he'd believe that Alison hadn't known about it then.

And what about Gina? He'd kept in touch with Wendy's mother. They spoke often. Well, not so often now, but for the first few years he'd phoned at least once a week to ask about Wendy's recovery. To hell with her father. It was Howard's fault Wendy had the accident. If he hadn't been pushing her so hard...

Seth took a deep breath.

There was no sense in going through all that again. It was over. So was what he'd once felt for Wendy.

Calmer now, he understood that neither Alison nor Gina felt under any obligation to tell him Wendy was returning. In which case, why had he gotten so upset? Wendy was the past. Joanne was the future.

His hands flexed on the steering wheel. Okay. Maybe she wasn't the future. Maybe what he felt for Jo wasn't what it should be. Maybe it was time to tell her that, before things got any stickier. Maybe...

The tires spun. Seth felt the truck slewing toward the cars parked along the curb. He managed to recover with only a fraction of a second to spare.

Maybe, he thought grimly, he needed to get his head together before he ended up breaking his neck.

He put on his signal light and pulled into an empty parking space just ahead. Climbing out of the truck, Seth turned up the collar of his old leather jacket and trudged toward Tubb's Café, just down the street.

The café was warm and steamy, fragrant with the aromas of coffee and freshly baked doughnuts. He slid onto a stool near the window, exchanged greetings with the college kid working the counter.

"Coffee," he said.

The kid poured him a mugful. Seth wrapped his hands around it, letting its warmth chase the cold from his fingers. Maybe it was irrational, but it pissed him off that nobody had thought to tell him about Wendy. Hadn't it occurred to Gina or Alison that he'd be interested? He'd loved her, once.

No. Damn it, no! He'd been infatuated, that was all. What nineteen-year-old kid who'd come out of nowhere wouldn't be infatuated with a beautiful girl? Wendy had been the town's darling. The guy she went with should have been a local product. The captain of the football team. A jock with varsity letters and a family that went back a hundred years. Instead, she'd fallen for him. No family, no background, no varsity letters on his jacket...

There she was.

The mug trembled in Seth's hands. He put it down on the counter, his gaze riveted to the window. Two people had just come out of a store. A man and a woman. Howard Monroe and Wendy. She was bundled in a dark-green anorak; her fiery hair was tucked up under a knitted ski cap so that only strands of it were visible against the pale oval of her face, and her eyes were hidden behind big, dark glasses. But none of that mattered. People hurrying past didn't recognize her, but Seth did.

He'd have known her anywhere.

His heart turned over as she began walking alongside her father. It was the first time he'd seen her on her feet. Until this moment, the damage she'd suffered had been confined to his imagination. Now he could see the reality of it. Instead of her former graceful walk, Wendy's hip and knee were stiff. Her limping gait after all those years of rehab, was evidence of the severity of the accident.

They reached her father's SUV. Howard held out his hand, but she shook her head and said something that looked like "I can do it." And she did, navigating the icy sidewalk toward the curb and the truck door with studied care.

Seth's eyes narrowed.

Why wasn't she using a cane? Why wouldn't she take her old man's hand? Why was she so damned thickheaded? She could fall. She could go down in the ice and snow and...

And it was none of his business.

Except it was. Wendy had meant something to him once upon a time, even if that time was long ago.

He got off the stool, dug out a bill, tossed it on the counter and zipped up his jacket. What was the matter with people in this town? Didn't anybody consider what it would be like for him to discover that she was back by stumbling across her?

He strode toward the door, slapped his hand against the glass. He wasn't going to let Wendy get away with treating him as if he didn't matter, the way she'd done nine years ago. He'd go straight up to her, grab her and shake some sense into her. Yeah, that was it. He'd march out of here, take her by the shoulders, shake her.... God, he'd pull her into his arms, tell her that it broke his heart to see her like this, her leg hurting, her dreams shattered....

"Mr. Castleman?"

He looked around. The kid who worked the counter was holding out a bunch of bills.

"You gave me a twenty," he said. "Here's your change."

Seth turned toward the street again. Wendy was getting into her father's truck. He watched Howard shut the door, then trot around to the driver's side and get in.

"Mr. Castleman?"

Seth swallowed hard and swung around. "Yeah. Thanks." He plucked a couple of bills from the kid's outstretched hand, left the rest behind. "Keep it," he said. It was the least he could do, considering that the boy had just kept him from making an ass of himself.

Wendy was back. So what? It didn't change a thing. Seth whistled through his teeth as he got into his truck and drove along Main Street toward Sawtooth Mountain Road. Yeah, they'd had a thing going for a while there. He'd thought he loved her, thought it enough to have flown to Norway the second her mother phoned in hysterics to tell him that Wendy had fallen during a practice run and nobody knew if she was going to make it or not.

His hands tightened on the steering wheel.

He hadn't wanted her to go to Norway to start with. He knew how much it meant to her that she'd made the Olympic team, but he'd wondered if she was really up for it. She had the talent and the determination, but those last few weeks, watching her…

He shook his head, thinking back, still seeing the exhaustion on her face, the dark circles under her eyes. She'd been tired all the time, and why wouldn't she be, the way her old man cracked the whip? As part of the American Ski Team, she had the best coaches in the business, but Howard had taught her to ski. He'd been her trainer from childhood on and he wasn't about to let that change. He'd still been coaching Wendy, taking her out on the slopes early in the morning, bringing her back late at night, working her and working her until she'd looked ready to collapse.

Seth saw less and less of her as the time for her departure drew close. She was worn out by the end of the day. The few times they did go out, Howard would come to the door, flash a practiced smile and say, "Don't forget, Seth. Our girl can't stay out too late."

As if he hadn't figured that out for himself, Seth thought, his jaw tightening. He'd been more concerned about her welfare than Howard, when you came down to it. He wasn't the one who had her skiing and lifting weights and doing leg lifts a thousand hours a day, her old man was.

But Howard was his girlfriend's father. He deserved respect. So Seth would nod and say yes sir, he understood, even though he didn't.

The road rose steeply ahead as it climbed the mountain. The plow and the sanding trucks had already been through. Seth downshifted, made it up and over the rise and into his driveway, but he didn't pull into the garage. Instead, he shut off the engine and sat quietly in the gathering darkness.

He'd never understood how Howard could push his daughter the way he had and not see what he was doing to her.

Seth had finally told Wendy that one evening.

"Honey," he'd said, "don't you think your dad's over-doing things?"

"He isn't," she'd replied. "He's just helping me."

"Yeah, but you're so tired...."

Wendy, curled against him with her face buried in his neck, sighed deeply and snuggled closer.

"Just hold me," she'd murmured. "I love being in your arms."

He'd held her tighter and pressed a kiss to the top of her head.

"You can be there all the time," he'd said huskily. "Just say the word and I'll drive us to Vermont. We'll go to the county clerk's office the minute it opens in the morning, get a license, and by noon, you'll be my wife."

Wendy had sat up and looped her arms around his neck. "We've been through this before," she'd said with a little smile. "You know I want to marry you, but—"

"But," he'd said, trying for a light tone, "first you want to bring back the gold."

"I just want to go to Lillehammer and do the very best I can. Is that so wrong?"

It wasn't wrong at all. He knew that, and he told her so. After a while, he just kept his mouth shut. He didn't want to quarrel with her, especially not with the Olympics so close. She didn't need any more stress. Besides, he knew he'd miss her terribly while she was gone, and he didn't want his memories tinged with bitterness.

Instead, he made the most of those last few evenings together.

Some nights they went to Pittsfield and took in a movie. Others, they just drove around for a while, maybe stopped in at the Burger Barn for a double order of the fries she loved.

But the best nights, the ones he'd never forgotten, were when they drove up Sawtooth Mountain and parked in the little clearing they thought of as their very own. He'd turn on the radio, find a station they both liked, and take Wendy in his arms.

"Seth," she'd whisper, her voice going all low and smoky, and he'd kiss her, gently at first, then with more passion. Her breathing would quicken and he'd undo her bra, slip his hands up under her sweater and cup her breasts, so silky, so warm, so sensitive to his touch.

Her soft moans were sweeter than the music coming from the speakers. The heat of her against his questing hand when he slid it inside her jeans was like flame. Together, they'd undo his zipper and she'd straddle him, kiss him as she lowered herself on him....

"Hell."

Seth shifted uncomfortably in his seat. Terrific. He was a grown man thinking about kid stuff that had been over for the best part of a decade, and he was turning himself on.

Impatiently, he climbed out of his truck and went into the house. The storm was over. Stars winked in the inky-black sky. It was going to be a cold, clear night. Maybe, he thought as he shrugged off his jacket and tossed his keys on the bird's-eye maple table near the door—maybe he'd phone Jo, see if she wanted to grab dinner at the little place they both liked all the way down near Lee.

And maybe it was wrong to ask one woman to dinner when you were having sexual fantasies about another.

Seth blew out a breath as he undid the laces of his leather construction boots and toed them off.

The day had begun so quietly. At nine, the only problem on his agenda had been how to fit in time to stop at Philo's and take down a Santa Claus.

That was how he liked things. Simple. Easy to figure out. He'd had enough complexity to last him a lifetime after Wendy's accident. All those endless, mind-numbing days when he'd paced the corridor of the hospital in Oslo, going crazy because she'd been unconscious and all he could do was sit by her bedside and clutch her hand. Then going even crazier because when she'd finally opened her eyes and regained consciousness, she'd turned away from him.

"She's not herself," Gina had told him. "She's just not herself yet, Seth."

Two terrible weeks later, Wendy still didn't want to see him. The flowers he'd sent her filled other rooms. The notes he'd written lay in the trash basket. She wouldn't take his phone calls. And, at last, a weeping Gina brought him a note in Wendy's own hand.

"I'm sorry," she'd written, "but I don't want to see you anymore. Please. Go away."

He hadn't wanted to believe it. She was upset. He understood that. She'd come close to death. Now she'd learned that she'd be in a wheelchair. Forever, the doctors said, though nobody who knew Wendy really bought that. So, okay. He'd swallowed past the lump in his throat, written her a last, long letter telling her that he would give her all the time she needed, that he wouldn't rush her, that he loved her with all his heart and always would. When she was ready, he wrote, he'd be there. Because he knew—knew—that she really loved him.

Seth walked slowly through the house to the dark kitchen. He snagged a cold bottle of ale from the refrigerator, unscrewed the top and took a long, soothing swallow as he made his way into the glass-walled living room with its view of the valley and the mountain ridge beyond it.

How wrong could a man be? He'd poured out his heart in that last letter and Wendy hadn't even opened it. She sent it back with a note scrawled across the flap.

"I don't want you waiting for me," she'd written. "I'm sorry, Seth, but the accident opened my eyes to the truth. What we had was just kid stuff, and now it's over."

Still, he'd hung in for a long time, telling himself she'd change her mind. The turning point had come months later.

He'd phoned Gina to find out how Wendy was and to ask when she was coming home.

"She's not," Gina had told him gently. "She needs some very specialized rehabilitation. There's a place in France, just outside Paris. She's decided to go there."

That was the day he'd finally admitted that the girl he'd loved had changed into a woman he didn't know. A little while later, he'd realized it was more than that. Wendy had gotten it right. What had been between them had been kid stuff. Hot, horny teenage sex that steamed up the windows and made your toes curl, but nothing more. She'd figured out the truth before he had, thanks to the jolt of reality the accident had provided.

He'd needed his own jolt of reality to get on with his life. At first he'd packed up his things, loaded them into his old pickup and taken off for parts unknown. He bummed around the country for a while, as aimlessly as when he'd turned eighteen—washing dishes in Tennessee, picking beans in Arkansas, clearing a fire trail in the Wasatch Mountains, until he woke up one morning and realized with a start of surprise that he was homesick for New England and Cooper's Corner.

Seth put down the empty bottle, tucked his hands in his back pockets and watched a fat ivory moon rise over the valley.

He'd headed for the Northeast, got an off-season job at a lumberyard. It sounded like something a guy with muscles and no particular training could do. He hoisted two-by-fours, cleaned up, delivered stuff to construction sites and carpentry shops. After a while, he realized he liked the smell of wood and the feel of it under his hands. The guy who owned the lumberyard was into carpentry, and Seth took to hanging around and watching him work.

One thing led to another. Before he knew it, he had a skill, not just a job. Now he had a thriving business and a home he'd built from the ground up, and the woman he'd been seeing for a couple of months had made it clear she'd be interested in a more permanent arrangement.

A smile curled his lips. He went back into the kitchen, put the empty ale bottle in the sink and reached for the phone. It wasn't too late to call Jo. Seeing her tonight might be just what he needed. She'd come to mean a lot to him. She was a good woman, bright and warm and kind....

Except she wasn't Wendy. His body, his being didn't catch fire when she was in his arms, and he never felt the sweet contentment that came of just holding her after they made love.

Seth cursed and slammed the phone back into its cradle.

He was wrong. It *was* too late to phone Joanne. It was too late to do anything except take a shower, climb into bed and try his damnedest to fall into an uncaring, dreamless sleep.

CHAPTER THREE

AT EIGHT O'CLOCK the next morning, Seth had a cup of strong coffee in one hand, the day's schedule in the other and the kind of headache that made a person consider decapitation as a cure—proof, as if he needed it, that life didn't always give you what you wanted.

Instead of the solid night's sleep he'd hoped for, he'd tossed and turned until the blanket and sheets were knotted. Eventually, exhaustion won, but instead of finding rest, he'd been drawn into a turbulent sea of bad dreams. Finally he'd said to hell with it and tossed back the covers. That was when he'd discovered that somebody with a sledgehammer had set up shop inside his skull.

Three aspirin, tossed down his throat as soon as he'd staggered to the bathroom, had yet to chase away the pain. A hot shower followed by a blast of icy water hadn't done it, either. Seth took a swallow of coffee, hoping a belt of caffeine would do the job. He had a nine-thirty breakfast appointment with a guy he'd met on the slopes a couple of days ago. They'd been the only two people crazy enough to take on Deadman's Run at dusk. Afterward, over brandy-laced coffee in the lounge, they'd introduced themselves.

"Rod Pommier," the guy had said, narrowing his eyes as if he half expected the name would elicit a reaction.

Seth had recognized the name—he read the papers—and he knew Pommier wanted privacy. That was fine. As far as he was concerned, the doctor was just another skier.

"Nice to meet you," he said. "I'm Seth Castleman."

They shook hands—Seth liked Pommier's firm, no-nonsense grip—and went back to talking about skiing. After a while, they talked about Cooper's Corner and how laid-back the town was.

"People seem friendly but not nosy, if you know what I mean," Rod said.

Seth smiled. "That's typically New England."

"I get the feeling that the president of the United States could show up with a pair of skis on and it wouldn't cause a ripple."

"Actually, it would depend on whether he was a Democrat or a Republican." Both men laughed. "But I know what you mean," Seth said. "This is a small town with an old-fashioned attitude. Don't get me wrong. Gossip's the lifeblood of the place, especially if you live here, but if you want to be left alone, nobody's going to bother you."

Rod looked up from his coffee. "Am I getting a message here?" he asked pleasantly.

"You mean, do I know who you are?" Seth grinned. "Sure. You're a skier who just happens to be a doctor in his spare time. Does that about sum it up?"

"It sure does," Rod said, and Seth could almost see him relax.

They bumped into each other on the slopes again. The second time around, Rod said he'd heard Seth was a carpenter. "And a guy who makes damned fine furniture," he added. "I'm staying at Twin Oaks. I admired a walnut table in the entry hall and Clint Cooper told me it was your work."

Seth nodded. "Yeah. That piece came out pretty well."

Rod smiled. "Clint told me you'd say something like that, but he says the truth is, you're good."

"Thanks."

"Hey, it's not immodest to admit it if you've got talent." The men's eyes met and Rod grinned. "The danger is in letting the rest of the world know it."

They shared a chuckle, talked some more, and then the doctor mentioned he'd been looking at an old ski chalet with a fantastic view. It was for sale but it needed a lot of work. He described the location and Seth said he knew the place.

"I've seen it from the road. From what I've heard it's sound, structurally, but the inside—"

"Is a disaster." The doctor sighed. "Yeah, I know. Dark, old, boxy. But there's nothing around here that has a view to match it. The sun just about lights up the top of the mountain. And I feel…comfortable, I guess, in this town." He paused. "I've been giving some serious thought to buying the place and rebuilding it. Gut the interior, get rid of all that dark stained pine and put in—"

"Beech and maple. Draws the light right in."

Rod raised his eyebrows. "Yeah. Exactly." He sipped his coffee, then tapped his fingers on the table. "Could you drive over one morning and tell me what you think?"

Seth smiled. "My pleasure."

They'd made an appointment for this morning. Seth had already cruised by the chalet a couple of times, getting the feel of it, and ideas had started coming. As many as could, anyway, until he saw the interior. He'd jotted them down in his notebook and was eager to discuss them with the doctor.

There was still another hour and a half until it was time to meet Pommier. Thankfully, the little guy with the sledgehammer had gone from trying to bash his way out of Seth's skull to merely tapping at it, so why stand around?

Seth drained the last of the coffee, rinsed the mug and put it in the sink. There were things he could do before he left. He could start stripping the finish from the old cherry rocker he'd picked up at a garage sale. Work on the chest he was making for his bedroom. Drive out to that farm near New Ashford, see if the owner had made up his mind whether or not he wanted to take down his barn and sell the hand-hewn beams and weathered old siding....

Who was he kidding?

He grabbed his jacket and keys and hurried out to his truck. There was only one thing that really needed doing this morning, and he damned well was going to do it.

GINA MONROE SAT at the old maple table in her kitchen, elbows propped on its scarred surface, hands wrapped around a steaming cup of herbal tea. On impulse, she'd taken the day off from her job as a teacher at the local elementary school. Now she watched with satisfaction as her daughter tucked into a stack of blueberry pancakes she'd sworn she could never finish when Gina served them to her ten minutes earlier.

Wendy forked up a mouthful dripping with maple syrup and melted butter. Gina smiled at the look on her face.

"Good?"

Wendy chewed, swallowed and dabbed at her lips with her napkin. "No," she said, straight-faced. "I'm just making a pig of myself to keep you happy."

Gina grinned and thought how wonderful it was to have her little girl home again. It was the same thing she'd been thinking for the last two days.

"Seriously, Mom, these are incredible."

"Well, we had a great blueberry crop last summer," Gina said modestly. "Your father couldn't keep away from the pick-your-own place just north of town."

"Is it still there?"

"Mmm-hmm. And Daddy bought boxes and boxes of berries. I made blueberry pie, blueberry tarts, blueberry vinegar, blueberry liqueur—"

"Whoa. Blueberry liqueur? That's a new one."

Gina smiled as she rose and went to the counter. "Your father gave me a course in herbal cooking as a birthday gift last year." She spooned some fresh herbs into an infuser and filled her mug with water from the kettle. "More coffee for you?"

"Yes, please."

She topped up Wendy's cup. "I have some pancakes left. Would you like a couple more?"

Wendy groaned and held up her hands. "I couldn't eat another bite."

"Just one, maybe?"

"Honestly, I'm full." Wendy pushed back her chair. "I'd almost forgotten what an American breakfast was like. That was absolutely delicious."

"I'm glad. Oh, don't get up, sweetie. Let me get those dishes. You just sit there and take it easy."

Wendy shook her head, collected her dishes and took them to the sink. "That's all I've been doing since I got back."

"It's all I want you to do."

"I'm not an invalid, Mother."

"Well, of course you aren't. I just enjoy fussing over you." Gina made a face. "And now I'm in trouble."

"Huh?"

"You just called me 'Mother.'" She took two cake plates from the cupboard and put them on the table. "That's always a danger sign."

"I don't know what you're talking about, Mom."

"See? Now I'm 'Mom.'" Gina smiled as she took out forks and arranged them on fresh napkins alongside the plates. "'Mom' is good. 'Mother' is a warning," she said, opening the oven. The scents of cinnamon and nutmeg drifted out. "You ready for some coffee cake?"

Wendy stared at her mother. "No. Yes. Is it that sour cream cake you used to make?"

"Uh-huh."

"In that case, maybe a sliver...and what in heck are you talking about?"

"I'm talking about you and the Mom-Mother thing."

Gina took the cake from the oven and put it on the table, then closed the door with her hip. "'Why must I wear my galoshes, *Mother?*'" she said in a little-girl voice. "'Why must I do my homework now, *Mother?*'" She laughed at the perplexed expression on Wendy's face. "Ever since you were tiny, I was 'Mom' when you were happy with me and 'Mother' when you weren't."

"Really?"

"Really."

"I didn't know I was that transparent." Wendy hesitated, watching as Gina sliced the cake. "Sorry. I didn't mean to snap just now."

"I know you didn't, sweetie." Gina looked at her daughter. "And I don't want to make you uncomfortable. You just need to remember that I haven't had the chance to fuss over you in a very long time."

"I know. And I really love having you fuss. I just…I guess I confused it with you thinking I wasn't up to doing things for myself, and I'm not very good at letting people help me."

"Not good? Dear, you bristle like a porcupine, but I'm not surprised. You always were so fiercely independent. It's what got you into trouble your very first day in kindergarten."

Wendy smiled. "Seriously?"

"Oh, yes. I'll never forget it. Your teacher cornered me when I came to pick you up." Gina's expression softened at the memory. "I'd just gone back to teaching. I was doing half days, paired with a new teacher. She took mornings so I could be home with you in the afternoons."

"Uh-huh. I remember."

"Anyway, I came to get you. And your teacher—"

"Mrs. Barrett."

"Right. Sally Barrett said she hated having to tell me, but you'd walloped some little boy."

"I didn't!" Wendy laughed. "I don't remember that at all."

"Well, it's true. Seems he'd been crying. Lots of the kids were. First day away from home and all that... Anyway, this poor little guy wanted his mother. You were sitting next to him and you were crying, too."

"I definitely don't remember that! I loved kindergarten."

"Yes, you did. But that very first day, you were teary-eyed, the same as the other children. Sally said the little boy looked at you—for comfort, maybe—and you said, 'What are you looking at?' or words to that effect, and he said he was looking at you because you were crying, and you said—"

"Oh, wow." Wendy giggled and covered her face with her hands. "It's coming back to me. I said he was a baby and he said if he was a baby, so was I, and—"

"And," Gina said, putting slices of cake on their plates, "you hauled off and hit him." She grinned. "Then he really had something to cry about, poor kid. Anyway, Sally Barrett read you the riot act. So did I. And when your father came home and I told him what had happened..."

"He said I'd done a bad thing." Wendy's lips twitched. "Then he picked me up, lifted me high in the air and said I was some piece of work."

"He was right. You were." Gina smiled. "You still are. Soft as velvet most of the time, but tough as nails when you have to be." Her smile tilted. "Which brings us to this operation."

Here we go, Wendy thought. She'd broken the news to her mother her first evening home. Gina had blanched, but she hadn't said much.

"Mom took it well," she'd whispered to her father when she kissed him good-night, but Howard had shaken his head and reminded her that that was her mother's way. When Gina learned something that upset her, she'd keep it to herself, turn it over and over in her mind, then talk about it when she was ready.

From the look in her eyes, she was ready right now.

Wendy caught hold of her hand. "Mom, I know the news that I want to have this surgery came as a surprise—"

"Surprise? *Shock* is a better word. Why did you tell your father and not me?"

"Because I knew you'd be upset," Wendy said gently. "And I was right."

"Of course I'm upset! I thought all those things—the hospital stays, the surgeries—were behind us."

"Yeah. Well, so did I. But this new technique—"

"Is unproven."

"It's not unproven, Mom. Dr. Pommier's performed this procedure on a lot of people."

"If he's the only one doing it, it's unproven and experimental."

"Any new technique is experimental. The bottom line is that what he does works."

Gina stood up, dumped the pancake griddle into the sink and ran the hot water. "It works for certain people, Wendy, and for only certain types of injuries. You and your father admit that."

"That's right. And as far as I can tell, I'm a perfect candidate." Wendy stood up and reached for a dish towel. "Look, I know you're worried, but—"

"You had the very best surgeons in Norway, and the best doctors at the French rehab clinic." Gina shut off the water, wiped her hands on her apron and turned around. "If any of them had thought there was more they could do, they'd have done it."

"Exactly. They did everything they could, but things have changed. This technique didn't exist back then."

"And what about the fact that this doctor says he's not taking on new patients? That you phoned him, sent him a letter, and he won't even discuss your case?"

Wendy tossed the towel on the back of a chair. "I knew I shouldn't have told you that!"

"You're probably right. You kept everything else from me, letting me think you were coming home—really coming home—when all the time—"

"I never said that, Mother. Never!"

"No. You didn't. But I thought...I thought—" Gina turned away, wrapped her hands around the rim of the sink as if that might help steady the turmoil inside her. "Aside from anything else," she said quietly, "you're not facing reality. Do you really believe you can change Dr. Pommier's mind simply by meeting him?"

"Of course not. But if I can talk to him, show him my records, explain how desperately I want to try this—"

"Why 'desperately'? That's what I don't understand. They said you'd never walk again but you did. You are. I mean, just look at you. You're on your feet, getting around on your own—"

"I limp. I can't ski—"

"For heaven's sake!" Gina's face flushed. "You're my daughter. I can't believe you're so...so foolish that you'd think people would judge you by the way you walk, or by what you can or can't do!"

"How about the way *I* judge me?" Wendy's voice trembled. She felt her eyes fill with tears and she swiped her hand across them, hating herself for letting her emotions show again. "Do you know what it's like to be reminded, every single day of your life, of what happened to you one morning a long time ago?"

"Oh, sweetie." Gina clasped her daughter's shoulders. "Is that what it's all about?"

Wendy shut her eyes. The scene in her head was as real as if it had happened yesterday. She saw herself early that fateful day, dragging out of bed. Tired, exhausted, muscles aching, barely making it to the bathroom before her stomach rose in her throat as it had done every morning since the ski team arrived in Lillehammer...

"Wendy." Gina cupped Wendy's face. "Darling, you can't possibly think you were responsible for the accident. The run was icy. Other skiers had wiped out before you in that very same place. You caught some ice, lost control...."

Gina couldn't bring herself to describe the rest. Wendy sighed and put her arm around her.

"I've gone over it a million times," she said softly.

"Then you know that it wasn't your fault."

Wendy nodded. She did, sometimes, when she was being logical. There were inherent dangers in racing down a snow-covered mountain at eighty or ninety miles an hour. When you stepped into your skis, you accepted that as a fact of life.

But...but maybe if she hadn't been so determined to win a medal, she'd have faced the truth that day—that she didn't feel well, hadn't felt well for a while. Maybe she should have told her coach the truth when he looked at her, frowned and said, "You okay, Monroe? You look kind of green around the edges."

"I'm fine," she'd answered. She wasn't. She'd felt rotten, but so what? If you wanted to win, you had to tough it out. She'd skied with aches and pains before. Everyone on the team did. She'd suspected she was coming down with the flu, like a couple of the men already had. She had all the symptoms. If she'd said, "You're right, coach, I feel awful," what then? He'd have sidelined her, and with the start of the Olympics just days away, she'd needed all the practice she could get....

So she'd lied. And she'd skied. And now, for the rest of her life, that quick, selfish decision would haunt her each morning when she limped from the bed to the bathroom. When she saw a snow-covered mountain and knew she couldn't ski it. She'd remember not just who she'd once been but what she'd once been. What she'd had, and could never have again.

"Wendy? Sweetie?"

Her mother's eyes were dark with worry. Wendy fought back the desire to fling herself into Gina's arms and pour out her heart. What would that accomplish? Then the pain would be her mother's, as well as hers, and she loved Gina too much to do that.

No. This was her problem. Hers alone. She would deal with it.

"Wendy?" Gina moistened her lips with the tip of her tongue. "I just want you to know that—that I don't agree with what you want to do." She held out her hands and Wendy took them. "But I'll stand by you, every inch of the way."

Wendy smiled. "I love you, Mom," she said softly.

"I know. And I love you, too." Gina gave her daughter a quick hug. Then she stepped back and smiled, even though her eyes were suspiciously damp. "Well," she said briskly, "that's that, my bristly, stubborn daughter. I have the feeling that doctor's in for a big surprise."

"Me, too," Wendy said, and her smile broadened.

"Did Daddy say when he'd set up a meeting for you with this Dr. Pommier?"

"He doesn't know, exactly. He'll have to wait for the right moment."

"Well, until that moment comes, I'm going to make the most of having you here." Gina brushed a curl from Wendy's brow. "What would you like to do today? How about driving down to Lee? Did you know they built a mall there?"

"A mall?" Wendy said, grasping eagerly at the lifeline her mother had tossed. "A real mall? With real department stores?"

"Better than that. Discount stores." Gina rolled her eyes.

"Veddy, veddy upscale, my deah. Wait until you see. Tell you what. I'll clean up here while you get dressed."

"I'll help you."

"I thought we'd settled all that. You're my baby, you're home and I'm going to do my very best to spoil you rotten."

"Sentenced to spoiling," Wendy said, and grinned. "Okay. It's a deal."

Gina watched her daughter start from the room. In for a penny, in for a pound, she thought, and took a deep breath.

"Wendy?"

Wendy turned and looked at her. "Yes?"

"I know you told me that you didn't want anyone to know you were going to be here, but…are you going to see Seth while you're home?"

Wendy's face paled. "Did you tell him I was coming back? Oh, Mother! I specifically asked you—"

"I didn't tell him anything."

"You just said—"

"All I said was, are you going to see him while you're here?"

"No," Wendy said sharply. "Why would I?"

"Well, I just thought…" Gina hesitated. "As a courtesy, I thought you might at least call him. He still asks about you, you know."

Wendy dug her hands into the pockets of her robe. Her fingers closed around a loose thread and she worried it between her thumb and forefinger. "Does he?"

"He used to call to see how you were. Even now, if we run into each other, he asks about you."

"That's very nice of him," Wendy said stiffly, "but Seth and I have nothing to say to each other. I'm a different person now, and so is he."

Gina gave a resigned sigh. "Okay."

"I don't want to talk to him. I don't want to see him. And if you should run into him—"

"Wendy." Gina put her hand on her daughter's arm. "Forget I mentioned it."

"We were kids, that's all. Two silly kids. The accident helped me realize that."

Wendy's eyes darkened. She looked down, and Gina held her breath. Her daughter seemed on the verge of saying something that would explain the change of heart that had taken place in her, but when Wendy raised her head, Gina knew the moment had slipped by.

"Let's not talk about the past," she said softly. "Okay?"

Gina nodded. She wanted to fling her arms around Wendy and tell her she'd make whatever was troubling her go away, just as she had when Wendy was little. But the bittersweet truth was that mothers lost that magical talent when children grew up.

"Okay." She smiled brightly and looked at the kitchen clock. "Hey, if we want to be the first ones there and pick up some real bargains, we'd better get moving."

"Right." Wendy smiled back, although her smile looked as phony as Gina's felt. "Give me ten minutes to shower and dress."

"You're on," Gina said.

She held her smile until Wendy left the kitchen. Then she sighed and began stacking the dishes in the dishwasher.

Her little girl—and that was what Wendy would always be, no matter how the years slipped by—her little girl was badly troubled. Gina kept looking for an explanation. Howard kept saying it was her leg, as if it was foolish to wonder about any other reason.

Maybe he was right, but Wendy had beat the odds. Wasn't that all that mattered? She was out of a wheelchair and walking, after most of the doctors had said she'd be an invalid for life.

Still, Gina supposed she could understand that Wendy would feel differently. People tended to define themselves by the things they did. She'd taken enough silly pop quizzes to know that. Who was Gina Monroe, if anyone asked? How would Gina Monroe describe herself? As a wife. A mother. A teacher.

Wendy would have defined herself as a champion skier. But was that all? It didn't seem possible that her daughter's self-image could be so one-dimensional. Wendy had loved to ski from the time she was a child, but there'd been more in her life than skiing.

At least, there had been after Seth Castleman came along.

Gina untied her apron, hung it on the back of the pantry door, then sat down at the table to finish her lukewarm tea.

Howard had bought their daughter her first pair of skis the Christmas she was, what? Four? Five?

"She's just a baby," Gina had said warily. "She could get hurt."

Her husband had smiled proudly as they watched their little girl stomp around the snowy yard. "She'll be fine. She can't possibly get hurt on the Ski Wee hills. You know that, darling. Those slopes are nothing more than bumps in the snow. Besides, our girl's a natural. Just look at her. She's got the makings of a champion."

He was right. Wendy had been born to ski. She was quick, graceful, a joy to watch. At eight, she'd won her first junior medal. At ten, she was taking winter vacation trips with Howard to Aspen. By the time she was twelve, skiing was all she lived for.

She was bright, thank goodness, so she did well in school, even though she didn't pay much attention to her studies. As for dances and parties and the sweet silliness young girls enjoy—those things didn't interest her. Gina closed her eyes, remembering how she used to long to be able to make the same complaints as other mothers of teen-age girls, but Wendy didn't spend hours tying up the phone, or plaster her room with posters of rock idols and giggle over boys.

And then, when Wendy was seventeen, she'd met a boy

on the slopes. She was practicing; Seth was running the lift. Gina didn't know what had happened that day, except that her daughter came home with high color in her cheeks and excitement in her eyes.

"A good day at Brodie, huh, punkin?" Howard said at dinner.

Wendy nodded. "Yes…terrific."

Something in the way she said it, or maybe in the quick rush of color that climbed into her face again, told Gina the truth.

Wendy had met a boy.

Gina kept her thoughts to herself. The phone began to ring with calls for Wendy, all of them from the same polite young man. Sometimes she came home a little late from school, and in the evenings, when she sat at the kitchen table doing her homework, Gina caught her staring into space with a dreamy look in her eyes.

Gina was glad. It had begun to trouble her, seeing Wendy lock everything but skiing out of her life. Her daughter still loved to ski, still skied almost all weekend, but for the first time, she balked at Howard's rigorous practice schedule.

Howard was perplexed.

"What's gotten into her?" he mumbled one evening when Wendy said she wasn't in the mood for a drive to Brodie for an hour's work.

"She's a teenage girl," Gina answered. "She just needs time for other things."

"Not if she wants to make it to the Olympics, she doesn't," Howard said, and not for the first time, Gina wondered whose goal that really was, his or Wendy's.

One evening at dinner, Wendy asked to be excused before dessert.

"Apple pie," Gina said. "Your favorite."

"I know, Mom, but…" She blushed. "I have a date."

Gina smiled. Howard stared.

"A date? With a boy?" Howard spoke in the same tone

he'd have used if Wendy had announced she had a date with a Klingon warrior.

"Yes." Wendy's blush deepened. "His name is Seth Castleman."

From that night on, everything revolved around what Seth said or did. Gina thought she'd never seen her little girl so happy. Howard thought he'd never seen her so distracted.

"She's going to lose her edge," he grumbled late one Friday night when he and Gina lay in bed, listening to the clock chime eleven and knowing Wendy had yet to come home.

Gina sighed and put her head on his shoulder. "She's in love, Howard."

"Don't be silly."

"The signs are all there."

Howard had snorted. "Puppy love, maybe. That's all it is."

Gina had been sure it was more than that—until the accident, when Seth flew to Norway to be with Wendy and Wendy wouldn't even see him. When she'd sent him a note that cut him out of her life.

The doorbell sounded. Gina glanced at the clock. Howard was the reading coordinator at the school where they both worked. He was meeting with the principal and she expected him home for lunch, but it was only ten. It had to be the UPS man with the books she'd ordered.

But it wasn't the UPS man. It was Seth.

"Hello, Gina."

She stared at him stupidly. Seth hadn't come to the house in a long time, and now, only minutes after they'd talked about him, he was here. She gaped at the young man before her, snow dusting his dark hair and leather jacket, as if he were an apparition.

"Seth? I didn't expect... I mean, what are you—"

"May I come in?"

Gina swallowed. "Actually," she said carefully, "this isn't a very good time."

"I know she's here."

"Seth." Gina glanced over her shoulder at the stairs. "I really don't think—"

"How come you didn't tell me she was coming home?"

There was anger in his voice, but she thought she could detect pain, too. "Oh, Seth…"

"You should have told me," he said gruffly.

The snow was coming down harder. And Mrs. Lewis, out walking her dog, had paused on the sidewalk and was watching the scene with frank curiosity. Gina swung the door wide and moved aside. "Come in, then. But only for a minute."

"Thanks." Seth stepped into the entry hall and stomped his boots on the mat a lot harder than necessary. He didn't give a damn just now about the snow he might track in on Gina Monroe's slate tiles. Driving here, he'd gone from ticked off to angry to plain furious. It was stupid, he knew, because Wendy didn't mean anything to him and Gina was under no obligation to tell him anything. Still, stupid or not, his temper was almost at the boiling point.

His anger started to abate as he looked at Gina's worried face. Calmer now, he wasn't even sure why he'd come. It was only that it was wrong that nobody had told him Wendy was coming home, warned him so he'd have been prepared for the shock of seeing her again.

"Seth." Gina looked up at him. "You can't stay. Really, I wish you could, but—"

"Yeah." He ran his fingers through his snow-dampened hair. "Look, I'm sorry. I just…I saw her, you know? And it was—it was a surprise. How come you didn't tell me?"

"Because…because—"

"Because I asked her not to."

Seth lifted his head. He stared past Gina and saw Wendy coming slowly down the stairs.

CHAPTER FOUR

WENDY CLUTCHED the banister and looked down at Seth.

This was the moment she'd feared, the one she'd known was inevitable ever since her father said it was probably going to take longer than he'd expected to get time alone with Dr. Pommier. The longer she stayed in town, the greater the risk that Seth would learn she was here. It was one of the reasons she'd come up with excuses yesterday, when her father asked her to go with him while he ran some errands.

"Are you concerned folks will ask you questions when they see you? About your plans and if you're home to stay, things like that?" he'd said, and then he'd answered the question himself. "Well, don't worry, honey. We won't tell them a thing until after you've seen Dr. Pommier and he's agreed to do that surgery. Okay?"

What could she have said after that? That she didn't want people to see her limp, or she didn't want to risk bumping into Seth? Either answer made her sound like a coward, so she'd smiled and said, sure, she'd go with him, now that she'd had a little time to get used to being back in Cooper's Corner.

But the thumping beat of her heart gave proof to the lie. She *was* a coward. She hadn't wanted to see anybody because she hadn't wanted to see pity in their eyes. But most of all, she'd been afraid of what she would see in the eyes of the man who'd loved the girl she used to be. She didn't want his sympathy any more than she wanted his rejection if he ever found out exactly how critical her injuries had been.

Looking down at him, Wendy knew with relief that she'd had nothing to worry about. What she saw in Seth's face was anger. Cold, controlled anger, and she knew, in that instant, that it was over for him, too.

Good.

So what if her pulse was rattling like a runaway train? That was normal when you saw a man who'd once been your lover, a man you hadn't seen or spoken to in nine endless years.

"Seth," she said carefully. "You're looking well."

"Hello, Wendy."

His voice was lower than she remembered. And he seemed bigger, though he'd always been tall and leanly muscled; standing next to him had made her feel feminine, almost delicate, even though her body was toned and hardened from years of skiing. He wasn't bigger, she realized. He was mature, a man instead of a boy. A ruggedly handsome man with a strong jaw and a beautiful mouth.

"How have you been?" There. Wasn't that good? Her voice was steady, her smile pleasant. So what if she left dents in the banister from gripping so hard? He'd never know.

"Fine." His gaze swept down her body, lingered on her leg, then returned to her face. "And you?"

"Oh, I'm—I'm well, thank you."

"Last I heard, you'd been putting in long hours at rehab."

Wendy glanced at her mother, the source, she was sure, of any updates. Gina seemed frozen in place, her hands clasped at her breast, her gaze moving from face to face as they talked, like a spectator watching match point at a tennis game.

"Yes, that's right. I still do."

"And it's obviously paid off. It's good to see you on your feet again."

The few people she'd talked with in town yesterday—in the general store, at the gas station—had carefully avoided making any reference to her leg. Did he think he was going to get to her by bringing up the past?

"Thank you. Mom," she said pleasantly, "if we're going to get to that mall—"

"Are you happy, living in France?"

"Very happy, thank you for asking."

"I was surprised to hear you were back."

"Why?" She turned to him again and smiled politely. "This is my home. Why wouldn't I come back?"

"Is this a visit? Or have you come home to stay?"

"Seth, really, it's very nice to see you, but—"

"You didn't answer my question. Why haven't you come home before?"

"Because I didn't want to," she said, holding the smile. "Anything else?"

"Wendy," Gina said sharply, "there's no need to—"

"That's okay, Gina. Wendy's right. Where she lives, what she does is none of my business." He stepped back and put a hand on the doorknob. "I probably should have called first."

What had happened to all that calm certainty she'd felt when she first started down the steps and saw him? Seth was just someone from the past. He was nothing to her now. Then why was the sight of him making her feel as if she was seventeen again and he'd just come to pick her up for their very first date? It had been snowing then, too, and he'd come inside the house just as she started down the stairs....

"Yes," she said, "you should have."

"Yeah." He cleared his throat. "Well, it's good seeing you again."

"Thank you."

"This is where you're supposed to say it's good seeing me again, too."

"Goodbye, Seth."

He turned away and opened the door. Then he hesitated. She saw his shoulders stiffen and suddenly he swung toward her, and she knew his anger had gotten the best of him.

"That's it? Nine years of silence, and all you can manage is 'Goodbye, Seth'?"

"I haven't anything else to say to you."

"Well, damn it, maybe you should. Maybe you should start with explaining why you treated me like a stranger after I flew to Norway to be with you. After a while, you might work your way around to 'I'm sorry, Seth.' How's that sound?"

"I don't owe you anything. You flew to Norway on your own. I didn't ask you to come."

His eyes bored into her as he reached behind him and slammed the door shut. The sound echoed off the walls. Out of the corner of her eye, Wendy saw her mother jump.

"No," he said bitterly, "you sure as hell didn't."

"Please leave."

"Great. It's still a dismissal, but this time there's a 'please' attached."

Wendy came down the rest of the steps. Her heart was still banging away but now it was with fury. Who did he think he was?

"Get out." She raised her hand, pointed at the door. "Get out of this house!"

"Wendy," Gina said, "Seth—"

"Oh, I'm going. I'm going, all right. I just wanted you to know that…that—" He clamped his lips together. "The hell with this," he muttered. "Gina? I'm sorry."

"No. Seth, it isn't your fault—"

He yanked the door open, stepped onto the porch into

the swirling snow and was gone. Gina shut the door, leaned against it and let out her breath.

"That poor boy."

"I can't believe he did that." Wendy was trembling. She wrapped her arms around herself and sank down on the bottom step. "Did he really think he could just...just barge in here and say..." Her head came up as her mother's words penetrated. "What?"

"I said—"

"I heard what you said, Mother. Do you mean to tell me you feel sorry for Seth?" She grabbed the banister and pulled herself to her feet. "You heard the things he said to me! How can you feel any sympathy for him?"

"You could have been more polite!"

"Polite?" Wendy barked out a laugh. "He came here uninvited, put me through an inquisition, acted as if I owed him something, and you call him a poor boy?"

"You *do* owe him something. An apology. I've never said that to you, not in all these years, but you treated Seth—"

"I don't want to hear it."

"Well, you're going to. That boy—"

"He's not a boy, he's a man. And if he thinks I'm going to grovel just because I had the courage to do what I knew I had to do—"

"That *man*," Gina said sternly, "dropped everything he was doing to fly to your side. And you—" She broke off in the middle of the sentence, breathing hard, eyes suddenly welling with tears. "Oh, honey. I'm sorry."

"That's all right," Wendy said stiffly. "Say what you have to say."

"No. Baby, I didn't mean..." Gina stepped forward and took hold of her daughter's shoulders. "You were right to concentrate all your energies on yourself. You had to. It's the only way you got through the accident. It's just that I saw how hurt Seth was. All through the years, I kept hoping you'd get in touch with him.''

"For what? I don't love him.''

"I'm not talking about love, baby, I'm talking about doing the right thing. You could have called him just to say, I don't know, that you appreciated what he'd done, that you hoped he was happy....''

"Is he?'' The words were out before Wendy could stop them. "Alison says he's seeing someone. Is he happy with her, Mom?''

"Oh, my,'' Gina said softly. "You still care for him.''

"No!'' Wendy wrenched free of her mother's hands. "You just finished saying I should have asked him if he was happy. Can't I ask it without you making it into something personal?''

"And it isn't?''

"Of course not!'' Wendy ran the tip of her tongue over her bottom lip. "Okay. You're right. I mean, I should have gotten in touch with him at some point. I just... It's hard, looking back, Mom. Can you understand that?''

"Yes, I guess I can. He reminds you of the past. And you only want to think about the future.'' Gina sighed. "And you're right. It's none of my business.''

"I didn't say that.''

"You didn't have to.'' Gina smiled. "I kind of got the message.''

Wendy's shoulders slumped. She sighed and put her arms around her mother. "Forgive me,'' she said softly. "I shouldn't be letting all this out on you.''

Gina returned the embrace. "And I shouldn't have jumped on you. No matter how much Seth might have wanted to see you, you were right. He *should* have called before coming here.'' She drew back and clasped Wendy's face. "I know it must have been a shock to see him again, after such a long time.''

Wendy nodded. "It was." She hesitated. "Mom, I know you think I treated Seth badly, but—"

"What I think," Gina said gently, "is that I have to keep out of this." Wendy sighed and sank down on the step again. Her mother sat down next to her. "Can I ask one question?"

"Of course."

Gina brushed a curl back from Wendy's forehead. "Did you break things off because you thought you might be in a wheelchair for the rest of your life?"

"That was part of it."

"Honey, you have to know that wouldn't have mattered to a man like Seth."

"There was more to it than that."

"I hope so," Gina said gently, "because that kind of decision wasn't yours to make."

"You're wrong, Mom. It *was* my decision. It couldn't have been Seth's. I knew he'd…he'd opt for the honorable thing. That he'd say my being unable to walk wouldn't matter, but it did."

"Wendy—"

"Don't tell me it's not true, Mother." Wendy's voice trembled. "I wasn't *me* anymore. I'm still not the person I was, the person Seth knew and fell in love with…." She bit her lip. "Seth and I had our time, and we lost it." She wouldn't cry. Wouldn't give in to the almost overwhelming desire to lay her head on her mother's shoulder and sob. She hadn't done that, not once, not even when she'd first awakened to a world in which pain was the only constant. Instead, she reached for Gina's hands and held them tightly in hers. "But that's not the reason I ended things."

"You decided you weren't in love with Seth."

"We were wrong for each other." It was the truth, in a way. "And I knew I had to do something about it."

"I understand. No, don't shake your head. I really do. Brushes with—with death make people see things differently." Gina gave a little laugh. "Oprah 101. But it's true. And I promise, that's the end of that. No more comments from me, I swear." She looked down at their joined hands for a long moment. When she lifted her head, her eyes were damp but she was smiling. "Okay," she said briskly, "it's time to take on the mall."

"Mom? Would you mind very much if we put it off?"

"No. Of course not. If you're tired—"

"I'm not. And before you ask, yes, my leg's fine. I just thought I might go out for a while, take a look around and see what's changed."

"In Cooper's Corner?" Gina grinned. "You're joking."

"Alison said there's a new B and B."

"Yes. And that's it, unless you want to count the new gum ball machine down at the grocery store. Why don't you call Alison and see if she's free for lunch? I'm sure you two still have lots of catching up to do. Take my car, go for a drive—the snow's not serious. It should be all done in another hour or two. Besides, my car has four-wheel drive. And those anti-lock brakes. Just remember, if you need to stop fast…" Gina rolled her eyes. "Good grief. I'm treating you as if you were a teenager."

Wendy laughed as she rose to her feet. "Yes, *Mother*," she said, putting deliberate emphasis on the word, "you are."

"Well, I'm not going to apologize. Being a nag is one of the perks of being a mom." Gina smiled. "Someday you'll find that out for yourself."

"Maybe," Wendy said, her smile tilting. "I guess we'll just have to wait and see."

She managed to hold the smile until Gina returned to the kitchen. Wendy wasn't in the mood for company, not even Alison's, but maybe her mother was right. Lunch might be fun. If nothing else, it would be a distraction.

She phoned the post office. Alison said yes, lunch sounded like a great idea.

"How about the Burger Barn? We never did get there the other day."

"Terrific." Wendy got her down parka from the closet, tucked the phone between her ear and her shoulder and worked her arm into a sleeve. "At noon? Is that good for you?"

Alison asked her to hold on for a second while she checked to see if the other clerk would swap his lunch hour with her.

"Yeah," she said, "that's fine. See you at noon."

Wendy hung up the phone, zipped her jacket, yelled a goodbye to her mother and headed out into the morning.

Maybe a drive and a bit of cold, clean air would help clear her head of memories that had no place in her life anymore.

SETH FELT LIKE James Bond.

Forget that. The suave Mr. Bond wouldn't be driving a country road, hanging four car lengths behind a blue Volvo driven by a woman he'd once loved. Correction. A woman he'd *thought* he once loved. No, old James wouldn't do such a stupid thing. He wouldn't have stood silent while Wendy all but pointed to the door and told him to get out of her house, either.

All right. Seth hadn't expected her to throw herself into his arms with joy. He'd only stopped by out of courtesy, to ask her how things were going....

"Liar," he growled, dropping back as the brake lights of Gina's blue Volvo blinked.

He'd gone to ask her the question that was still stuck in his craw after all these years. Why? Why had she treated him like dirt when he'd flown to Norway to be with her? Why had the flame that had burned so brightly between them turned to cold ashes? What had happened to all the plans they'd made?

He'd deserved better than Wendy's refusal to see him,

that cold note of dismissal and the endless silence ever since.

He'd gone to see her for answers, answers she damn well owed him. Instead, she'd stood on those steps, looking down at him with ice in her eyes, and what had he done about it? Nothing.

"Nothing," he said, his jaw tightening.

Instead, he'd stomped out to his truck and slammed the heel of his hand against the steering wheel with frustration. His cell phone had rung just then and a good thing, too. It was Rod Pommier, phoning to ask if they could meet this afternoon instead of this morning. Yes, Seth had said, that was fine.

It sure as hell was.

How could he have talked intelligently about beams and ceilings and rebuilding a chalet when all he wanted to do was go back to the Monroe house, confront Wendy and ask her if she really thought she could screw around with a man's head and get away with it not once, but twice in a lifetime?

Just about then, Wendy came down the steps, opened the garage door and drove out in Gina's Volvo wagon. Without thinking about it, Seth had started his truck, waited until she reached the end of the block, and pulled out after her. He'd been following her ever since while she drove, seemingly without plan. They'd gone through the village, turned onto Route 7, driven north for a while....

The Volvo's brake lights winked. The right turn signal went on. She was pulling into the lot at the Burger Barn, a place he hadn't been in since...was it really that long? Since they'd dated.

He checked his mirror and turned in after her. She wouldn't recognize his black pickup, but it was just a little past 11:45, too early for the safe anonymity of the lunch crowd that would start flocking here pretty soon. Seth kept his head averted when he drove past her and parked at the far end of the almost empty lot.

What now? She didn't seem to be getting out. Yeah. She was. He saw her door open, saw her step out, shut the door and pull up her hood.

His heart climbed into his throat.

The snow had changed to big, lazy flakes that left a white layer on the ground. There could be ice beneath it. He'd watched Wendy in town the other day and seen how she limped. The footing was probably dicey, but he could just imagine her reaction if he suddenly came barreling out of nowhere, grabbed her arm, told her to hang on to him for support.

He sat still, gripping the steering wheel until his knuckles whitened, watching her make her way toward the Barn, his entire body on alert in case he had to throw open the door and race to her side. When she reached the restaurant and went in, Seth let out his breath, cursed himself for being a fool, reached for the key still in the ignition…

And stopped.

What was he doing? He'd gone to see her this morning, followed her through half the valley after she'd told him to get lost, and now he was just going to turn around and drive away? The hell he was.

He wanted closure.

Nine years before, he'd taken every dime he'd managed to save, sunk it into an airplane ticket and flown straight to Wendy because he'd thought she needed him.

She hadn't.

It had taken him a long time to get his life back together after that. It was a hell of a thing to think a woman loved you and then have her send you a note—a note, damn it— that told you she didn't.

Closure, Seth thought, his jaw tightening. He not only wanted it, he deserved it.

He took the key from the ignition, got out of the truck

and strode toward the restaurant. The warm scents of grilled hamburgers and fried onions met him as he stepped inside. He pulled off his gloves, looked around and saw her sitting in a booth way at the back. She was reading the menu, her head slightly bent, auburn curls falling forward over her shoulders, and he walked toward her quickly, wanting whatever small advantage he might gain through surprise.

"Wendy."

Surprise? Shock was more like it. She looked up, face draining of color, the menu falling from her hands.

"Seth? What are you doing here?"

"The same thing I was doing before. I'm here to see you."

"To see…" She swallowed. With grim pleasure, he saw her struggling to regain her composure. Slowly, color washed up under her skin in a wave of pale pink. "Well." She swallowed again, reached for the leather gloves and purse she'd put on the seat beside her. "Well, unfortunately, I was just—"

"Leaving?" He smiled tightly. "I don't think so. You just got here."

Her eyes widened. "How do you know? Did you—I don't believe it! You followed me."

"Yes. And I'll damn well follow you again, up and down this valley if I have to."

"Keep your voice down!" She looked around. The only other customers were at the front. Nobody was paying any attention to them. Frankly, he wouldn't have cared if the entire town marched in at that moment. Clearly, she did.

"You keep running away, I'll just keep going after you."

That did it. Her eyes snapped with anger. "You're crazy."

"Maybe so, but the choice is yours. You want me to tag after you, I will. Up and down Route 7 and from one end of Main Street to the other. I can always park my truck in your driveway and camp out."

"For heaven's sake…!" She glared at him. "Sit down."

"An intelligent decision," he said as he slid into the booth across from her. "But then, you always were bright. I was the one who wasn't."

"I don't know what that's supposed to—"

"Hi," a voice said cheerfully. "You folks ready to order?"

Seth looked up. A waitress had materialized beside their table, a notepad in her hand and a smile on her lips.

"The onion burger is today's special. Two patties of beef, smoked cheddar, fried onions—"

"Coffee," Seth said.

The waitress lifted her eyebrows. "Right. And you, miss?"

"I don't want anything."

"She'll have coffee, too."

"Listen, Seth…" Wendy glanced up at the waitress and flushed. "Coffee's fine."

The waitress pursed her lips and scooped up their menus. "You got it."

Seth waited until she'd walked away from the table. Then he leaned forward. "Only a stupid son of a bitch wouldn't have realized you were leaving him, not just Cooper's Corner."

Wendy looked blank. "I don't know…" She stared at him and then she laughed. Really laughed, which only sent his anger up another notch.

"You think that's funny?"

"You think I went to Norway rather than simply break things off with you?" She sat back as the waitress served their coffee, her laughter dying as soon as the girl left. "You know what, Seth? If you believe that, you're right. You really are dumb."

"You know damn well what I mean. When you left here, I thought things were fine between us. And then, wham, you didn't even have the decency to slam the door in my face. A Dear John letter, for God's sake. Until then, I thought people only did those things in bad movies.''

His face was dark with anger. Wendy could see the faint, rhythmic tick of a muscle in his jaw. For a second, she wanted to reach across the table, put her fingers against that telltale pulse, tell him...tell him—

"All right."

"What's that supposed to mean?"

"It means I...I shouldn't have done it that way. But I was in a hospital bed, remember? I wasn't up to having conversations with visitors.''

"I wasn't a visitor, damn it. I was your lover." Seth leaned forward, his voice low and rough. "Do you have any idea what it was like? Being here, a million miles from you, getting that call from your mother, knowing you'd been hurt, knowing that you might—that you might be dying?"

"This is history. And I've already apologized. That's what you wanted, wasn't it? To hear me admit I was wrong? I should have told you I was ending things...except, if you think back, I tried. I refused to see you. I didn't open your notes...."

She wrapped her hands around the mug, hoping some of the coffee's warmth would seep into her icy fingers. She didn't regret what she'd done. What choice had there been? Seth was over her. She was over him. But she owed him this moment.

"I'm sorry," she said quietly. "I was wrong. I know it's years too late, but...but thank you for coming."

He made a sound that might have been a laugh. "I didn't want your thanks, Wendy. I just wanted you to look at me. Tell me how glad you were to see me." His voice turned husky. He cleared his throat, reached for the cream and poured some into his coffee. "What's that old song?" he said with a quick smile. "Something about not always getting what you want, right?"

"You're right about the note, too. I should have had the courage to face you and tell you I was ending things."

He looked up from his coffee, and all at once he seemed young and vulnerable. "That you wanted me out of your life."

"It wasn't easy," Wendy said. She swallowed past the lump in her throat. "I want you to know that."

"Yeah." He stirred his coffee, then put down his spoon. "But you did it." He lifted the mug to his lips, took a sip. "And you were right," he said briskly. "I mean, we were just kids. What do kids know about what they really feel or want?"

She felt a little tug at her heart. "Not much." She took a deep breath. "Okay?"

Was it? He wasn't sure, but he'd come for closure and that was what she was offering.

"Sure." Seth held out his hand. "Friends?"

"Friends."

She smiled and put her hand in his. His fingers, warm and callused, tightened around hers. An electric tingle of remembrance shot through her. Their eyes met and held. Then he let go of her hand and reached for his coffee.

"I hear you're a teacher."

"Mais oui," she said, still smiling, still feeling the current running from her fingers straight through her blood. "And you're a hotshot carpenter."

She was doing her best to lighten the conversation, Seth realized. He could help her, now that they'd settled things. They'd been friends long before they'd been lovers. It would be nice to be friends again—and they could be, now that his anger was gone.

"That's me." He grinned. "Seth Castleman, Cooper's Corner's best carpenter."

"I bet."

"Hey, I can't lose." He dropped his voice to an exaggerated whisper. "I'm its *only* carpenter."

They both smiled, waited, then spoke at the same time.

"So," Wendy said.

"So," Seth said.

They laughed. "You first," he told her.

"No, you go ahead. What were you about to say?"

"I was going to ask what brought you home."

A visit, she started to say, but he smiled, a crooked tilt of the mouth she'd never forgotten. Her heart gave that funny little lurch again, but there was nothing but pleasant interest in his gaze. Good. That was good. That was all she felt, too. It meant they could be, well, perhaps not friends, but friendly. In that spirit, she decided to tell him the truth.

"I'm here to meet someone. Well, to introduce myself to him." Seth looked puzzled. She leaned closer. "Have you ever heard of a surgeon named Rod Pommier?"

He blinked and sat back. "Pommier? Yeah, sure I've heard of him. Actually—"

"Actually, what?"

I know him. The words were on the tip of Seth's tongue, but he bit them back.

"A person would have to be dense not to have heard of the guy. He made the papers, the cover of all the magazines a while back...." He stared at her. "You want him to operate on you?"

"That's right." Wendy's face seemed to light from within. "He's developed a technique that could change my life. It's a bonding thing. I don't understand most of it but—"

"Change your life how? You're walking. That was the big thing, wasn't it? That you got back the use of your leg?"

"I want to ski again," she said, as if he should have been able to figure that out for himself.

"Can't you?"

"Is that your idea of a joke?"

Her voice had turned cold. He knew somehow he'd made a mistake, but about what?

"No. Of course not. Look, I know you walk with a limp—"

"That's very incisive."

"Wendy. Damn it, all I meant was… I still ski and—"

"Yes," she said. Her tone had gone from cold to frigid. "I'm sure you do." She grabbed her gloves and purse and began to rise. He reached out and caught her wrist. "Please let go of me."

"Will you stop being an idiot? I'm trying to tell you that when I'm on the slopes, I see people with all kinds of handicaps."

"Handicaps." Ice crystals rimed each syllable.

"You know what I mean. I just assumed—"

"Assumptions are always a mistake."

"Will you stop looking at me that way?"

"How about you let go of my wrist?"

"Look…" He sat back, telling himself that he wasn't going to get anywhere by losing his temper again. "I'm just surprised, that's all. If you miss skiing—"

"*If* I miss it?" She gave a bitter laugh. "You really don't know me at all, do you?"

His eyes narrowed. "I guess not, because I figured you'd have been back on the mountains for a long time by now."

"Where? How? On the beginner's slope?"

"No, of course not. They held a race at Brodie last winter for people with disabilities." He saw her flinch at the word. "For people who are challenged."

"Don't play with the truth, Seth. For cripples. Isn't that what you mean?" She glared at him, her breathing quick. "Do you really think I could be satisfied with that?"

"These people don't stay on the beginner's—"

"Damn it, you know what I'm saying! No, I haven't skied since my accident. Why would I? I don't want to poke along, watching out for each bump. I want to ski the way I once did. To fly down a mountain. To compete.''

The words fell between them, heavy as stones. So far, Wendy thought, the only person who knew how she felt was her father, and he sure hadn't looked at her the way Seth was looking at her now.

"You're kidding."

"I'm dead serious. If Pommier can fix my leg—"

"Pommier isn't taking on new patients, or did I read those stories wrong?''

"He says he isn't. But I'm convinced if I can just get him to see me—''

"How are you going to manage that?''

Wendy hesitated. "I—I have an in.'' Her voice quickened and she leaned forward eagerly. "Don't you see, Seth? If he operates, if it works, I can get back in shape within a year. Two, max.''

"Wendy, come on. Those are huge if's. Besides, even if the guy could work this miracle—''

"It's what he does. I've read every word written about him. Pommier can do it.''

"I've read a lot about him, too. The surgery's risky.''

"Life's full of risks.''

Seth put down his coffee mug and ran a hand through his hair. "Maybe I just don't get it. Why would you want to ski competitively again? You've been there, done that. You have the medals to prove it.''

"Not Olympic gold.''

"You still have your legs," he said harshly. "Isn't that as good as Olympic gold?''

They stared at each other in taut silence. Then Wendy reached for her things. "I should have known you wouldn't see this my way. The only person who understands is my father.''

"Does he, now," Seth said, his voice flat.

"Yes. Yes, he does. I'm going to get my chance to talk to Dr. Pommier, thanks to him."

Seth's mouth thinned. "Ah. So that's your 'in.' Your old man. It figures."

Her head came up. "What's that supposed to mean?"

"Your old man will do anything to get that gold. He pushed you like crazy, ran you right into the ground. You got to Norway so worn-out that it's a wonder you didn't fall down as soon as you got off the plane."

"You think the accident was his fault?"

"That's what I just said."

"You're wrong."

"I don't think so." Seth hesitated a moment, then went on. "And while I'm at it, I'll tell you something else. Your father was glad you ended things between us."

"That's not true!"

"He saw me as a kid with no future, getting in the way of his pursuit of an Olympic medal."

"It wasn't his pursuit, it was mine. And you're dead wrong about the accident." Wendy's voice shook. "It was my fault. All mine."

"Yeah, right." Seth dug out his wallet, took out a bill and tossed it on the table. His anger was back and he knew he'd never get rid of it until he placed it where it belonged, square on the jaw of Howard Monroe. "He's got you brainwashed."

Wendy's eyes flashed. "You have no right to say that."

"I have every right. That last night, on Sawtooth Mountain, you lay in my arms and said you loved me. You said you had to get the dream of winning out of your system." Seth got to his feet, his face white, his eyes hot. "But you were lying. You already knew you were going to break up with me, Wendy, whether you won that damned medal or not. That accident just made it easier for you. You had the perfect excuse to shove me out of your life."

"You bastard! You...you unfeeling, self-centered son of a—"

"Hi, everybody. I hope I'm not interrupting anything."

They both turned. Alison was standing beside their table, smiling nervously and twisting her knit cap in her hands.

"Look, you guys, why don't I go outside, drive around for a while, say, fifteen minutes or so and—"

"No," Wendy said sharply.

"Hell, no," Seth said, even more sharply. "I was just leaving. So long, Wendy. Have a nice life."

Wendy watched as he strode to the door, yanked it open and stepped out of the Burger Barn and, she devoutly hoped, out of her life.

CHAPTER FIVE

RODNEY POMMIER, M.D., F.A.C.S., had come to Cooper's Corner to get away from all those initials dangling after his name.

Not that they didn't matter to him. He'd worked hard to get them and he was proud of them. He'd just never figured being a medical doctor and a Fellow of the American College of Surgeons could also turn a man into a celebrity.

A very unhappy celebrity.

Rod had wanted to be a doctor ever since he was a kid. That his path through life had been all but laid out for him in a different direction by generations of Pommiers had made reaching his goal all the sweeter. When he was growing up, it had been expected he'd go to McGill, take his degree in finance and management and, as his father put it, come on board at Pommier Investments.

Well, he'd tried.

Rod sighed as he stood on the sagging porch of the old cabin he'd just bought, and looked out at the view.

He'd absolutely tried. But after a year of struggling to give a damn about cost analysis and price earnings ratios, he'd given up, flown home one weekend and announced that he was going to become a doctor, not a financier. He'd stood in his father's wood-paneled study, ready for the war that was sure to come. Instead, after a couple of minutes of stunned silence, he'd gotten a smile, a handshake that turned into a hug, and all the best wishes he'd never expected.

"It's time a Pommier went out into the world and did something else with his life," his father had said.

That was what Rod had done.

He loved medicine. Loved his work. *Newsweek* said he had the arrogance of all top surgeons, that he played God in the operating room. He didn't see it that way. He was a man with a talent for looking at broken bones and torn muscles as parts of an intricate puzzle. It would have been as wrong to deny that talent as it would have been to misuse it....

Which was why he was here, skiing in the snowy Berkshires, instead of back in Manhattan seeing new patients.

Rod sighed again and leaned his elbows on the porch railing.

His discovery of the regenerative matrix technique, a TV reporter had gushed, had opened a door into a new field of orthopedic medicine. Well, yeah. Maybe so, but it was still too soon to know exactly what lay beyond that door. Not everybody would benefit from the surgery. Some might even be damaged by it. "First, do no harm," said the Hippocratic oath. After a while, Rod had wearied of trying to explain that, especially since far too many people thought he just wasn't interested in taking on patients who weren't rich or famous.

The truth was, most of his patients were neither. He chose people based on how well he thought they'd respond to the new technique, not for any other reason. But after he attended a couple of functions run by New York's upper crust and his name and face began appearing on the Sunday society pages of the *Times,* the world was sure it knew all it needed to know about him. Rod had only attended the damned parties because his department chairman had urged him to go.

"For the good of the hospital," she'd said, and it had taken a while before Rod realized that what she really meant was for the charitable donations that his appearance could engender.

Before he knew it, he was a media darling. That was bad enough, but even worse were the endless calls and letters, the people who buttonholed him in restaurants and supermarkets, every last one of them wanting him to perform his miracle on them—and, damn it, he didn't perform miracles. He was a surgeon, and the surgery was risky, delicate and sometimes dangerous, though nobody seemed to want to hear that. The proverbial straw that broke the camel's back came the morning the director of his hospital's board asked him to come by for coffee.

After a few minutes of banal conversation, the man got to the point. There was great interest in the hospital, thanks to Rod's new procedure. NBC was interested in doing a series of interviews. They'd like to meet with Rod in his office, in his home; they'd like to put a camera into the operating room....

No, no and no, Rod had said coldly. He turned to leave, but the director called him back. There was one other thing. The board was wondering, could he see his way clear to increasing the number of surgeries he was doing? For the good of medicine, the director added hastily.

Rod explained that he was doing the optimum number now. He was only operating on patients he was sure would benefit from the technique and he needed more follow-up studies before he'd present a paper to the *New England Journal of Medicine*.

"I admire your caution, Doctor," the director had said, with an unctuous smile. "But there's a fine line between prudence and denying patients the right to be helped. Surely you see that."

What Rod saw was that he needed to rethink his professional life. Other hospitals had been making offers; he'd wanted to stay where he was out of loyalty, but wasn't integrity supposed to accompany loyalty?

He went back to his office, told his secretary not to make any appointments for him from mid-December through mid-January, called his travel agent and asked her to find him a place where he could ski and take it easy and not be anybody's media darling.

That was how he'd ended up in a town so small it didn't even appear on some maps, where nobody shoved a mike or a camera in his face, or asked for his autograph as if he was a rock star.

Rod grinned. He was feeling better than he had in a long, long time. Oh, yeah, some people knew who he was, and he suspected one or two of them were working up to mentioning it for reasons of their own—like Howard Monroe, who skied with the local club. But Rod had developed good antennae; he knew when it was time to say "no, thanks" to an offer of coffee.

He liked it here in Cooper's Corner. Owning a piece of it made him feel good, even if the piece he owned needed work.

A cold wind swept across the face of the mountain. Rod went back into the cabin and took his anorak from the battered sofa where he'd tossed it. He glanced at his watch— 3:05. It would be dark soon, and cold as the arctic. He'd had the electricity turned on, a plumber had checked the pipes and a heating guy had delivered oil right after he'd closed on the deal this morning. The lights worked—he'd checked first thing—and so did the plumbing, but the oil burner wasn't doing anything except making noise.

He stepped out on the porch again.

Shadows were creeping from the edge of the woods, but the narrow road that led up the mountain was still plainly visible. A truck turned onto it. Had to be Seth Castleman, Rod thought, checking his watch again. They had a three-fifteen appointment, and he knew he'd be on time. Castleman was a first-rate carpenter, a fine cabinetmaker and a man who took his responsibilities seriously. If he said he'd meet you at three-fifteen, that was when he met you.

Meeting your obligations was a trait Rod admired. His good mood slipped a notch. That was why he'd have to head back to New York pretty soon, another week or ten days at the most. He hadn't scheduled any new patients but he knew there were people wanting to see him.

Surgery—no neon lights, no cameras, no hoopla—was what he did and what he wanted to get back to doing.

Seth's truck pulled into the driveway. That was another thing Rod had arranged for this morning: a guy with a snowplow to clear the drive. And a good thing, too, considering that more snow was predicted for tonight.

"Hey," Seth called, smiling as he got out of his truck.

"Hey," Rod said, and grinned. He went down the steps, hand outstretched. "Welcome to Pommier's Folly."

Seth chuckled as they shook hands. "Yeah. I heard you really bought the place this morning."

Rod rolled his eyes. "Is there anything that stays confidential in this town?"

"Nope," Seth said cheerfully, "there isn't." He looked at Rod. "Not unless it's really important. Folks tend to respect personal privacy."

Rod nodded. He knew what Seth was telling him. That was one of the reasons he liked it in Cooper's Corner. He was pretty sure almost everybody had figured out who he was—he'd registered under his real name at Twin Oaks, and even though the town was small and out of the way, it bristled with as many TV antennaes and satellite dishes as any other place.

"Anyway," Seth said as they climbed the porch steps and entered the cabin, "if you don't want folks to know what you eat for breakfast, you'd better tear your empty box of cornflakes into little pieces and flush 'em down the toilet."

Rod sighed. "Not this toilet."

"Doesn't work?"

"No. Well, the one in the half bath down here does, if you give it enough time, but the plumber said the one upstairs is a lost cause."

"Hey," Seth said lightly, "it's not like you wanted to keep that pink commode, right?" He unzipped his jacket, put his hands on his hips and took a slow walk through the main room. "You did get Pete Lehigh to come in and take a look, didn't you?"

"The structural engineer? Yeah. He said, same as you, the place is basically sound." Rod watched Seth's face, trying to read his reaction to what he saw. "Well? What do you think?"

Seth took in the boxy dimensions, the metal avocado cabinets visible beyond the Formica breakfast bar, the phony overhead beams and the green shag carpeting.

"Exactly what I thought the first time I saw it," he said, deadpan. "The view's fantastic."

"The well's good, too. Don't leave that out." Rod grinned. "Every little bit counts, right?"

"Uh-huh. Just as long as you don't mind spending the rest of your life redoing the interior."

"Myself, you mean?" The doctor sighed. "Yeah, that's what I said the last time we talked, right? Well, that was just an idea. A crazy one."

"Not so crazy. If you really like working with wood, hammering, sawing, that whole thing can be—"

"Relaxing. Rewarding." Rod walked over to a sofa upholstered in orange corduroy, winced at the sight of it and dropped down on the end cushion. "The truth is, I don't have the skill, even if you were to provide the design and the know-how and half the muscle."

"You're going to bring somebody in."

"I am, yeah. Someone who has the talent to do the work and the ability to act as a general contractor, oversee dealing with the new plumbing, the burner that I suspect is dying...."

Seth nodded. They'd talked about a sort of do-it-yourself project, with Seth providing help, but he wasn't really surprised by the doctor's decision. Disappointed, yes, but not surprised. He'd figured Pommier would realize that his wistful talk of working with his hands was just that. The guy was here, taking time off from the real world, but the real world was where he belonged. And it would take long hours to do this job right—refinishing the handsome wood floor buried beneath the rug, restructuring the rooms, making cabinets and built-in furniture.

He and Rod had talked long enough for Seth to understand what the other man wanted—a quiet, peaceful place where he could recharge his energies—and then Seth had made some suggestions, done a few quick sketches, and Pommier had responded with enthusiasm. A day later, he'd phoned and asked, cautiously, how Seth would feel about Rod doing some of the work himself. He had a buddy in New York, another doctor, who was into woodworking as a hobby and kept telling him how relaxing it was. Seth had listened, said bluntly that as long as Pommier agreed to leave the finer stuff—the furniture—to him, he saw no problem doing it that way.

Then he'd done some daydreaming about the project even though he'd known, deep down, that it wouldn't happen.

Pommier had come to his senses. He'd obviously realized he wouldn't have the time. And he was a big-city guy with money. It was only natural he'd want to bring in somebody from New York or Boston.

"Well," Seth said, smiling, "thanks for letting me know." He came toward Rod, hand outstretched. The doctor got to his feet. "And good luck."

"Yeah. You, too—and believe me, you're gonna need it more than I will." He grinned and clasped Seth's hand. "Heck, I'll just write the checks. You're the one who'll deal with the headaches."

"Headaches?" Seth said, frowning.

"You're guaranteed to have quite a few, turning this sow's ear into a silk purse."

Seth stared at Pommier. "Are you saying you're hiring me as your general contractor?"

"Who else? And before you ask, I checked around. In fact, I talked with Clint Cooper again just last night. No question, you're the man to do the job. Is it a deal?"

"You bet it is."

The men smiled, shook hands, then stepped apart. "Well," the doctor said, "that's done." He strolled across the room, rolled his eyes at the avocado refrigerator and pulled the door open. "Ugly," he said, "but at least it works." He reached inside, held up two bottles of ale. "I figured we'd want to celebrate. Okay with you?"

"Sounds like a plan."

"Great. I'd offer you a glass, but the thought of drinking ale out of something the color of a lime—"

"Say no more." Seth took the bottle Pommier held out.

"Success," Rod said.

The bottles clinked lightly as the two men touched them together. They drank, swallowed, and Seth cleared his throat.

"I want to thank you for this opportunity... Hell, I sound like the speaker at some Chamber of Commerce dinner."

"Forget it. Besides, you may not feel like thanking me once you get started on this project. The more I see of this place, the more I wonder if my head was screwed on straight when I said I wanted to buy it."

"It's a great location, and the basic structure *is* sound. You'll save a small fortune on construction by redoing instead of starting from scratch."

"Yeah, so I keep telling myself." Rod smiled. "Anyway, you're the one who's going to be sweating through this. Me? Well, right now, I'm planning a little trip to Vermont. Then I'll come back here for a while before returning to New York. After that, I'm just going to drive up weekends, stay at Twin Oaks, stop by here and make you a little nuts once in a while, asking if I can drive in a nail or two.''

"It's your house. You can drive in nails anytime you like.''

"Don't let any of my residents hear you say that. Some of them are convinced surgeons are supposed to be like virtuoso piano players. Doing anything that might risk injury to your hands is a crime against medicine and humanity.''

"And you don't agree?''

Rod shrugged. "Injury's always a possibility, I guess, but I can't imagine living a life totally free of risk. What would be the point?''

"I've heard that philosophy before,'' Seth observed quietly.

"But?''

"But, having the risk bite you in the tail isn't quite the same as imagining it.''

Rod hitched a hip onto one of the vinyl-covered counter stools. "You speaking from personal experience?''

"Just an observation.''

"Right. Well, it's true, I suppose. I guess some of us have to learn the hard way.'' Both men took a drink of ale. "Got to admit, you don't strike me as somebody who's avoided risk.''

"I didn't say I avoided it, just that it's a dangerous way to live.'' One corner of Seth's mouth curved upward. "It took me most of my teens to figure that out.''

"You grew up here?''

Seth shook his head. "I grew up in New York.''

"The city? I'd never have believed it.''

"I lived there until I was eighteen.''

"How come you moved up here? Oh, hell. Listen to me. Sorry, Castleman. I'm the one who's big on privacy, and here I am, asking questions. It's just that I'm so accustomed to meeting people who've gone in the other direction. You know, you grow up in, I don't know, Oshkosh, and when you hit the magic age, you pack up and head for New York.''

"Is that what you did?''

"Well, I wasn't raised in Oshkosh.'' Rod tilted the bottle to his mouth. "I'm from Canada, originally. Went to college there, then med school, applied for residency in New York, settled in and never looked back. It just felt like the right place.''

"Not for me. I was born in Brooklyn but I...I shifted around a lot. By the time I finished high school, I'd had about as much of the city as I could stomach. College wasn't on the horizon, not then, but I'd been up in these parts once when I was a kid. Went to summer camp not far from Cooper's Corner for two weeks with a community youth group. Came back with the same bunch on a winter ski trip, one of those inner city things....''

"Like I said, it's none of my business.''

"I don't mind talking about it.'' Seth flashed a quick grin. "I'm a success story. No, I mean it. A couple of my high school teachers would have bet I'd end up in a place with a view of steel bars and barbed wire, but something about this area got to me. I graduated high school, came up here, figured maybe I could find some kind of job before moving on across the country. But I liked it here. The mountains. The sleepy little towns. Plus, I turned out to be pretty good on skis and Jiminy was hiring people....''

A sudden image flashed into his head. Wendy, the day he'd first met her. One of her ski bindings had come loose and she'd sat down on a bench to fix it. He hadn't known that; he'd just figured she was a snow bunny, busy adjusting her skis rather than facing the terrors of the slope. He'd watched her for a couple of minutes, his gaze taking in the long legs encased in black spandex, the riot of dark red curls peeping out from beneath a black knit cap. Finally, he'd put on his best Hey, I'm a Sexy Stud smile—it had worked wonders on lots of girls that winter—strolled up and used what had by then turned into the easiest pickup line in the world, tailor-made for snow bunnies.

"Hi," he'd said. "Would you like some help?"

She'd looked up, and the intensity of those blue eyes had almost struck him speechless. Almost, but not quite. He'd mustered enough presence of mind to add that he was pretty good on skis. He smiled when he said it, in a self-deprecating kind of way that made it clear what he really meant was he was damn good. And, if she liked, he'd be happy to help her adjust her skis, and then take her to one of the easy runs, where he'd show her some basics.

Those gorgeous blue eyes had widened with something halfway between amusement and amazement.

"Thanks," she'd said, very politely, "but I'll be fine."

And by the grace of whatever god had been watching, before he'd dug himself any deeper by saying he'd be glad to show her how to get on and off the chair lift, some dude in an anorak like hers had come along, ignored him, smiled at her and said the team was waiting for her.

The team? When she'd gotten to her feet, Seth had wanted to dig a hole in the snow and crawl in because emblazoned on the back of her jacket and on the dude's was a downhill skier, obviously going a zillion miles an hour.

All New England Ski Team, the logo under the little figure said.

"Castleman?"

Seth blinked. Rod Pommier was looking at him, eyebrows lifted.

"Sorry." Seth cleared his throat. "I was, uh, I was remembering what it was like, coming up here…"

"And deciding to stay. That was the big thing, wasn't it? I mean, some decisions are tough. Whether to stay in a place or leave it, whether to do something you believe in even when you think people are using you...." The doctor gave a quick laugh. "Sorry. I guess it's always hard to make the right decision, but it's got to be even harder if you're an eighteen-year-old kid."

"Yeah." Seth shrugged. "Well, as I said, I kind of liked the town. And I met some people I liked, too."

"A girl." Rod nodded wisely. "Sure. You were eighteen and you met a girl. That was what almost kept me back in Canada. Come to think of it, it's how I knew I wasn't really in love with her. If I had been, I'd never have left. That's why I'm figuring it was a girl who kept you in Cooper's Corner."

Seth thought about denying it, but what was the point? They were talking about the past, and that was where Wendy belonged. Yes, he'd loved her once, but he didn't love her now. Maybe looking back would help keep things in perspective...or maybe, at the very least, it would stop him from waking up and going to sleep thinking about her, which he'd been doing all damned week, despite the bitter words they'd exchanged a couple of hours ago.

"You're right," he said after a minute, "it was a girl."

"Let me guess. Seventeen. Pretty. A cheerleader at the high school."

Seth stood up, crossed the room and ran his hand over the fireplace mantel. "Nice." He rapped it lightly with his knuckles. "Oak. Probably local."

"The girl?"

"The mant—" He looked at Pommier and laughed. "Yeah, she was local. And seventeen. And definitely pretty. In her senior year of high school. But she wasn't a cheerleader. She was a skier. A champion skier."

"Oh, hell." Rod folded his arms over his chest. "Wendy Monroe?"

"Yes." Seth frowned. "How'd you know?"

"Well, how many pretty teenage champion skiers could a town this size have produced a decade ago? I skied with some guys from the Cooper's Corner ski club. They were talking about a girl named Wendy Monroe, said she'd come home again after ten years.''

"Nine."

"Whatever. She was a big name, I gather, back then."

Seth nodded. He put one foot up on the hearth and tucked his hands into the back pockets of his jeans.

"Made the Olympics, too," Rod said.

"Yeah."

"Actually, I recognized the name right away. Unless I've got her mixed up with someone else, I'm pretty sure she wrote to me a few months back."

"You haven't got her mixed up with anybody," Seth said, his tone giving nothing away. "It was Wendy."

"You knew about it?"

"Not then. I hadn't heard from her in a long time. But I saw her last week and she told me she'd been in contact with you."

"Well, that's one way of putting it. She asked me if I'd see her. I said I wouldn't."

"End of story."

"That's right. I'd already decided not to take on new pa—" Rod scowled. "What a coincidence," he said slowly. "The lady writes to me, I come here on vacation and she turns up after all these years away."

Seth didn't answer. Rod gave a slow, thoughtful whistle through his teeth.

"And now it turns out that the guy who's going to do the work on my cabin is her boyfriend."

"Former boyfriend," Seth said quickly. "As in the ex from another...." His eyes narrowed as the other man's words sank in. "What is this? You think I'm in some kind of conspiracy with Wendy Monroe?"

"I think," Rod said carefully, "we need to get this out in the open." He paused. "We're partners when it comes to this project, Seth. And I'd like us to be friends, as well, but you have to know that I don't let my professional life get mixed up with my personal life.''

"If you knew me a little better," Seth said coldly, "you'd know that you just insulted me. You think I've been cozying up to you so I can ask you a favor for Wendy?'' The men glared at each other. Then Seth grabbed the gloves he'd dumped on the counter. "Get yourself another carpenter. I'm out of here.''

"Wait a minute.''

"No." Seth swung away from the door. "No, *you* wait a minute, Pommier. I didn't come to you about this project, remember? You came to me. And I resent the hell out of you thinking I'd play that kind of game.''

"You misunderstood me," Rod said quietly. "Or maybe I said it wrong. Look, man, you have to understand. People have been camping on my doorstep in New York, even bribing the guy who runs the elevator in my building.'' He laughed. "Sorry. You don't need all that laid on you. Okay. I apologize. I just meant... I guess I was saying that I'm not going to change my mind. I already gave your girlfriend my answer. I'm not taking new patients.''

"You've got a short memory, Doc. I told you, she's not my girlfriend. And I'm not sucking up to you for favors for her or anybody else.''

"Damn it.'' The doctor rubbed his hands over his face. "I really screwed up, didn't I?''

"Yes," Seth said sharply, "you did. I don't give a damn if you're a surgeon or Mickey Mouse. You either trust me or we can part company, here and now.''

Pommier nodded. "You're right." He gave a low, unhappy laugh. "Guess I seem paranoid, huh?''

Seth took a long look at the other man. "No," he said after a few seconds. "You just seem like a man who's been hounded into the ground.''

"Still, that's no excuse for seeing a conspiracy everywhere.''

"Yeah." Seth took a deep breath. "Well, I suppose it's only natural, if people are driving you nuts—"

"Remind me to tell you about the eighty-year-old grandmother who smuggled herself into my office in a laundry cart."

"Are you serious?"

"Unfortunately, yes. She'd heard I worked miracles—her word, not mine—and the miracle she wanted was to look like she was twenty again."

Seth laughed, and Rod did, too.

"I'm sorry, man," he said, clearing his throat. "I really am. I never should have implied what I did. I know you're not the kind who'd ask for a favor."

"You're wrong," Seth said quietly. "I might ask, but I wouldn't come at you from the back. If I wanted you to take Wendy on as a patient, I'd say so. I'd give you all the reasons I thought you should do it and count on the fact that you'd make the right decision."

"If you and she were still involved, you mean. Okay. Fair enough."

"Wrong. It has nothing to do with my relationship with her."

"No?"

"I've read about your surgery, Doc. I know it's still somewhat experimental. Risky. Right?"

"Right. I make that clear to each patient, but—"

"But they want it anyway."

Rod nodded his head. "Yeah. And I can understand it. If you can't walk or live a normal life, the risk is worthwhile."

"What if you *can* walk? If you can do everything you once did except pin a number on your back and go down a slope at ninety miles an hour? What if you could live with that, but the person who's been driving you since the day you were born can't?"

"Is that the situation with Wendy Monroe?"

Seth paced across the room. "I'd bet my last dollar this is her father's idea, not hers."

"Well, it's too bad. That she can't stand up to him, I mean."

"She just doesn't see it. She's got this image of herself as a failure unless she can get back into competitive skiing."

"That's how you see it, huh?"

"That's how it is."

"And you see her, how? Forgetting about skiing? Settling down here and doing something else with her life?"

Seth swung toward him. "What's that supposed to mean?"

"Just that it's interesting you're ticked off because you think her father is making life choices for her, and here you are, doing the same thing."

"That's nuts."

"Hey, you said it yourself. If you wanted to ask me to do you a favor and see Wendy Monroe you would, right?"

"So?"

Rod shrugged. "Then you told me you weren't going to, because she shouldn't have the surgery."

Seth's lips compressed. "I didn't say that."

"Maybe not." Rod grimaced. "Listen, man, we're off the subject. Your specialty is cabinetry. Mine is orthopedics. I'm not licensed to be a shrink."

"And a good thing, too, because you've got it all wrong." Seth softened the words with a smile. "So," he said briskly, "what's next? You want a contract drawn up or you want to work this on a handshake?"

"A handshake is fine with me."

The men shook hands.

"Okay," Seth said, "that's done. All we need now is a plan of work. What you want. How much you want to spend. That kind of thing."

"I've got some ideas. If we could get together, say, tomorrow morning...?"

"Sorry." Seth shook his head. "I'm full up tomorrow."

"This evening, then. We could grab a bite at Tubb's."

"Sure." Seth started to zip up his jacket. He walked toward the door, then stopped. "Damn. I almost forgot. I can't make it tonight."

"Heavy date, huh?"

Seth smiled, as if that were the answer. It was simpler that way. Truth was, he was taking Jo to dinner because he'd run out of excuses not to see her. She'd phoned several times over the last few days, suggesting they get together. He knew he needed to end things between them soon, if not tonight. He'd just been putting it off because he was a coward.

Jo deserved a guy who was looking to settle down, and that guy wasn't him. A man who couldn't get another woman out of his head, even if he didn't want her there anymore, had no right to be seeing someone as good, as decent, as kind as Joanne.

"Well," Rod said, "no problem. I'm heading to Vermont for a while—somebody told me about a couple of killer ski runs up there—but I'll call you when I get back. We'll get together then."

"Okay. Fine." The two men walked to the door. Rod shut off the lights and they stepped out onto the porch. The sun had set and the darkness was almost complete.

Seth looked into the sky and turned up his collar. "Snow before morning."

"That's what the weatherman says."

"Well, for once he's gonna be right. If it's okay with you, I'll touch base with Bob Ziller, ask him to take a look at that furnace and the heating system. There's usually trouble when it's been turned completely off for a while."

"You're the man in charge. You think something needs doing, do it."

"Great. Well, see you later."

"Right."

They trotted down the steps, booted feet crunching noisily on the packed snow. Seth headed for his truck, Rod for his SUV. At the last second, Rod turned around.

"Seth?"

Seth swung toward him. "Yeah?"

"You think I'm some rich kid who slid through college and med school on my butt?"

"I don't think about it at all," Seth replied honestly. He grinned. "Disappointed?"

"Not a bit." Rod grinned back. "But it's true. I *was* a rich kid."

Seth laughed. The doctor was okay. "There's a point to this, right?"

"I didn't have to work my way through school, but when I was an undergrad, I wrote a column on finance for the campus newspaper."

"Great," Seth said dryly. "I'm very impressed."

"One day, a girl who did one of the other columns got herself tossed out of school."

"The trials and tribulations of the rich."

"We were desperate, so I said, okay, I'd fill in for her. I ended up doing her damned column for a month, until they finally got somebody else."

"Pommier, I'm sure this is all fascinating stuff, but I'm freezing my tail off. Plus, I have to go home and get ready to—"

"Yeah, yeah. You've got a date. You already told me. The thing is, you've got a date with the wrong girl."

"What?"

"I said—"

"I heard what you said. I'm just trying to figure out what you're talking about."

"The column I wrote for the girl who left school? It was called 'Aunt Agatha's Advice.' Ever hear of it?"

"Mercifully, no."

Rod opened the door to his truck, got inside and put down the window. Seth did the same.

"I'm just giving you my credentials so you'll know the truth of what I'm about to tell you."

"And that is...?"

"You're not over this girl, Castleman. This Wendy Monroe."

"Ten minutes ago you were an orthopedist, not a shrink."

"I'm still an orthopedist." Rod flashed a smile. "I'm also a former Aunt Agatha, and I'm telling you, you have a thing for Wendy."

"You're wrong."

"I'm right. One hundred percent."

Seth searched for a clever comeback, but all he could come up with was the memory of Wendy, sitting on that bench at Jiminy Peak the day he'd first set eyes on her.

"You're wrong," he said again, but so softly that he knew Pommier couldn't hear him. He turned the key to fire the ignition, and drove off into the rapidly encroaching night.

CHAPTER SIX

GINA MONROE WAS WORRIED.

She was ecstatic to have her daughter back home, but she could see that Wendy was unhappy. The lunch with Alison hadn't improved things. If anything, Wendy had come home looking even more depressed.

"Hi, honey," Gina said when Wendy came in the door. "Did you have fun?"

"Yes."

That had been Wendy's entire answer. Just "yes," and Gina hadn't believed it, not for a minute. Her daughter had looked emotionally drained. Gina had wanted to follow her to her room, take her in her arms and ask her what was wrong, but instinct had warned her not to. When Wendy reappeared a couple of hours later, she'd still looked upset. Her mouth had been turned down, her eyes had been shiny with…what? Tears? All Gina knew for certain was that her little girl was unhappy, but about what? Surely not about Seth. Wendy had shown nothing but anger when she'd dealt with him that morning.

After a couple of days, Wendy seemed better, but she was still quieter than usual. Gina knew better than to ask questions. Instead, she whispered her concerns to Howard as they sat reading in bed one night.

"I'm worried, Howard," she said softly. "Wendy's unhappy. She says she's fine, but she's not."

"Well, of course she's not happy, honey. Her leg—"

"It's more than that."

"She's impatient, that's all. She wants to meet Dr. Pommier. I'm doing everything I can to get five minutes alone with him, but—"

The last thing Gina wanted to discuss was Dr. Pommier. She and Howard were on completely opposite sides of that issue.

"I'm sure you're doing your best," she said carefully.

"Oh, I am. We just never seem to be in the same place at the same time." Howard sighed. "He's driven up to Vermont to ski a couple of times, and now that he bought a house here—"

"What house?"

"Not a house, exactly. The old Sullivan place, up on Dragon Mountain. Seems like he's up in Pittsfield, checking out kitchen appliances and such, more than he's in Cooper's Corner."

"How do you know all that?"

"I bumped into Clint at the hardware store before I came home. He mentioned it." Howard's voice took on an edge. "Would you believe Pommier's turned the whole job over to Seth Castleman?"

"Yes. I would. Seth's talented, Howard. And he's a good organizer. Just look how he's built up that business of his."

"I suppose."

Gina closed her book and put it on the nightstand. Howard had always been polite to Seth when he was dating Wendy, and Seth had been respectful to him, but she'd sensed the tension between them.

"Wendy's too young to tie herself down," Howard would say, and Gina would remind him that she'd been exactly their daughter's age when she'd started dating him. But she'd known he wasn't really talking about Wendy being too young. He was talking about her burgeoning success as a skier, and its inevitable end if she married Seth.

There was no reason to get into that discussion anymore.

Wendy's career was over, and so was her relationship with Seth.

Howard put his book aside. "I'm going to try to talk to Pommier at Twin Oaks."

Gina frowned at the change of subject. She didn't want to get into this discussion, either, but there wasn't much choice, not with both her husband and her daughter so determined to buttonhole the doctor.

"What do you mean?"

"I'll find a pretext to stop by there one of these evenings. Maybe I'll get lucky and the doctor will be sitting in the gathering room."

"I don't know what you expect to accomplish. Dr. Pommier's already told Wendy no."

"He read a letter she sent him. That's a lot different from actually talking to her."

"I just want to go on record that I still think this is a bad idea," Gina said stiffly.

Howard reached for her hand and squeezed it. "It's what our girl wants, honey."

"That doesn't make it right. There are a dozen things she could do with her life besides ski." Gina tugged her hand free and looked at him. "She's got a quick mind. And she's creative. Remember those pictures she used to draw? Those stories she used to write?"

Howard sighed. "Wendy could do a lot of things. She will, someday. But first she wants to—"

"I *know* what she wants, Howard. What if it turns out it's not possible?"

"Then she'll have to accept the inevitable. She'll need our support either way," he said gently. "Isn't that right?" The springs creaked as Howard settled under the covers. "I'd never let our girl do anything that would be bad for her. The doctor will tell us if he thinks the operation is right or wrong for Wendy." He ran his hand up and down Gina's arm in slow, comforting strokes. "Don't you think I'm worried about the risks, too?"

Gina looked at him. "I know you love her as much as I do. That's why I can't understand—"

"It's because we come at this differently. I can put myself in Wendy's place. I remember what it's like to have a shot at big-time skiing, and I never even got as close as she did. I never made the nationals, but Wendy—"

"Big-time skiing isn't everything."

"You're right. It isn't. It's doing whatever you can to reach for a dream that's everything. And if getting back on skis is our daughter's dream, I'm going to do my very best to help her achieve it."

"No matter what the cost?" Gina said bitterly. It was the first time she'd let the full extent of her anger show. She saw the shock on her husband's face and didn't know who she'd shocked the most, him or herself.

"Gina, how can you say that? Didn't I just tell you I'm worried, too? My God, do you really think I'd encourage her to go ahead with an operation if the doctor says he's not one hundred percent sure it's safe?"

Nothing in life was safe. Hadn't Wendy's fall proved that? Gina almost said as much to Howard, but she knew she'd already hurt him enough, that he was torn between wanting to protect Wendy and wanting her to be happy. She sighed, put her arms around him and held him until he fell asleep. Then she rose quietly, slipped on her robe and went down the hall to Wendy's room. She stared at the closed door, then leaned her forehead against the cool wood.

Howard was right. Wendy was upset because of her impatience to meet the doctor—and yet there was more to her withdrawal. Gina was sure of it. Something else was worrying their daughter.

The next evening, Howard said he was going out for a while. To Twin Oaks, Gina suspected, though he didn't say

it. She made some popcorn, put the bowl between Wendy
and her on the sofa in the family room and clicked on the
TV. She surfed the channels until she found a news show.
After a while, she hit the mute button, put her feet up on
the coffee table and looked at Wendy.

She'd planned how to approach this. Subtly. Carefully.
She wouldn't say anything to put her daughter on the defensive.

"Wendy? What's troubling you, baby?" So much for
subtlety. Still, she was glad she'd finally asked the question.

Wendy looked at her, then back at the silent picture on
the TV screen.

"Nothing. I mean, nothing but what's been troubling me
all along. I wonder if Daddy's ever going to find a way to
talk to Dr. Pommier."

In for a penny, in for a pound, Gina thought. "I know
about that. But I think something else is upsetting you.
Something more personal."

Wendy lifted her eyebrows. "What could be more personal than my leg?"

Gina ignored that. It had been offered as a diversion and
she wasn't going to be diverted. Not tonight.

"You've been awfully quiet since you had lunch with
Alison." She paused. "I thought seeing her would do you
a world of good, but you came home sort of down, and
you're still down."

"I'm probably just tired. The flight home—"

"That was a week ago."

"Well, the change, you know? From one place to another—"

"Did you and Alison talk about Seth?" More subtlety,
Gina thought unhappily. She couldn't believe she'd blurted
that out, but the idea had popped into her head without
warning. One look at her daughter's face and she knew
she'd hit the mark.

"Why on earth would we talk about Seth?"

"Well, you'd just had that…that little blowup with him so I just thought… I wondered…"

"No need to wonder. We didn't talk about him. End of story."

"I'm not prying, sweetie. I'm just worried about you."

"Well, there's nothing to worry about. Seth is history. I'm over him. He's over me. He's involved with someone and that's fine. Oh, don't look so stricken, Mother." Wendy rose to her feet and limped across the room. She grabbed a magazine from the small wooden rack, limped back and sat down again. "People in this town know what you eat for breakfast. Did you think I wouldn't find out about Seth's girlfriend?"

"Oh, baby. That explains why you're upset."

"I am not upset. Why would I be?" Wendy snapped open the magazine. "I don't want to talk about Seth. Okay?"

"Okay."

Mother and daughter remained locked in silence, Gina pretending to watch TV, Wendy pretending to read, until Howard returned an hour later. Wendy looked up, her face alive with expectancy, and Gina knew her daughter figured he'd gone to find the doctor.

But Pommier hadn't been at the bed-and-breakfast, not in the public rooms at any rate. And Gina, though consumed with guilt, kept thinking, *Please, please, let the doctor go back to New York.*

There was no such thing as risk-free surgery. Besides, despite what Wendy said, Gina wasn't at all sure that not being able to ski was the heart of the problem. Something more was troubling her daughter, something that wasn't as visible as her limp but was every bit as disturbing.

Maybe what she and Wendy needed was the chance to spend some time together. Alone. Sort of a girls' night out, the way they used to when Wendy was in high school. They hadn't managed to have them often—not anywhere near often enough—because of Wendy's grueling schedule. But every now and then they'd taken off together, just the two of them, for dinner somewhere special, and they'd talk and laugh and have fun.

A girls' night out. Definitely. Gina picked up the phone and made reservations. She wasn't going to give Wendy the chance to say no.

GINA HAD CHOSEN the restaurant with care. The food at the Purple Panda was delicious, the place itself was charming and it took more than forty minutes to drive there.

She wanted to have lots of time to chat with Wendy. There was something about riding through the night on dark country roads that tended to loosen a person's tongue.

Wrong, she thought as they sped along the dark roads. Wendy hadn't said more than half a dozen words during the entire trip. Gina kept up a one-sided conversation, babbling away about nothing in particular and getting back mostly "uh-huh" and "um-hmm" in response.

It was a relief when they finally reached Stockbridge and drove past the big, stately homes that lined both sides of the wide street, which narrowed as it approached the town green.

"Well," Gina said brightly, "here we are." She slipped the Volvo into a parking space. "I'm really looking forward to dinner tonight. You'll love this place, and we can just sit back and relax. Everything's been so, um, so rushed lately.…"

"I can just imagine. Exams are coming up soon, right?"

A complete sentence, at last. But Gina had to stop and think. "Exams?" she said as they got out of the car. "Oh. Oh, you mean at school. Math quizzes and English essays. Right. My kids are all excited."

Wendy made a face. "They're terrified, Mom, not excited."

"Of what? They'll all do fine. If anybody's terrified, it

should be me.'' She took Wendy's arm as they stepped onto the sidewalk. ''Careful. The street's probably slippery.'' The night was cold, the air crisp; a thin skim of frosty snow crackled under their boots. ''When I think of the endless hours I'll have to put in, marking all those tests...''

''I could help you with them.''

''Yes, you could.'' Gina laughed. ''You don't really expect me to be polite and turn down such an offer, do you?''

''Actually, I've been thinking about some kind of job.''

''A job? But—'' *You won't be here long enough to hold down a job,* Gina thought. Or was her luck turning? Had Wendy changed her mind about what she wanted?

''I know what you're thinking. I won't be here very long.'' The Purple Panda was just ahead. The door was trimmed with tiny bells that tinkled merrily when Wendy pulled it open. ''But Daddy mentioned that the people who own Twin Oaks—''

''Clint and Maureen,'' Gina said as the door swung shut behind them.

''That's it. He said they were thinking about finding someone to help out evenings.''

''Doing what?''

''Oh, nothing very complicated.'' Wendy peeled off her gloves and put them in her pockets. ''Answer the phone, hang around the gathering room to serve coffee or tea or wine. They just got their liquor permit.''

''Well,'' Gina said cautiously, ''you might enjoy it. You know, getting out, meeting some people from out of town—''

''Meeting Rod Pommier, if I'm lucky.''

''Oh, Wendy.''

''Oh, Mother,'' Wendy teased. ''Come on, get that look off your face. Mmm, this place is handsome. When did it open?''

Gina knew when she was being taken on a detour. ''Last summer,'' she said, and sighed.

"And what's that luscious smell?"

"Cloves. Maybe allspice."

"Allspice. Isn't that what you used to put into that incredible beef and beer thingy?"

Detoured and derailed, Gina thought, but that was okay if it meant getting Wendy to think about something other than whatever was making her look so glum.

"It's known as *boeuf carbonade,* if you please, my darling daughter." Gina took Wendy's hand as they eased through a knot of people toward the hostess. "After all these years of eating French cooking, you should know there's a difference between a 'beef thingy' and something *française.* And no, that's not allspice in *carbonade,* it's thyme."

"Yeah, yeah, yeah." Wendy rolled her eyes. "You just like to remind people you're a fancy cook."

"Not me!" Gina laughed and turned to the hostess. "The name's Monroe. I reserved a table for two."

"Good evening, Ms. Monroe. Your table will be ready in just a few minutes. Would you like to wait at the bar?"

The bar was crowded, too, but they were lucky and snagged two high-backed stools. Gina ordered a glass of white wine. Wendy ordered merlot.

"Pretty place." Wendy ran a finger lightly along the top of the bar. "Zinc. Reminds me of Paris."

"The food will, too. Well, maybe not quite Paris, but it's good. I convinced your father to come here once, right after it opened." Gina smiled as the bartender put their glasses of wine in front of them. "Thanks. Where was I? Oh. That time I came here with your father. 'This is it?' he asked me when he opened the menu. 'Soups, salads and homemade bread?' I pointed out that some of the soups were more like stews, but he wasn't fooled, not for a minute."

Wendy grinned. "Not Daddy's idea of a meal, huh?"

"He was a good sport about it, but as soon as we got home, he went into the kitchen and put together one of those sandwiches of his. Two slabs of rye bread, mustard, mayo—''

''—and whatever isn't nailed down.'' Wendy sipped her wine. ''He still eats those things?''

''He does,'' Gina said, continuing with their light, breezy chat, even as part of her looked on in delighted surprise. Maybe this girls' night out hadn't been such a bad idea. Wendy was smiling; she was animated. Driving here, Gina figured they'd sit through their meal in silence, but it looked as if the evening might turn into a success.

Idly, she twirled the stem of her wineglass in her fingers. ''Have I told you how lovely it is, having you home?''

''Only a couple of thousand times,'' Wendy said with a little smile.

''It's such a joy, waking up in the morning and knowing you're right down the hall, that I don't have to wonder how you are or where you are, that I don't have to look at the clock and think about what time it is in Paris before I call you.''

''Mom.'' Wendy took her mother's hand. ''It was the same for me.''

''Was it? Paris is such a glamorous city....''

''But it wasn't home. Honestly, I'm glad to be back.''

It was true, Wendy thought in surprise. She was happy to be back. And happy to be here tonight. All week, her mother had begged her to tell her what was wrong, but how could she when she didn't know herself? She'd felt...what? A heaviness within her breast. A sort of melancholy that just wouldn't go away.

She'd told herself it was because she was edgy and impatient about meeting Dr. Pommier, but down deep she'd known it wasn't entirely that.

Her mother kept saying she needed to get out, do things. Well, maybe she was right. There was something pleasant about being out tonight, surrounded by the sound of laughter and the smell of good food. Maybe she'd been silly to

worry so much about what people would say when they
saw her. Or to worry about how she'd feel, seeing Seth.

Nothing. That was what she felt. He just made her angry,
that was all. He was so stubborn. So mule-headed. So
damned arrogant and self-righteous—

"Ladies? Your table is ready."

"Wonderful," Gina said. "Sweetie? You ready?"

"Absolutely," Wendy said brightly. Her mother picked
up her glass, slid from the stool and followed the hostess.
Wendy fell in behind her.

The hostess led them through the long, crowded room to
a table near the fireplace. Their server would be along in
just a minute, she said, and placed their menus before them.
Gina shrugged off her coat and let it drape over the back
of her chair. She looked at Wendy, who did the same thing.

"I love sitting back here. You get a view of the entire
room this way. Isn't it lovely?"

"Very." Wendy opened her menu. "What's good?"

"Everything." Gina smiled, supposedly at the menu, but
really at the pleasure of seeing her daughter without a frown
puckering her forehead. "Try the black bean soup, if you
want something that'll really warm you up. Or the cheddar
cheese bisque."

"Mmm. That's for me. The cheese bisque." Wendy
closed the menu and cleared her throat. "Mom? Thanks for
bringing me here."

"Don't be silly. It's my pleasure."

"You know what I mean. I've been such a mope, and
you know what? You were right. It's good getting out."

"To the big city," Gina said, and laughed.

The waiter took their order. The women drank their wine,
munched on salty breadsticks and had the kind of free-
roving conversation they hadn't had since Wendy had come
home.

Since the accident, Gina thought, and felt the unwanted

blur of tears. She blinked them back but it was too late. Wendy had noticed.

"Mom? What's the matter?"

"Nothing," Gina said.

They looked at each other. Then they began to laugh.

"Talk about role reversal..." Wendy sat back as the waiter served their salads. "You were crying," she said softly.

"No. Well, maybe just a little." Gina picked up her fork and stabbed an endive leaf. "I was thinking how nice it is, having dinner with my favorite daughter."

"Your only daughter," Wendy answered, and they laughed again at the old joke. They ate in silence for a few minutes. "Mom?"

Gina looked up. "What, dear?"

"There was another English teacher in the school where I taught in Paris." She put down her fork and folded her hands in her lap. "Actually, I don't think I've told you much about my work there. The method I used, I mean. Have I?"

Not a word, Gina thought. "No," she said, "you haven't."

Wendy nodded. "Well, what I'd do was give my students a few weeks of the basics. Vocabulary mostly, with a little bit of grammar tossed in."

When the waiter appeared with their soup, Wendy sat back a moment until he'd served them.

"After that," she continued, once he had gone, "we'd just talk. It worked really well, and one day the other teacher asked me if I could show her my plan book. I said I didn't have one, that I used the 'deal with it as it comes' method. And she said, 'Ah, of course. Deal with it the way one deals with life.'" Wendy swallowed dryly. "I want you to know I'm trying to do that. Deal with it as it comes— and I know you're opposed to what comes next."

"I just want you to be sure that having the operation is the right thing, Wendy. Can you understand that?"

"Yes. Absolutely. But the thing is, Mom, this is *my* life. I need to deal with it in my own way. I need to be me again."

"Oh, baby, you *are* you! Just because you got hurt—"

"I didn't just get hurt," Wendy said fiercely. "I let everybody down. My team. My town. My coach. You and Daddy."

"Never, Wendy! And surely, never me."

"Yes, you. But most of all, the person I let down was…" *Seth.*

At first she thought she'd actually said his name, but her mother was still looking at her, waiting for the rest. Wendy clamped her lips together, horrified at how close she'd come to a truth nobody could ever know.

"Wendy."

Her mother reached across the table for her hand. If she touched her…God, if she touched her, it was all going to come tumbling out—that she hadn't just disappointed them all, she'd destroyed the one dream that really mattered. Not the one her father thought she cherished, but the true dream, the secret dream…

"I'm all right," Wendy said. She put her spoon on her plate, her napkin on the table, then pushed back her chair. Gina started to rise, too. Wendy shook her head. "No. No, thank you, Mom, but—but you don't have to come with me. I just…I have to go to the ladies' room. You stay here. I'll be—"

Seconds ago, she'd thought of Seth. Now, as she stood up, she saw him. She could almost feel the blood drain from her face.

"Wendy?"

And it was silly, wasn't it? Hadn't she just told Gina her motto? Deal With It As It Comes, because there wasn't a way in the world you could prepare for life ahead of time.

"Baby, please, what is it?"

You could never plan on anything...but maybe, just maybe, in an area as small as this tiny piece of New England, she should have been smart enough to have at least anticipated coming face-to-face with Seth seated two tables away, holding hands with the woman who'd replaced her.

It wouldn't have helped.

Nothing could have prepared her for how she'd feel to see him with another woman, or for the sharpness of the pain that knifed through her heart.

CHAPTER SEVEN

THE LADIES' ROOM was empty, except for a whimsical toy panda dressed in a purple ski suit that sat on the marble vanity, smiling at Wendy as she ran cold water into the sink and splashed handfuls of it on her face.

After a few seconds, she shut off the water, lifted her head and looked at herself in the mirror. A woman with suspiciously bright eyes and blotchy skin stared back at her.

The stuffed panda was still smiling.

"What are *you* looking at?" Wendy grumbled, and doused her face with more cool water.

It was ridiculous to be so upset at seeing Seth with another woman. He had a new life. So did she—or she would have, once she had the operation. One of the risks in coming back to Cooper's Corner had been the probability of seeing Seth, and it had already happened twice.

She'd survived both encounters.

So what if this was a little different? He was on a date. Well, that was his prerogative. It was perfectly normal for him to be here with a woman, deep in conversation, so deep that he hadn't noticed her sitting just a couple of tables away.

"I'm fine with that," Wendy said to the panda.

She tore a paper towel from the dispenser, soaked it in cold water and pressed it to her face. Her cheeks felt as if they were on fire. She couldn't go back out there like this, skin hot, eyes glittering as if there were tears in them.

The past was the past. If she had a dollar for every time she'd said that the last few days...

"I'd be a millionaire," she told the panda, just as the door opened. A teenage girl shot her the kind of look any sane person would give someone conversing with a panda wearing a purple ski suit. Wendy thought about explaining, decided against it, took a steadying breath and left. Outside in the narrow hall, she paused, curved her lips into a smile and stepped into the dining room.

The first thing she saw was her mother's white, pinched face.

The second was Seth, leaning across the table and holding the woman's hands, focusing so intently on her that he was oblivious to everything else.

"There you are," Gina said, when Wendy reached their table and sat down. She scooted forward and leaned in close. "Oh, baby, I saw."

"Saw what?" Wendy asked calmly, picking up her spoon. The soup, so delicious moments ago, tasted like wormwood. "Mmm. This is wonderful."

"Wendy, did you hear me? I know what upset you. I saw Seth."

"Do I look upset? Eat your soup, Mom."

"If you weren't upset, why did you run off like that?"

Wendy looked at Gina. "I admit I was...surprised. I'm fine now." She spooned up some soup. "The soup's getting cold."

"Wendy, this is silly. We wanted to have a fun evening. Let's just get our check and go someplace else."

"No!" Wendy leaned forward, voice pitched low. If she left now, she'd be running away, and why on earth should she run? She'd found her resolve in a one-sided dialogue with a toy panda and she was going to keep it. "You were the one who kept telling me I needed to get out and do stuff, Mom. Well, here I am, out with you, having dinner, and I'm not going to split just because an old boyfriend is here with his date.''

Gina looked unconvinced. "Are you sure?''

"Yes, absolutely." Wendy smiled, shoveled another spoonful of soup into her mouth and choked it down. "Come on. Talk to me. Tell me about school. Do you still have the same horrid principal, or did the board finally get rid of her?''

"We have someone new," Gina said, with obvious reluctance.

Wendy nodded, asked another question. Her mother answered. The topic was an old one; Wendy knew Gina had been one of the teachers who'd lobbied for a change. If she got her mother talking about it, maybe she'd carry the conversation.

It took a few minutes, but it worked. Gina was passionate on the subject of giving good teachers administrative support, not dictums, and she got caught up in the topic. Unfortunately, Wendy didn't. She tried hard, but her attention kept wandering to Seth and the scene playing out at his table. It was like cruising past an accident on the highway. You didn't want to look but you just couldn't help it.

She couldn't see much of the woman, only her slender back, straight shoulders and long, straight, silky blond hair, the kind that she probably never had to gel or blow-dry into submission. She was undoubtedly pretty, too. Pretty girls had always hung around Seth when they were going together. He was oblivious to his appeal, as if he'd never looked in the mirror and noticed that he was good-looking. He'd been as polite and friendly to the ski bunnies who asked for his help getting up on their feet as he was to the experienced skiers whose bindings seemed to be too loose whenever he was in sight.

Wendy had teased him unmercifully.

"Hi, Seth," she'd say in a simpering whisper. "Could big ol' you help little ol' me? Pretty please? I want to do a snowplow. Oh, no, don't show it to me. Put your arms around me and demonstrate.'' Then she'd bat her lashes. ''I'll learn a lot faster that way.''

Seth would tease her right back. ''At least all of that goes on in front of you,'' he'd say. ''What about all those guys who look at you as if you were a mug of hot soup on a cold day when you're off skiing in Vail and I'm here in New England?''

''I don't have time to flirt,'' she'd say with mock indignation. ''I spend those days working.''

''Yeah?'' he'd say. ''What kind of work?''

Which would be her cue to give him a come-hither smile and slip her arms around his neck.

''Not this kind,'' she'd purr, and then she'd kiss him, and the teasing would give way to passion.

The truth was, they'd both had eyes only for each other, right from the beginning. The differences between them— she longed for Olympic gold and he for a quiet life with her—hadn't mattered. They'd loved each other enough to get past those things.

''...visit my classroom,'' Gina said, ''and you'll see...''

What Wendy saw was that they'd been too young to realize that it wouldn't have worked. They were too different. Hadn't what happened to her proved that? Her dream had destroyed his. One bad fall and their future together had ended.

Years before, she'd taken the first step toward setting them both free. She'd sent Seth away, and look how well it had worked. He'd moved on, gone from holding down a casual job on a ski slope and tucking in occasional business courses to becoming a skilled craftsman. In a part of her heart, she'd always known she'd have held him back. Her career would have had to come first, had they married.

Now he'd found someone to love. A woman who held his attention as she'd once held it.

"Mom?" Wendy interrupted Gina in midsentence. "What's her name?"

Her mother glanced at the other table, looked quickly away and pushed aside her soup bowl.

"Who?" she said, with an innocent lift of her eyebrows.

"Mother…"

Gina sighed. "Joanne. Joanne Cabot. And don't ask me for details because I don't know anything more."

"What does she do? Does she live in Cooper's Corner? How long has Seth been seeing her?"

"She's a legal secretary. She lives in New Ashford and he's been seeing her for two or three months."

Wendy almost smiled. "You don't know anything more, huh?"

"No. Not a thing."

"Yeah, well, I'm glad he's happy."

"Are you?"

"Yes. Why wouldn't I be? I—I cared for him once, re-member?"

But *she* wasn't happy. The ugly truth was that it hurt to see the warmth in his amber eyes as he looked at another woman the same way he'd looked at her that last night they'd been together, when he'd asked her to give up Lil-lehammer and marry him.

Seth, she thought, *oh, Seth.*

He glanced up as if he'd heard her, and his eyes widened with shock. The woman with him—Joanne—must have no-ticed because she turned around, looked over her shoulder and saw Wendy.

Her face drained of color. She pulled her hands free of Seth's. He said something. She answered. He spoke again and she stiffened.

Wendy pushed back her chair.

"Wendy," Gina said with quiet urgency, "what are you doing?"

"I'm going over to say hello to Seth and his girlfriend," Wendy replied calmly.

"I don't think that's a good idea."

"It's the right thing to do, Mother. They just saw me. They're not happy about it, and that's silly. There's no reason for all of us to be uncomfortable. We're adults."

It was a lie. An adult wouldn't hear her pulse hammering in her ears as she rose to her feet and walked past the fireplace. An adult wouldn't feel her lips tremble as she smiled.

But Seth wasn't smiling. He was glowering, and he stood up just as she got to his table.

"Hi," she said brightly. "I just noticed you sitting over here and I thought I'd—"

"Wendy." His voice was low. "Your timing's bad."

Wendy's hard-won smile faded at the edges. "So much for being adult," she started to say, but Joanne made a strangled sound, shot to her feet and hurried toward the door. Seth snarled an oath, dumped a handful of bills on the table and went after her.

Wendy could almost hear the silence; she could feel people trying not to stare. She wanted to crawl away, to become invisible. Instead, she walked back toward her mother. Gina was already standing in the aisle with Wendy's coat in her arms.

"Go on," Gina said quietly. "I'll meet you outside."

Wendy nodded, kept her eyes straight ahead and made her way to the door.

"How was everything?" the hostess asked as she brushed past her.

"Fine," she answered. What else could she say? Surely not that she should never have come home, not even for the hope of five minutes alone with Rodney Pommier.

She stepped out the door into a night that was black as ink and cold as only these hills could be in midwinter. The darkness and the cold were welcome. One wrapped her in blessed anonymity; the other was a balm to her hot-cheeked humiliation. She yearned for her own car so she could escape, but she had to wait for her mother.

Wendy turned up her collar, put on her gloves and headed around the side of the building, away from people and the bright fairy lights that adorned the door and windows of the restaurant.

She'd spent half the flight from France to the U.S.A. suffering over how tough it was going to be to face people who'd known her when she was whole, how awful it would be to have them look at her, and know they were pitying her.

The bittersweet truth was that nothing was as old as yesterday's fame. Nobody had stared at her...

Until now.

She bit back a moan.

Every eye had been on her. The entire restaurant had watched her embarrassment, watched her endless walk to the door in defeat.

"Wendy."

Her hand flew to her throat. She whirled around and saw Seth stepping out of the shadows.

Despair, rage, humiliation...a dozen emotions swept through her. Seth was the cause of them all.

"Get away from me!"

"Wendy, please. I know you're upset—"

"Upset? Why would I be upset? Just because you made me look like a fool?"

"I'm sorry."

"I don't give a damn if you're sorry or not."

Seth's hands clamped onto her shoulders. He stepped around her and planted himself in her path.

"Grow up," he said roughly. "You're the one who came to my table. You're the one who caused a difficult situation to get worse."

"What I did was grown-up. You behaved like a—a spoiled child."

Seth's hands tightened on her. "I knew you were there."

"That's why I went to your table. I just wanted—"

"From the minute you walked into the restaurant and all through dinner, I sensed you. Damn it, don't look at me that way. Is it so crazy to think I wouldn't know you were near me?" His mouth thinned. "But I concentrated on Jo. It was the right thing to do."

"How nice for you both," Wendy said with a polite smile. "Now, please, get out of my way."

"I didn't dare look at you. I knew I'd never stop looking, once our eyes met."

"You know what, Seth? There are names for a man who takes one woman to dinner and—and comes on to another." Wendy peered past him. "Where's your girlfriend? What excuse did you give for leaving her in your truck while you came after me?"

"Jo left. She came in her own car."

"Well, be sure and tell her I didn't mean to upset her and that she doesn't have to run when she sees me. The field's clear. It has been for a long time."

"Damn it, Wendy!" Seth's eyes were dark with anger. "Will you listen to me?" He took a deep breath. "The reason I was less than gracious when you showed up was because of Jo."

"Really?" Wendy said sweetly.

"She's a wonderful woman."

"Terrific."

"She's kind and generous and—"

"And she loves animals. You know what, Seth? I'm not very interested in a rundown on her character."

"She cares for me. A lot. And…" He took a breath. "And I just broke up with her."

"That's too damned…" Wendy's eyes widened. "You what?"

Seth let go of her and ran his hands through his hair, something she recalled him doing whenever he was upset.

"That's what you walked in on," he said grimly, "me taking half the meal to work up enough courage to tell her so long, stay well, it's been nice but it's over. I'd gotten just past that point when you came along."

Wendy sagged back against the brick wall. A spurt of elation swept through her, followed quickly by the knowledge that it was wrong to feel anything but compassion for a woman she didn't know and a man who'd once been her lover.

"I'm sorry. I had no idea…"

"She wanted…she wanted more commitment than I could give. She deserves better than that. It had become an issue and we'd been drifting apart." It was close enough to the truth. Seth wasn't sure what had gone wrong; he only knew that saying any more would be saying too much. "And then I got to the worst part, where I told Jo that I thought it would be best if we stopped seeing each other. I looked up and there you were, big as life, standing next to the table."

"Seth." Wendy put her hand on his sleeve. "I'm so sorry. I just wanted to do the right thing. I mean, I saw you and—and Joanne, and I thought about how we'd probably keep tripping over each other and that I couldn't run away each time…."

She stopped, caught her breath as she realized what she was saying, how much she was saying, but it didn't matter. Seth hadn't been listening. He was looking at her in a way that made her heartbeat quicken.

"Nine years," he said. "Nine long, endless years you stayed out of my life, and all of a sudden, here you are."

"I came back to Cooper's Corner, not to you."

"Every time I turn around, you're there."

"Every time *you* turn around?" Wendy's chin came up. "Don't think you can lay this on me! *I* didn't come bursting into *your* house. *I* didn't follow *you* to the Burger Barn. And tonight, when I tried to do the...the polite thing—"

"Aren't you going to ask me what Jo said when I told her we weren't going to see each other anymore?"

"I am not! Frankly, I don't much—"

"She said, 'Is it because of Wendy Monroe? Is it because she's back and you never got over her?'"

"I hope you told her the truth. I'd hate to think you used me as an excuse to break up with the woman."

Seth closed his hands around her wrists. "You are some piece of work, you know that?"

"Let go."

"You think you're the only one whose world turned upside down when you took that fall? I've got news for you, lady. My world took a pretty bad hit, too, but you never gave a damn about that."

"Okay. That's enough. I don't have to stand here and listen to this garbage!"

Wendy pulled free and started toward the restaurant. Seth went after her, caught her arm and turned her toward him.

"You want to get on with your life? Well, so do I. But I can't. And if you're honest, you'll admit that you can't, either." He moved closer to her, his shoulders blocking out the night, this man who had once been her lover but who had become a stranger. "That's what I told Jo. I said I didn't know what in hell I felt for you, but my life has to be on hold until I find out."

Wendy was trembling. From the cold, she told herself, surely not from the feel of Seth's hands, from the emotions she could see warring in his eyes.

"We need to settle things, Wendy."

"We did settle things." Her voice was a papery whisper and she cleared her throat and started again. "We broke up."

"No," he said bitterly, "*we* didn't break up. You broke us up."

"It's the same thing."

"The hell it is! When you left Cooper's Corner, you were my girl. Then you took that fall and you didn't want to know me." His hands tightened on her. He stepped closer, cupped her elbows, drew her to him. "I've waited a long time for answers, but, by God, I'm going to get them."

"The answers you want belong to the past."

"That's the trouble," he said gruffly. "I don't know what's in the past and neither do you."

"You're wrong—"

"Am I?"

She saw the warning flash in his eyes and she put her hands up to ward him off, but his mouth came down on hers, hard and hungry, just as it used to on those hot nights in his cold truck up on Sawtooth Mountain, and even as she told herself she didn't want this, she felt the need for him ignite deep inside her.

He felt it, too. She knew he did, because his mouth softened on hers and his kiss became tender and sweet, and suddenly she was eighteen and he was nineteen, and nothing mattered but each other.

She trembled, moaned Seth's name. He groaned, thrust his fingers into her hair, kissed her again and again, and she opened her mouth to his, caught up in the moment, in the memory, in a dream.

Somewhere in the distance, a door opened and closed. Voices carried on the still night air. "Good night," people called. "Drive safely." Footsteps crunched on the snow-crusted pavement.

"Come with me," Seth whispered against Wendy's mouth. "Sweetheart, come with me."

"Wendy? Wendy? Where are you?"

Lost, Wendy thought. *Oh God, I'm lost!*

"Wendy? Are you out here?"

"My mother," she gasped, twisting her face away from Seth's.

"I don't care." His voice was thick with desire. "Come with me."

"I can't."

"Yes. You can. You can do whatever you want, sweet-heart. We're not kids anymore. We don't need anybody's permission to be together." He gathered her closer in his arms. "Nothing's changed. Not a thing, in all these years."

"You're wrong." Wendy slapped her hands against Seth's chest and pulled back in his arms. "Everything's changed. Haven't you figured that out yet?"

"Wendy? Wendy! Oh, there you are. I've been calling and call—" Gina's eyes widened. She looked from one flushed face to the other. "Oh. I'm sorry. I had no idea... Look, why don't you two just—I mean, I'll drive home and you two can..."

"That's all right, Gina." Seth's voice was cool. "Wendy and I were just catching up on old times. Isn't that right, Wendy?"

Wendy lifted her chin. "Good night, Seth."

She waited for him to say goodbye but he didn't. He just went on looking at her while her throat constricted and her heart beat faster and faster, and then he took a step toward her, as if they were alone in the universe instead of standing on a street corner with an audience of one.

"This isn't finished," he said quietly.

"It was finished years ago."

"I used to think about the kind of woman you'd grow up to be."

"This is all very interesting, Seth, but my mother and I—"

"Your mother's on her way to her car."

"All the more reason for me to say good-night."

"Not yet," he said gruffly. "Not until we get things set-tled."

"We'll never settle anything this way. And I don't want

to quarrel whenever we see each other.'' Wendy tried a tentative smile. ''Can't we just be friends?''

''Friends?'' He caught her by the wrist, moved closer until they were a breath apart, until she had to tilt her head back to meet his eyes. ''We have too much history just to be friends. When we talked in the diner, you handed me some garbage about knowing it was over between us. I prettied it up with how we'd only been kids. And you know what? Not a damn bit of it was the truth.''

''Does it really matter, after all these years?''

''Yeah. Yeah, it matters. I was a kid, head over heels in love, so crazy about you that I was happy to wait for you until there was nothing to keep us apart. No coaches. No crowds. No you flying off to Colorado and me staying behind. I used to daydream about it, you know? The time we'd finally be together.''

He was right, and that made it even worse. He'd never demanded anything of her except her love, and what had she given him in return? Oh God, if he knew the truth…

''Seth.'' Her eyes swam with tears. ''Please. Let's just say goodbye.''

''Winning that damned medal was all you talked about, all you lived for, but I figured okay, I could understand it. I could deal with it because we had a future all planned. That was what I hung on to. What it would be like when you married me, when we settled down and had kids.''

The pain that shot through her at his words was almost unbearable. Wendy clamped her lips together, certain she was going to tell him her awful secret…certain when she did he'd hate her even more than he had for the last nine years.

Instead, she wrenched her arm free. She'd had years to prepare for this moment and she'd been doing fine until she'd been foolish enough to let him kiss her.

''That's exactly why I broke off with you.''

''What are you talking about?''

"That future you had all planned." She took a deep breath, dug her hands into her pockets to stop their shaking. "I lay in that hospital bed in Oslo, staring at the ceiling. You know how they say your life flashes in front of you when you're dying? Well, what flashed in front of me was the future I wasn't going to have."

She dragged another breath into her lungs. The winter night was turning as frigid as the look in Seth's eyes. She could almost feel her heart turning to ice, too.

"And that was when it came to me. The future I wasn't going to have had nothing to do with the one you wanted. Settling down. A house in the country. Kids." She heard her voice quaver and she curled her hands into fists, felt the sharp bite of her fingernails into her palms. "Those dreams were yours, not mine. I wanted to ski until I was too old to pick up a pair of poles. And...and I didn't know how to tell you that."

She saw his face go white. *Don't stop,* she told herself fiercely, *just keep going.* She didn't want to do this but it needed doing. He didn't want to believe they had no future, but she knew better. How else to convince him except like this?

"What saved me then was determination. I swore that if I lived, I'd find a way to compete again. I knew you'd try to talk me out of it, and I decided to do what I had to do, for my own survival. It was better to break things off cleanly than to let them drag on. If I hurt you in the process, Seth, I'm sorry."

She watched the color come back to his face, watched his eyes and mouth harden.

"So what you're telling me," he said, "is that there never was a future for us."

"It isn't that simple."

"The hell it isn't. It's as simple as a dumb kid spinning dreams for a girl who never shared them."

"I didn't know, not until the accident."

"Sure you did. That's why it didn't mean a damn to you when we spent weeks apart, while you were off skiing in some tournament your old man said you needed to win."

"My father has nothing to do with this."

"He has everything to do with it!" Seth's eyes narrowed, and the fury she saw burning in their depths stole her breath away. "Amazing, isn't it? There were two men in your life. Me and your father. Each of us saw a future with you in the starring role. The difference is that I wanted you for yourself. He wanted you so he could live out his own dream through you."

"That's ridiculous!"

"He still wants that. This damned risky surgery—"

"Don't start that again! It's my choice. My life."

"Yeah. It is. And it's a good thing you figured it out before I trapped you here, in a dull existence you never wanted."

"No. Oh, Seth, I didn't mean—"

She put her hand on his arm. He pulled back as if she'd burned him.

"Hey, no problem. In fact, I'm glad it's all come out. Jo accused me of still carrying a torch for you. She said that was the real reason I was ending our relationship, and you know what? Maybe she was right."

"Seth. Please—"

"Seeing you again set me back. Stupid, but everybody knows that old habits are hard to change." His mouth narrowed. "I got it right the other day at the Burger Barn when I said we were just kids. We didn't know the difference between love and sex."

"That's not…"

"Not what?" His words were sharp and quick.

Wendy shook her head. *Not true,* she'd almost said, but what was the point? He was hurting her because she'd hurt him. Until this moment, she hadn't realized just how badly.

"Never mind. It doesn't matter. I think we've said enough, don't you?"

She didn't wait for an answer. Instead, she began to walk away as quickly as she could manage.

Seth saw her limp, and his heart began to ache at the sight. Not all wounds were visible. Sometimes the ones nobody could see were the most painful of all.

He went after her.

"I'm not done," he said gruffly.

"Yes, you are," she said without stopping. "We have nothing more to say to each other."

"I think you'll want to hear this."

What Wendy wanted was to find a place where she could curl into a ball and weep, but there wasn't a way in the world she'd ever let him know that. She turned around, head high, and looked at him.

"What more could you have to say that I'd want to hear?"

That you're still in my blood.

The words were right there, on the tip of his tongue, but Seth didn't say them. It wasn't true. It couldn't be, not after the things she'd told him tonight. Still, the sight of her pale face, her eyes shimmering with unshed tears, made him long to draw her into his arms.

"Wendy." He cleared his throat. "I'm sorry. I didn't mean it to end like this."

"No." Her voice trembled. "Neither did I."

"Listen." He ran a hand through his hair, searching for words. "About this surgery—"

"Please, Seth. Not again!"

"Wait." He reached out and clasped her hand. She hadn't put her gloves on; her fingers were icy against his. "If you decide, really decide that you want it—that *you* want it, not your father—"

"He has nothing to do with it. What will it take to convince you?"

Seth gave a quick, uncertain smile. "That's just it. I don't know what it will take. But when you're sure you know what you want, let me know."

"Let *you* know?" Wendy tugged her hand away. "Why would I do that?"

"For old time's sake, okay?" He took a step back. "Until then, babe, I'll see you around."

Babe? *Babe?* So much for feeling she'd wounded him. The word, his arrogance, even the way he turned and strolled off infuriated Wendy. She wanted to go after him, grab him by the scruff of his neck and shake him until what few brains he had rattled in his head.

"Do you honestly think I'd come to you for approval to get on with my life? Seth? Damn you, answer me!"

He raised a hand and waggled it without looking back.

"Seth? Seth!"

From the corner of her eye, she saw the headlights on her mother's car blink on and off. Wendy glared after Seth's retreating figure. Then she started toward the Volvo, her pace quickening with each step.

She wasn't looking back, either. Not anymore.

CHAPTER EIGHT

CLINT COOPER SQUATTED next to Seth, protected from the bite of the wind by the walls of the woodshed behind Twin Oaks. Firewood lay scattered all around them; above, snow fell lightly through what, until the evening before, Clint had thought was a perfectly good roof.

Seth ran his hand along the edge of a rafter that had supported the roof, and frowned. He poked at a couple of the logs and turned them over. Finally, he stood, took off his gloves and slapped them against his jeans-clad legs to rid them of snow.

"Well?" Clint got to his feet and tucked his hands into the pockets of his coat. "What do you think?"

Seth heard the impatience in Clint's voice. He'd called him a couple of hours ago, sounding upset. Maureen had gone out to the shed the night before for some wood, and a section of the roof had collapsed on top of her.

"Is Maureen okay?" Seth had asked.

Clint said she had a couple of bruises and that she'd been a little shaken by the accident.

"But she keeps insisting she's fine," he'd said wryly, and then he'd asked if Seth could stop by and see about repairing the shed. Seth had said he would, but ever since he'd gotten here, Clint's questions had dealt more with how the accident could have occurred than with fixing the woodshed.

Seth decided it was time to confront that, head-on.

"Come spring, I can fix the shed easily enough," he said,

watching Clint closely. "But I get the feeling there's more to your question than how long it'll take me to get that roof back up."

Clint hesitated. "You might say that, yes." He looked up at the empty space. "The thing is, I can't figure out why the roof would give way."

"Snow can be really heavy, Clint. You know that as well as I do."

"There wasn't any more weight on that shed than usual. Less, maybe. I shoveled it off just a couple of days ago."

"Still, stuff like this happens."

Clint sighed. "Does it?"

"Sure. You're dealing with wood. This shed was built a while ago, near as I can tell. There are termites and carpenter ants, hungry little buggers that can weaken a piece of wood over time. A building can go all to hell if it isn't maintained properly, especially with lots of snow, icy rain... I've been working over near Williamstown. There's a farm I pass each day. Old place, with lots of small outbuildings. Monday, this little structure that looks like it might have been a pumphouse was fine. Tuesday, I drove by, noticed that a section of it had collapsed." Seth smiled. "Welcome to the country, pal."

"Yeah." Clint nodded. "I guess I feel guilty, that's all."

"About what?"

"About the roof coming down on Maureen instead of me. She always insists on bringing in the wood, but I'd noticed that there were only a few logs left by the fireplace in the gathering room and said I'd do it. Then the phone rang and I got sidetracked." Clint's mouth turned down at the corners. "If I'd only ignored that telephone..."

"You guys run a B and B." Seth smiled. "Ignore that phone enough and there won't be anything to run."

"You're right. I just feel...well, I'd rather this hadn't happened at all, but to have it happen to my sister..."

"Did she notice anything wrong before the accident?"

"No. She just opened the door, stepped inside the way she's done hundreds of times..." Clint looked up at the hole in the roof again "...and just like that, the roof came down and took the whole wall of logs with it."

"But you said Maureen's okay, right?"

"She's got some bruises on her shoulder and a mild concussion. Nothing serious, thank goodness. Doc Dorn stopped by, checked her over, then convinced her to go for an X ray." Clint rolled his eyes. "It took a lot of fast talking, but then, you know my sister."

"She's lucky. Damn lucky. Those logs are heavy."

"I know." Clint's jaw tightened. "She could have been badly hurt. As it is, if she'd been trapped under the logs much longer..." His voice trailed off. "It was bitter cold last night."

Seth nodded. "Yeah. It's a good thing you found her when you did."

"Tell me about it." Clint rocked back on his heels and peered at the roof again. "So, you figure it was the weight of the snow, huh?"

Seth picked up a splintered piece of the two-by-four brace that had held up the logs. "I can't think what else it could have been."

"Just an accident, right?"

Seth looked at him. Clint's expression was impassive, but something in his tone was troubling.

"Do you have reason to think it wasn't?" he asked quietly.

Clint opened his mouth, then shut it again. "No. Of course not."

The denial wasn't convincing. "Because if you do," Seth said, "you might want to contact the police."

"There's no reason. I'm sure this is just what you said it was. Too much snow on the roof." Clint slapped his hand against one of the walls. "So, what do you think?" he said briskly. "Should we repair it or rebuild it? This shed's got to be, what, almost as old as the house?"

"Darned close."

"Uh-huh." Clint clapped him on the back. "Tell you what. Come on up to the house. We'll have some coffee and you can explain the pros and cons of repairing the roof as opposed to building a new shed."

"Does that coffee come with homemade scones?"

Clint laughed. "It does."

"In that case, it's a deal."

The men walked slowly up the hill toward Twin Oaks. Seth craned his neck and looked back at the ice-bound river, then at the snow-covered hills surrounding them.

"One heck of a view," he said.

"Yup. The Cooper that built here sure knew a nice piece of land when he saw it."

"So did you and Maureen," Seth said, smiling. "Took you, what, ten minutes to fall in love with the place and decide to move here?"

"Move *back* here, you mean."

"Right. I keep forgetting you lived in Cooper's Corner as a kid."

"Yeah." Clint opened the back door and motioned Seth to move ahead of him. "I was here till I was nine, and all those years, I don't ever recall a woodshed roof collapsing because of the snow. But then, I was only a kid. I guess I didn't pay much attention to those things." He toed off his boots, shrugged off his coat and hung it on a peg beside the door. "Take off your jacket," he said as he washed up at the utility sink, "and sit down."

Seth glanced down at his feet. "My boots are going to leave tracks on the floor."

Clint grinned. "That's one of the benefits of a stone floor. Nothing ruins it. Go on. Take a load off while I pour us some coffee."

"Sounds good." Seth took his turn at the sink. "If you

have some paper and a pencil, I'll work up a rough estimate of building a new shed.''

Clint took a notepad and pencil from the counter and put them on the table. ''What about fixing up the old one?''

''Well, I'll give you a rough idea of that, too, but it probably makes sense to start from scratch.''

While Seth made his calculations, Clint poured coffee and piled scones on a plate.

''Okay. Here's what I figure it'll cost you, both ways.'' Seth turned the pad toward Clint, who frowned as he read the numbers.

''So cheap?''

''Of course.'' Seth reached for a scone from the plate Clint had placed on the kitchen table. ''You'll do it yourself. Zero labor costs.''

''Hey. I didn't mean—''

''Come on, man. You know you're just looking to put me out of work.'' The men grinned at each other.

''Hey, Castleman,'' Clint said in a Western drawl that would have made John Wayne proud, ''are you tellin' me this town ain't big enough for the two of us?''

Both men laughed. They'd fallen into the friendly routine ever since Clint and his sister inherited Twin Oaks and decided to convert the old house to a bed-and-breakfast. Clint was an architect by training and had always gone in for hands-on participation in the projects he designed. He was a more than competent carpenter, but he cheerfully admitted he couldn't hold a candle to Seth when it came to things like cabinetry or furniture making.

''Okay. Thanks for the estimate.''

''No problem. I can even give you a couple of recommendations to some lumberyards where you can buy well-seasoned wood.'' Seth bit into the scone and rolled his eyes. ''Did you ever think about opening a restaurant, adding a little class to the valley? I know, I know. Cooking's just a hobby, but you're damned good.''

"That's just what we need, all right." Clint smiled, amused. "A gourmet restaurant to compete with the ones in Lenox. I was surprised enough when that new place opened in Stockbridge. What's it called? The Purple Panda?"

"Yeah. Something like that."

Clint looked at him. "What?"

"Nothing. I just…I was just remembering that I ate there the other night."

"And? How was it?"

A sudden image of Wendy's face, pale and distraught as she looked up at him in the darkness of the parking lot, flashed through Seth's mind.

"It was—it was okay, I guess."

"Not exactly what you hoped for, huh?" Clint shrugged. "Well, that's life. Lots of things aren't quite what you hope they'll be."

Seth nodded. "No," he said softly, "they aren't." He looked up. Clint was eyeing him with concern. "Hey," he said briskly, pointing his finger at a glass-fronted cabinet. "I just noticed—is that new?"

Clint smiled. "Maureen picked it up a couple of weeks ago. Nice, huh?"

"Very. You've done great things with this room."

"Well, she gets all the credit. She was right. I mean, we both agreed to keep the stone floor, but pulling down the wallboard was Maureen's suggestion."

"Who knew we'd find that great fireplace, and all this old brick?"

"Our guests seem to like it, the feeling that you can step back in time without giving up twenty-first century comforts."

"Bookings are good?"

"They're great. First the leaf peepers, now the skiers. We're off to a good start." Clint pointed to Seth's cup. "How's the coffee?"

"Your one failing in the kitchen, right?" Seth teased. "It's good enough so I figure it must be Maureen's."

"She insisted on making it," Clint confessed. "I wanted her to stay in bed, but no way would she do that."

"She's feeling better today?"

"Yeah. Almost a hundred percent, she says. But she'll need to get off her feet every now and then for a few days—when I can convince her to do it." He hesitated. "Is there a way for me to build the new shed so the roof's really tight?"

Seth studied his friend closely. "Clint, what's on your mind?"

"Nothing. I guess I was a city boy for a lot of years. You live in a big city, you learn to be suspicious of damn near everything. Besides, what do I know about snow on a roof?"

"A lot, I'd bet." Seth kept his eyes on the other man's face. "An architect would know about rafters and roofs and bearing loads."

"Theory isn't the same as reality."

"That's true. These scones, for instance." Seth reached for another buttery biscuit. "They don't taste anything like the ones I buy at the supermarket."

"Yeah, well, don't buy 'em there. Stop by here and take home a doggy bag whenever you like." The men ate and drank in silence for a couple of minutes. Clint got up, went to the stove, got the coffeepot and topped off their mugs. "You know, when Maureen and I first talked about opening this B and B, if anybody had asked me how to keep a houseful of guests happy, I'd have said, 'Give 'em comfortable rooms and good food.'"

"Why do I hear a 'but' coming?"

"But," Clint said, "I'd have been wrong. Nice rooms, homemade breakfasts are part of it, but there's more. People are on vacation. They want to feel as if they've gotten away from their real lives."

"Meaning?"

"Meaning they need TLC. Tender loving care."

"Ah. A piece of chocolate on the pillow at night."

"More than that. A pot of coffee on the sideboard in the gathering room. An urn of tea, maybe another one filled with hot water and some packets of hot cocoa, especially in the evening when they feel like sitting around and winding down. A glass of wine, some crackers…"

"Yeah. I heard. The license came through, huh?"

"Yup. And it's worked out just fine. All we're serving is wine, brandy and cognac, but that's what folks want when the fire's going in the gathering room."

"Well," Seth said, crumpling his napkin and putting it on his plate, "it sounds as if you've got the TLC thing under control."

Clint grinned. "We've just got one problem. We're making our guests feel comfortable, but we're shorthanded. I want Maureen to take it easy for a while—and if you quote me to her, I'll deny everything."

Seth laughed. "Your secret's safe with me."

"Actually, I've hired someone to come in evenings. You know, take phone calls, pour some *vino,* make sure the coffee's hot, chat with guests who feel like chatting—"

"And leave alone the ones who don't."

"Uh-huh. Like Rod Pommier. The guy sure keeps to himself."

"Well, I can understand it," Seth said "The media drove him crazy in New York. Anyway, he's not around now, is he? He told me he was going to spend a few days in Vermont."

"Right. I forgot, you're doing that chalet he bought. How's it going?"

"Terrific. Pommier's the best kind of client."

Clint laughed. "An absent one."

"No, seriously. The guy knows what he wants and what he doesn't want. He trusts my judgment and he can afford to make that chalet into something special." Seth took a swallow of his coffee. "So, did you run an ad in the paper for help?"

"Didn't have to. You know how it is in this town. Say something to someone, the wind picks it up and it spreads. Matter of fact, she starts tonight."

"Well, that should help smooth things for you."

"Oh, it will. Now, if I could just find a way to keep Randi and Robin occupied for more than five minutes at a clip...."

"Maureen's twins?" Seth's eyebrows rose. "Yeah, I'll bet. Those little girls have more energy than a tornado."

"That they do, and here's another reality bite. It's tough to say 'no' or 'in a minute, sweetheart' to three-year-olds."

"In other words, you need a baby-sitter." Seth thought about Clint's twelve-year-old son. "What about Keegan?"

Clint shook his head. "Keegan already helps out with the girls, and he's got homework. The thing is, the girls are late-to-bed types. Always have been. From six to seven o'clock is when their energy levels are highest. I just need a breather once in a while. You know, find some way to keep one eye on them and one eye on business."

"And a hell of a picture that makes, Cooper." Both men chuckled. Seth lifted his mug and drank the last of the coffee. "How about if I lend a hand?"

"You?"

"Hey, I'll have you know I'm great with kids. I volunteer an afternoon each weekend at Ski Wee—the ski program for kids, up on the mountain. And Randi and Robin know me. They like me."

"Like you? They worship you. They're out with Maureen or they'd be doing everything but climbing inside your toolbox."

"Wrong. Randi *did* climb into it last time I was here. So, what do you think about me coming by to help out for a while?"

"I don't know, Seth. That's an awful lot to ask."

"Okay. You're right. It is too much to ask." Seth's lips twitched. "You'll just have to pay me…say, a couple of scones a night."

Clint tried to look serious. "Well, I don't know. I don't always have scones on hand. Could we negotiate? Would you settle for blueberry muffins? Or banana bread? That's what's on the menu for tomorrow's breakfast."

Seth stood up and put out his hand. "You drive a tough bargain, Cooper."

"Yeah," Clint said, clasping Seth's hand in his, "so do you, Castleman. Seriously, though, this is great. But don't feel you have to come by all the time. Two evenings…" He grinned. "Three evenings a week would be terrific."

"No problem."

"I mean, I know you have other things to do with your nights."

Seth's smile faded. "Not really."

"What about Jo Cabot?"

"That's over."

"Hey, I'm sorry. I thought you and she—"

"So did I, for a while, but then I realized I wasn't…she wasn't…" He cleared his throat and reached for the toolbox he'd brought with him. "Got to run. I promised a guy over in New Ashford I'd stop by and give him an estimate on an extension."

"Sure."

The men walked to the back door. Seth took his jacket from a wooden peg and slipped it on.

"Well, I'll see you whenever you get the chance to stop by."

"How's tonight sound?"

"It sounds great. Maybe this place will seem less like bedlam with my nieces driving you nuts and somebody in the gathering room letting the guests do the same thing to her." Clint winked. "Only kidding. Guests at Twin Oaks never drive anybody crazy."

"But if they do," Seth said, "don't let it be the owners, huh? Who'd you hire, anyway?"

Clint stepped back as Seth opened the door.

"Oh," he said, "we hired the Monroes' daughter. Her name's Wendy. Do you know her?"

"Yes," Seth said calmly, as if his gut hadn't just tried to tie itself into a knot, "I do."

"She's perfect for the job. She was a champion skier— had a nasty accident that ended her career, poor kid. I guess you know that."

"Yeah." Obviously, Phyllis and Philo Cooper were slipping if Clint didn't know that Wendy had once been Seth's girlfriend.

"She's been living in Europe. Gives her a nice sophisticated touch. Besides, if people have questions about skiing in these parts, she can answer them. She made a point of saying she didn't expect to be in town very long, but I figured, what the heck, maybe she'll change her mind."

"I wouldn't count on it," Seth warned.

"Maureen said the same thing. Well, at least this gives us time to look for another person."

"Right." Seth zipped his jacket and put on his gloves. "See you later, Clint."

"Fine. Oh, and Seth?"

Halfway down the porch steps, Seth looked back over his shoulder.

"Thanks. You can't imagine what this means to me. You offering to come by in the evenings."

"I'm sure I'm going to enjoy every minute of it," Seth said, and half expected a bolt of lightning to strike from the cloudless sky and turn him into a puddle of melted flesh and bone.

GINA STOOD IN THE DOORWAY of Wendy's bedroom, watching as her daughter slipped on her new black cashmere turtleneck, then ran her hands down the front of her equally new white wool pants.

"You look lovely, sweetie."

"Thanks." Wendy caught Gina's eye in the mirror and smiled. "I'm glad we finally got to that mall."

"Me, too. Wasn't it fun?"

"It was great."

Was "great" overdoing it? Maybe, but it made Gina smile back at her. The smile was definitely preferable to the look her mother had been giving her lately, the wary kind parents usually reserved for small children in potentially dangerous situations.

"Gina? I can't find any cookies. Gina? Honey? Do you know where the cookies are?"

Her father's voice rose plaintively up the stairs. Wendy smiled. Her mother sighed and rolled her eyes.

"Honestly," she said, "men can be such babies."

"Gina?"

"I'll be right there, Howard." She stepped into the room and gave Wendy a quick hug. "See you downstairs."

"Okay."

Wendy sat down on the bed and pulled on a pair of well-worn hiking boots. Of all the things she'd figured on dealing with during her visit here, the one thing that had never crossed her mind was how difficult it would be to have left her parents' home a teenage girl and returned to it an adult.

"Where are you off to?" her father said in the evening if she put on her coat and headed for the door, and she'd have to explain that she and Alison were taking in a movie or going for a drive. It was silly but she resented it. It was like stepping back a decade—except now, her father didn't smile, tell her to enjoy herself, and then remind her, as if she'd ever forgotten, that she had to be up early for practice.

Wendy went to the dresser and picked up her brush.

Still, dealing with her father was easier than dealing with

her mother. Gina probably asked her if she was okay a dozen times a day.

Wendy sighed and ran the brush through her hair.

Actually, she couldn't blame her. The scene her mother had stumbled across outside the restaurant the other night had to have been unsettling, to say the least, and Wendy knew she hadn't improved things by refusing to discuss it.

"I'm here if you want to talk," Gina kept saying.

What was there to talk about? She'd made a fool of herself, or maybe it was Seth who'd made a fool of her. Either way, she was determined to put him out of her mind, not just out of her life.

Wendy checked herself one last time in the mirror, then made her way down the stairs. Her father and mother were in the kitchen. Gina was pouring coffee; Howard was seated at the counter, munching on oatmeal cookies and reading the paper.

"Okay." Wendy put on her jacket and plucked her mother's keys from the hook on the wall where house keys and car keys hung. "I'm on my way."

Her father looked up. "You sure you want to go ahead with this job, Wendy? I told you, Gil—the orthopedist I ski with—Gil says Pommier's gone up to Vermont for a few days." He frowned. "I don't know what he expects to find on the Vermont slopes that he can't find here."

"Longer, steeper, more challenging runs," Wendy said lightly as she slipped on her coat. "Daddy, honestly, this is perfect. When Pommier does get back, he won't be able to avoid me." She smiled. "I'll serve him coffee or tea or whatever he wants to drink until he'll agree to give me five minutes of his time just to get rid of me. Besides, I really want to do some kind of work. I'm not accustomed to doing nothing all day."

"Nothing?" Gina snorted. "An entire afternoon doing leg lifts and riding on that stationary bike isn't my idea of 'nothing.'"

''See you guys later,'' Wendy said quickly, and headed out the door.

Outside, she paused just long enough to take a deep breath of the cold air. The night was a dark colander, with stars piercing the inky bowl of the sky. That last night she'd spent with Seth, nine years ago, had been just like this, the air crisp, the stars dazzling against the endless darkness.

Wendy got behind the wheel of Gina's car and backed out of the driveway.

Main Street was silent. It had been that night, too, with nothing but the sound of the tires on the wet road and the soft music coming over the truck radio.

They'd driven to their special place on Sawtooth Mountain, and all the way there, Seth kept asking her if she was cold. How could she have been cold, when she'd known what would happen as soon as he parked? As soon as he took her in his arms and kissed her? Touched her? As soon as he opened her jacket and she opened his shirt, her fingers trembling, her heart racing, and...

...and why was she thinking about Seth?

Too much time on her hands, that was why. The best thing she'd done was find herself a job. She'd fill at least a handful of empty hours each day by doing something useful and pleasant. What could be unpleasant about chatting with guests, or taking phone calls, or seeing to it that the coffeepot was full?

''People will want to ask you things,'' Clint Cooper had advised her. ''About the area. You know, what there is to do, places to see, to ski.''

He'd said it so naturally, so easily, that she realized he'd never thought she might be self-conscious about who she'd once been and who she now was.

Maybe he didn't know.

A minute later, she'd found out that he did.

She'd said yes, she'd love the job, providing he understood she couldn't tell him how long she'd be available.

They'd started to chat about the town, the mountains, the place where she'd lived in Paris—Clint knew the city pretty well, it turned out. Then he'd said matter-of-factly that he'd heard she'd skied every slope between here and the Canadian border before her accident, and had she managed to get in any skiing since she was back?

She'd been stunned. It had taken a couple of seconds for her to manage an answer.

"But I can't ski," she'd said. "My leg..."

"Oh." Clint had looked chagrined. "Sorry. I just thought...I mean, I've known several people with disabilities who were still able to..."

His sister had come along just then and the conversation had mercifully turned to other things, but Wendy still wondered how he could have asked her such a thing. Ski? Ski disabled? What was the point in standing on top of a mountain if you couldn't fly down its face with your heart pounding as the edges of your skis bit into the turns and the trees rushed by on your way to the finish line?

Wendy turned onto Oak Road. On the village green she could make out the statue of the Cooper's Corner Minuteman, softly illuminated by lights set around the base, standing stoically on his pedestal as he had for more than a century.

She slowed the car, signaled and made a right into the Twin Oaks driveway, followed it uphill to the lot and parked among several other cars and trucks.

The house was gaily lit. Clint had explained that they'd been open only a few months but business was good, and some of the locals had taken to dropping by the gathering room in the evenings.

Wendy turned up her collar, trudged up the steps to the porch, started to reach for the bell and then realized that all she had to do was open the door.

She took a deep breath, dusted some snow that had fallen from the trees off her shoulders, turned the knob...

And walked straight into Seth.

CHAPTER NINE

SETH WASN'T SURPRISED by the stunned look on Wendy's face when she saw him. What he hadn't expected was his own reaction, a kind of one-two punch of elation, quickly followed by anger. Elation at the sight of her, so feminine and beautiful, her cheeks turned crimson by the cold, and anger over the swift realization that he didn't want to think that way about her anymore.

Wasn't he supposed to be past that? Surely he could greet her politely.

"What are you doing here, Seth?"

So much for politeness. She'd posed the question the same way one of his foster mothers had when she'd found him in her kitchen, getting a glass of water in the middle of the night. 'What are you doing here?' she'd said. He'd been just young enough to wonder how come she couldn't see the answer for herself. He'd had to think about it before he understood that what she really meant was what was he doing in her life?

Well, he wasn't a kid anymore. He got the meaning of Wendy's question and answered it as he'd learned to back then, when contempt was his only defense.

"Hello, Wendy." He let his smile underscore his sarcasm. "It's a pleasure to see you, too."

The door was still half-open. The smell of spices, the sound of soft, happy voices drifted into the night. He stepped forward and pulled the door closed; she responded by taking a couple of steps back, as if they were partners in a dance and only they knew the steps. A memory came to him, quick and unwanted, of all the times they'd really danced together, his arms tight around her, her head on his shoulder, the scent of her hair teasing his senses....

Damn it, what was the point in remembering? Everything they'd once meant to each other—assuming they'd ever meant anything to each other—was long gone. He'd embarrassed her, though, and he took bitter pleasure in the way her color deepened.

"Sorry."

An apology? Score one for the home team, he thought, and decided to let her off the hook.

"Yeah, well, no problem." The night had a frigid bite. Seth put up his collar, tucked his hands deep into the slash pockets of his leather jacket and eased back against the doorjamb. "It's a small town." He flashed a quick smile. "I guess you're going to have to figure on us running into each other every now and then."

Wendy nodded, even managed something that approximated a smile, and he figured she was grateful for the lifeline he'd tossed her.

"Are you doing something for Clint?"

"Am I... Ah. You mean, did some emergency carpentry job come up at the B and B?" He shook his head. "Nope. I'm visiting. Clint and Maureen are my friends." She nodded again. So much for casual conversation. Seth cleared his throat. "Clint says you're going to be working here," he said.

"That's right. Well, for a while, anyway. For as long as I'm in town."

"For as long as it takes you to buttonhole Rod Pommier and talk him into that operation."

Her smile disappeared. "Clint's expecting me. Good night."

"Wait." Seth clasped her elbow as she started past him. "Wendy. I'm sorry. I shouldn't have—"

"No. You shouldn't."

"Yeah." He hesitated. "Look, there's no way we can avoid seeing each other."

"You already said that."

"What I mean is, you'll be here evenings and so will I."

She stared at him. When Clint said some of the townsfolk had taken to dropping by Twin Oaks in the evenings, she'd somehow translated that to mean people her parents' age.

"Clint's shorthanded," he told her.

"Yes. I know. That's the reason he hired me, but—"

"But what does that have to do with knowing I'm going to go on turning up like a bad penny?" He heard the bitterness in his voice and tried to soften it as he explained. "Maureen has twin daughters. They're sweet kids. Smart, cute, and a real handful. She needs a break and they're too much for Clint to handle at the same time he's trying to run Twin Oaks, so I traded keeping them busy an hour or two in the evenings for some of Clint's baking."

If he'd expected to coax a smile from her with that, he'd been mistaken. Her face went blank.

"You?"

She said it the way he figured she would have if he'd mentioned offering to fly to Mars.

"Yeah. Me. Why is that so surprising?"

"Well, I just didn't think—I mean, men don't usually—"

"I'm not 'men,' I'm me." His voice roughened. "Maybe that was always your problem, Wendy. You categorized me far too easily."

Her eyes glittered. With tears or with annoyance? He couldn't tell, but then, he couldn't tell much of anything about her anymore.

"Please," she said softly, "let's not do this."

"No." He felt a muscle knot in his jaw. "You're right. Let's not." He drew a breath, then let it out. "I like the twins. They like me. I like Clint and Maureen. What I'm doing is no big deal."

Wendy nodded. "Well, that's very nice of you."

"Like I said, it's no big deal."

Another silence fell between them. Then Wendy made a point of tugging her cuff back and checking her watch.

"I'd better get inside. I'm supposed to start work at six, but I thought I'd come in early tonight, you know, get a feel for things."

"Sure."

Silence again. Then she held out her hand. "Well, good night."

He looked at her hand, thought about telling her she hadn't seen the last of him tonight, that he was only going to fix the windshield wipers on his truck. But she would realize that shortly.

For now, it was sufficient to accept the peace offering and clasp her hand in his.

"Good luck tonight."

"Thanks." She smiled. "I have the feeling I'm going to need it. You could tuck what I know about being a hostess into a thimble and still have room left for a finger."

"You'll be fine. Twin Oaks draws a friendly crowd. Just be sure and sneak one of Clint's chocolate chip cookies before the guests scarf them all down."

Her smile broadened. She was more at ease now. He liked that, knowing she wasn't uptight just because she was talking to him, just because he hadn't yet let go of her hand.

"He's a terrific baker, huh?"

"Terrific doesn't even come close."

"That's what my father told me."

Her father. "Well, it's nice to know your old man is right about some things," he said, and cursed himself when he saw her face harden and felt her tug her hand free of his.

"Goodbye, Seth."

He stepped to his left. She stepped to her right and they found themselves facing each other again.

"Sorry," he said, and backed out of her way.

That was where she'd always wanted him, he thought as he watched her walk into the house.

Out of her way.

WENDY NEEDED A MOMENT to compose herself.

Couldn't she and Seth spend five minutes together without ending up quarreling? He was so damned self-righteous, so convinced he knew what was best for her. She'd almost told him that, accused him of being as bad as her father....

As bad as her father? No. Her father understood her. Seth didn't.

What bad luck to run into him now. She'd told Seth she was worried about being a hostess, but the truth went lots deeper than that.

What would it be like, mingling with people who'd never known her before the accident? Strangers would have no reason to pity her when they saw that she limped. But then they'd also have no way of knowing the quick, graceful woman she'd once been.

And how would she react when guests at Twin Oaks asked her questions about skiing? About the local slopes? She'd put up a brave front for Clint when he'd mentioned that part of the job; she'd done the same thing when her father brought up the subject at dinner last night.

"I still agree that working at Twin Oaks is the best way to get ahold of Pommier," he'd said, "but I wonder, honey, are you sure you'll be comfortable talking about skiing?"

That had upset her mother. "Of course she'll be comfortable talking about skiing," Gina had said sharply. "Why would you even think such a thing?"

"I know it's difficult for you to understand, Gina," her father had replied, "but when you've been so close to the top that you can taste it, well, it can be hard to admit it's not going to happen."

Her mother had clamped her lips together, risen from the

table, marched into the kitchen and almost immediately reappeared, her eyes bright with anger.

"Maybe what's even more difficult," she'd said in a tone Wendy had never heard her use before, "is admitting you never were that close to the top, Howard."

Wendy closed her eyes. That had brought things to a stop, all right. Blood had rushed to her father's face. He'd said nothing, just put down his knife and fork and left the room. Her mother had plopped into her chair, shoved aside her plate and knotted her hands together. Wendy had sat in silence, wishing she were a thousand miles away.

She'd grown up hearing her father talk about how close he'd come to the Olympics, and the rewards that followed when you came home with a medal. When she was little, she'd hung on every word, fascinated by his stories, puffing with pride when he'd say that she had his talent and more. Her mother had always cheered her on but, come to think of it, she'd never said much about her husband's stories.

And Gina's loss of temper at dinner was rare. Rare? The truth was Wendy couldn't recall it ever happening before.

Eventually, her mom had muttered something about not being very hungry. Wendy had said she wasn't, either. Together, they'd cleared the table and washed the dishes. Then Wendy had gone to her father's study.

"Daddy," she'd murmured, unsure of what to say next. But her father had looked up from the papers on his desk and spoken before she could come up with anything else.

"The waiting has made your mother understandably anxious," he'd told her calmly. "She's upset because we don't know if Pommier will agree to the surgery, that's all."

She's upset because she thinks the surgery's a mistake, Wendy had almost said, but why make a difficult situation worse? Instead, she'd hugged him and told him she understood. Then she'd gone up to her room, where she'd found Gina waiting for her.

"I didn't mean to hurt your father's feelings," her

mother had told her. "He was a fine skier. You get all your talent from him. I'm just... Don't let him pressure you into anything, sweetie. Okay?"

Wendy had hugged her, the same as she'd hugged her father. She'd said the same thing, too, that she understood. And reviewing it all now as she stood inside the doorway of Twin Oaks, she assured herself that she *did* understand. Her father was only being supportive. He wasn't trying to live his life through her, as Seth seemed to think.

Did her mother think that, too?

"Hi."

Wendy looked up. Clint Cooper was smiling at her from the archway that led to the front parlor, a room he and his sister had dubbed the gathering room.

"Hi." Wendy smiled in return. "Sorry if I'm late."

"You're early. It's only a quarter to six."

"Oh. Well, that's good. I thought I'd get here a little ahead of time so you could show me the ropes, but I, uh, I was held up."

"Yeah, I can imagine. Still snowing, huh?"

"Right," she said quickly, gratefully. "It's really picking up and there's that dip in the road on School Street where there's a mean stretch of black ice."

"Uh-huh. In New York City, you get potholes. Here, you get black ice." Clint grinned. "Sometimes I think I ought to write a letter to the mayor of New York and tell him I'm sorry for all the times I cursed him over those potholes. I'd rather deal with them than with a thin sheet of ice that's almost invisible on a dark asphalt surface."

Wendy smiled again. Too much smiling and her new boss would think she was crazy, but it was better than crying, which was what she'd felt like doing, if only for a moment.

"I know. I'd almost forgotten what a New England winter was like."

"Our guests love it. The snow, the cold, even the roads..."

Most of 'em think this town is straight out of the nineteenth century.''

''Well,'' Wendy said with a little laugh, ''I won't try and change their minds, I promise.''

''Great.'' Clint nodded toward the reception desk. ''Come on. I'll show you where to stow your things and then I'll give you the dollar tour.''

''Okay.''

''And I'll introduce you to the coffee urn. Maureen picked it up at a garage sale. It's thirty years old if it's a day, and she loves it. Unfortunately, the only person it loves is Maureen. If you can figure out how to make the darned thing purr, I'll give you a raise.''

Wendy laughed, this time with ease. Working here might be fun, not simply a way to meet Rodney Pommier or fill the endless hours.

Clint led her to a small office behind the reception desk.

''Hang your parka there, put your purse, whatever, in this drawer, and oh, by the way, welcome to Twin Oaks. We're happy to have you here.''

''I'm happy to be here,'' she said, and meant it.

There was lots to learn, but it was all easy stuff. Clint showed her how to register guests in case he wasn't available, and what to say when people phoned with questions about Twin Oaks and its accommodations. He pointed out the cabinet where he kept the supply of brochures about the Berkshires so she could refill the wooden racks near the desk when they were empty.

He showed her where to find the coffee, tea and cocoa, gave her a quick rundown on what wines, brandies and cognacs were available, and pointed out where they kept the nuts and dried fruits that filled the bowls scattered about the gathering room.

''We put out cheese and crackers, too, around eight o'clock. You'll find the cheese in the fridge, the crackers in the pantry. And I almost always put out a couple of baskets of cookies, too.''

"Chocolate chip?"

"The specialty of the house," Clint replied, and smiled. "Ah. You talked to Seth, huh?"

"Seth?"

"Seth Castleman. He said you two knew each other." Clint frowned. "Oh, damn. Did I put my foot in something?"

"No, not at all." Wendy deliberately turned her attention to the individual packets of hot chocolate heaped in a straw basket. "Seth and I are...we used to date, but that was a long time ago."

"Good." Clint groaned. "There I go again. I don't mean good that you guys are history, only that I'm relieved it won't be a problem for you to spend so much time together."

"It won't be." What exactly did "so much" mean? Once a week? Twice? Wendy thought about asking and decided against it. "No problem at all."

"That's terrific. Seth's become a good pal, and I have to admit, having him around for the kids—did he tell you about my nieces? They're twins, bright, beautiful three-year-olds...but they can wear you to a frazzle."

"And Seth's...good with them?"

"Good? He's terrific. One look and you can see he's a man who should have a houseful of his own someday."

The casually spoken words were like a knife to the heart. "Yes. He should." She smiled brightly to hide the wound. "How about standing by while I make some coffee? Just to be sure I've got it right."

"Good idea. Okay, let's take out a filter first..."

"Got it. And the coffee's in here, right?"

"Yup. We have different flavors, by the way. Sometimes we make up a small pot of vanilla or raspberry almond—"

"Uncle Clint!"

Wendy looked up as two little girls flew down the stairs
faces lit with excitement. Chestnut curls bobbed beneath red
velvet ribbons; blue-green eyes sparkled with excitement as
the children ran to Clint, who bent down and swept both
of them into his arms.

"Speak of the devil," he said, and grinned. "Here they
are, my twin tornadoes."

One of the twins giggled. "We're girls, not tomatoes."

"You are, too, tomatoes," Clint teased. "That's why you
have red bows in your hair."

"No, it's not," the other twin said. "We like red—and
Mommy does, too."

"Uh-huh." Clint shifted the children in his arms and
smiled at Wendy. "These terrors are either tomatoes or tornadoes, your choice, but they're definitely my favorite
nieces."

"Silly Uncle Clint. We're his *only* nieces."

"An' even if we wasn't, we'd be his favorites 'cause
we're the bestest nieces anywhere. Right, Uncle Clint?"

"Right," Clint said solemnly. "Say hello to Miss Monroe, you guys."

"It's Wendy," Wendy said. "And I'm delighted to meet
you."

"We're delighted to meet you, too," Robin said politely

Randi observed Wendy with care. "Are you Uncle
Clint's girlfriend?"

"No." Wendy laughed. "I'm not."

"Mommy says he could use one."

"Your mother's full of helpful ideas," Clint said, and
sighed. "What else did she say?"

"That we can stay down here for a little bit if you say
it's all right." Robin's smile was beguiling. "Is it all
right?"

"She says it's time we drove *you* crazy for a while,"
Randi added helpfully.

"I'll bet." Clint gave each girl a resounding kiss on the

cheek, then put them down. "Okay, ladies. I'd be delighted to have your company for a while, but you have to behave."

"We always behave," Randi said, wide-eyed.

"And the moon's made of green..." Clint looked past Wendy and sighed. "Uh-oh."

"Uh-oh, what?" Robin asked.

"Uh-oh, you guys will have to be very, very good while I take care of the gentleman heading for the desk. Mr. Collier," he added, for Wendy's benefit. "He checked in yesterday with his wife. Nice people but, uh, a little high maintenance."

"What's high main'ance?"

Clint laughed. "You'd think I'd have learned to watch what I say by now, wouldn't you? Wendy, I hate to ask, but could you keep an eye on the girls? Not for long. Seth should be back in just another few minutes."

"He's coming back?" Wendy heard the edge of distress in her voice and smiled hastily. "I mean, I saw him at the door before. He said he was leaving."

"He just went out to check his windshield wipers. One of them was sticking, and he figured it would be better to see what he could do about it now rather than later. They're predicting heavy snow for..." Clint waved his hand. "Yes, Mr. Collier. I'll be right there." He looked at Wendy. "Are you okay with this?"

Was she okay, knowing she was going to have to see Seth again tonight?

"Of course," she said, with what she hoped was conviction.

"You sure?"

"Positive. The girls and I—"

"They're not girls," a gruff voice intoned, "they're monsters. And I'm a knight, come to break the spell put over them by the wicked witch."

"Uncle Seth!"

Wendy swung around. Seth was coming toward them, his cheeks ruddy from the cold, his dark-brown hair tossed by the wind, and her heart thumped in a way she wished it wouldn't. She didn't want to feel this way, didn't, didn't, didn't....

"Hi."

She cleared her throat. "Hi."

"I see you've met Doc and Grumpy." Seth swept the twins into his arms as the children broke into giggles.

"We aren't Doc and Grumpy!"

"No?" He furrowed his brow. "Well, then, who are you? Oh. Wait a minute. It's coming to me..... You're Goofy and Pluto."

More giggles, punctuated by little fists pummeling Seth's chest.

"You know our names, Uncle Seth."

"Hmm. Mickey and Minnie? Ernie and Bert?" Hands tugged at his hair. "Ouch. Okay, I give up. They're Robin and Randi, and if you're not careful, they'll run you ragged."

"What's ragged?" two voices said in unison.

Seth put the children on their feet. "It's what happens to people when you guys don't behave yourselves."

"We always behave!"

"Yeah." He ruffled the girls' hair. "You do if you want a treat before you go to bed later. Like, say, your Uncle Clint's chocolate chip cookies and milk."

"Yum."

"Yum, indeed." Seth clasped the girls' hands and looked at Wendy. "How're things going?"

"Fine," she said, and wondered if she was going to make a fool of herself and cry just because Seth was so good with kids. She forced a smile. "Clint walked me through everything and finally turned me loose so I could try making some coffee." Why was he looking at her that way? She thumbed the hair back from her eyes. "Do I have a smudge on my face or something?"

"Or something."

His voice was soft. It made her knees tremble, and that was the last thing she wanted.

"Do you need me?"

Trembling knees, and now a trembling heart. "Sorry?"

"Do you need me to help with the coffee? Fill the urn, whatever?"

"Oh. Oh, no. I can—I can manage."

Seth nodded. "Yeah. Okay. Well, if you change your mind..."

"I'll let you know."

He smiled at her and she couldn't keep from smiling back. "Great," he said, still in that soft voice. Then he cleared his throat and looked down at Randi and Robin, who looked back at him with anticipatory glints in their eyes. "Okay, crew. Let's go build that Lego city we talked about."

"A castle," Robin said, jumping up and down. "I want a castle with a drawbridge."

"An' a dragon," Randi added excitedly. "Can we make a dragon, too?"

"We can make anything you want," Seth said. His eyes met Wendy's. "That's the thing about Lego. You want to build a dreamworld, you can. Reality never intrudes."

"What does that mean, Uncle Seth? Ree-al-uh-tee?"

Seth tore his eyes from Wendy's. "It means that you can build all the castles you want, but that doesn't guarantee you'll ever get to live in them."

"Oh," Robin said softly. "That's sad."

Seth cleared his throat. "Yeah," he said, and led the twins away while Wendy watched and blinked hard to keep back the tears burning in her eyes.

THE COFFEE MACHINE WAS easy to operate, once Wendy figured out its idiosyncrasies.

While the coffee dripped through the filter, she replenished the supply of tea bags, made sure the hot water urn was full, and got a fresh platter of cookies from the kitchen. A middle-aged couple came by and bombarded her with questions about the town's craft shops.

All of it was pleasant and easy to handle, which was good, because Wendy couldn't seem to keep her attention focused. She kept glancing over at Seth and the twins, sitting cross-legged in a little circle in a corner of the big room, a Lego castle rising before them.

A castle you could build, but not live in.

Blindly, she turned away. The coffee was ready; she filled a mug, blew on the hot black liquid and took a cautious sip.

"Good?" a man in a ski sweater and cords asked pleasantly.

Yes, she assured him, it was, and would he like some? She poured a cup for him, then for the people who'd inquired about the craft shops. A young couple who just had to be on their honeymoon came in, and Wendy chatted a bit with them.

Eventually, she was alone again. She looked at the corner. The castle was taller. A wall was going up around it. Seth was talking to Robin, smiling at Randi…

He was so good with kids.

What was wrong with her tonight?

She walked to the brochure rack and straightened brochures that didn't need straightening, trying not to pay attention to the children's soft voices and occasional laughter.

What kind of B and B encouraged children to play in the gathering room, anyway? It was a ridiculous arrangement. Three-year-old kids belonged in bed at this hour, even if they were sweethearts.…

Who was she kidding? The twins weren't bothering anybody. Every now and then, someone looked up and smiled at the sight of those two burnished chestnut heads and that one dark one, bent over the Lego blocks.

The dark head that belonged to a man she'd once loved. Oh, how she had loved him. With all her heart, all her soul.

Seth looked up and their eyes met. She felt as if he was looking deep inside her, past the false smiles, bitter words, anger and pain. That he was looking into the deepest recesses of her heart, where the truth lay quiescent, waiting to be awakened.

She loved him still. She'd never stopped loving him and never would. God, oh God. How could she have denied it for so long? She was still in love with Seth.

The sudden bleat of the telephone made her jump. She grabbed for it, clutched it with almost painful desperation.

"Good evening," she said, though her heart was pounding. "This is Twin Oaks. How may I help you?"

Someone wanted a reservation for next weekend. Yes, she said, of course, and she checked the book the way Clint had shown her, wrote everything down, did it all right even though she was shaking, even though she'd just made the one discovery she hadn't permitted herself to make in all these long, empty years.

She loved Seth Castleman.

She'd never stopped loving him, despite all her protests, her determined conviction that the Wendy who'd left for Norway wasn't the same Wendy who'd come home to Cooper's Corner.

Her body had let her down and now, so had her heart. How could it still belong to Seth? There was no future in loving him, not for her, certainly not for him. Even if there were, if by some miracle she could be the wife he'd once wanted, Seth didn't love her anymore.

She'd seen to that, hadn't she?

The phone trembled in her hand. The voice at the other

end was asking about area attractions and she said, still calmly, that there were lots of things to do and see in these mountains.

Finally, mercifully, the conversation dwindled to silence.

"Thank you for calling Twin Oaks," she said brightly. "We'll see you next weekend."

She hung up, shaking. She didn't dare turn around. What would Seth see in her eyes?

Clint came strolling up. "Everything okay?"

"Fine." She smiled at him, or hoped she did. "I just took a reservation for next weekend. I entered it in the book."

"Great." He paused. "You okay?"

"Oh, I'm fine. Fine." She cleared her throat. "Actually, now that you mention it... Would it be all right if I took a break? Just for a couple of minutes."

"Hey, you don't have to ask permission. You need a break, take it."

"Thanks. I just didn't... Thanks."

She'd have to pass Seth and the twins to reach the bathroom, but that was all right. She wouldn't look in his direction. He surely wouldn't look in hers. She might even have imagined that instant when their eyes met a little while ago.

The bathroom was unoccupied. Thank goodness for small favors. Wendy let out a breath she hadn't realized she'd been holding and put her hand on the door.

"Wendy?"

Her heart stood still. Seth had come up behind her. She turned slowly toward him, while butterflies swarmed beneath her breastbone.

"Yes?"

He smiled, a slow, lazy smile she felt straight down to her toes. "Are you busy?"

"I—I am, yes." She waved a hand toward the bathroom door. "I was just going to take a break...."

"I noticed." He stepped closer, curled his hand around her arm. "The thing is," he said softly, "I need you."

CHAPTER TEN

THERE WAS A TIME when Seth used to tease her about being able to read her mind. Could he still do it, so many years later? Did he know what she'd been thinking only moments ago? That it was still true, that all she wanted, all she'd ever wanted, was him?

"Wendy? Did you hear me?"

His voice was low, his eyes locked to hers. She didn't trust herself to speak. He was barely a breath away. All she had to do was reach out, cup his face in her hands, bring his mouth down to hers.

"Uncle Seth? We have to go *now*."

The small voice was taut with urgency. Wendy blinked and looked down. Robin and Randi stood on either side of Seth, clutching his hands and shifting from foot to foot.

Shifting from foot to foot? Oh. The twins had to go to the bathroom. That's what this was all about. Seth didn't need her; the kids did.

"You want me to take the girls to the bathroom?"

"Would you? I'd do it myself but I've never dealt with…" He blushed. "You know, the mechanics."

A minute ago she'd wanted to kiss him. Now she wanted to bang her head against the wall at her sheer stupidity. But his embarrassed smile reached her and she took pity on him. He was a man confronted by something he was totally unprepared for, just as she'd been unprepared for the foolish thoughts that were nothing but the imaginings of her own silly sentimentality.

"No problem," she said, and held out her hands to the girls. "Come on, kids. Let's go to the ladies' room."

"It's not a ladies' room." Randi piped up as Wendy bumped the door open with her hip. "Mommy says it's a unaset room."

"A unaset..." Wendy smiled. "Unisex. Right. That's what it is. Okay. Let's get you guys unbuttoned."

She helped two pairs of overeager little fingers work their way through buttons and snaps. There was only one commode and Randi volunteered to wait, making the offer with solemn courage. After they were done, all the snaps and buttons had to be done up again. Finally, Wendy lifted each child to the sink for a round of hand-washing.

Randi gave her a curious look. "Do you have little girls of your own?"

"No," Wendy said, forcing an answering smile, "I don't."

"She doesn't have little girls," Randi whispered to Robin, as if Wendy weren't there.

"You'd be a good mommy," Robin said, with all the wisdom of her three years.

Wendy took the cloth towel from the child and tossed it into the wicker hamper. Gently, she smoothed Robin's tumbled chestnut curls from her forehead.

"Thank you," she said softly.

"You could have a baby. Maybe with Uncle Clint for the daddy."

"Or Uncle Seth. He'd make a good daddy, too."

Wendy's throat tightened. Did you laugh or cry at stuff like this? Laugh, she decided, or at least smile. She gave each child a quick kiss and pulled the door open.

"Come on, you two. Let's find your Uncle Seth so he can help you finish building that castle."

"We already did." The little girls beamed at Seth, who was leaning against the reception desk, arms folded, feet crossed at the ankles. "Right, Uncle Seth? Didn't we finish the castle?"

"Right down to the moat." Seth scooped the twins into his arms. "And a great castle it is, strong and safe from goblins and witches and dragons."

Two heads nodded with enthusiasm.

"Did you thank Wendy for helping you?"

The twins looked at her. "Thank you, Wendy."

"You're very welcome."

Randi looped an arm around Seth's neck. "Can we go for a walk?"

"It's late. I think it's bedtime for you guys."

Robin stuck out her bottom lip. "But it's snowing."

"Uh-huh. All the more reason not to take a walk."

"Walking in the snow is fun. It's all squishy."

Seth grinned. "Squishy is always good," he told Wendy, who smiled back at him.

"And it's pretty. Snow is like fairy dust, Uncle Seth. So, please, can we go? Please? Just for a little walk?"

Seth looked into the two pairs of blue-green eyes, knew he was a goner and gave a deep sigh. "A very little one, okay?"

"Yay!"

"But you have to check with your Uncle Clint first."

"Check what?" Clint said, hurrying past them with a box in his arms.

"The terrible twosome want to take a walk in the snow." Seth shot Clint a speaking look. "A short walk. Very short."

"Yeah, sure. Sweaters, hats, boots, snowsuits, gloves." He grinned. "It'll take you longer to dress 'em than to walk 'em."

"Okay, kids, you heard the rules. First we get dressed. Then we take a short walk."

"Uncle Seth?"

"What, sugar?"

Robin tucked her thumb in her mouth. "We like Wendy," she said shyly. "Can she come, too?"

"Oh. Oh, no," Wendy said quickly. "I mean, I couldn't possibly. I—I have—"

"Wendy can't come with us," Seth told them. "She has more important things to do."

Wendy bristled. "I never said that!"

"More important than a walk?" Robin asked plaintively.

"It's not that." Wendy took the child's hands in hers. "I'm...I'm busy, honey. I have to help people with things here."

"What things?" Randi said innocently.

What things, indeed? There weren't that many people in the gathering room. Locals didn't show up much on weekday evenings, Clint had told her. Except for the middle-aged couple sipping coffee as they played chess in front of the fireplace, the room was empty.

"Just things," Wendy said after a minute. "I'm working tonight. Otherwise, I'd go with—"

"Go where?"

Clint, retracing his path from the storeroom to the desk, paused and raised his eyebrows.

"Wendy says she'd like to go for a walk with Uncle Seth and us, but she can't 'cause she's working."

"Don't be silly." Clint smiled at Wendy. "Of course you can go. The coffee's done—it's perfect, by the way, lots better than I ever make it. Everybody's settled in. If you feel up to torture by twins, go for it."

"The reception desk," Wendy said quickly. "If someone phones—"

"I'll handle it."

"Say yes, Wendy! Say you'll come. Please, please, please?"

She looked at the two hopeful faces. And at Seth, whose face bore no expression at all.

"A walk sounds lovely," she said, and tried to ignore the way her heart lifted at the smile that curved Seth's lips.

CLINT WAS RIGHT. Getting the children into their gear took a long time.

"It's not easy to turn kids into Pillsbury Dough Boys," Seth announced as they worked the girls' legs into pants, their feet into boots. They pulled on sweaters, jackets and hoods. They buttoned, zipped and fastened, tugged on mittens and burst out laughing when the children waddled to the door.

"Heaven help us if they fall down."

"Not to worry." Seth grinned. "I can always attach a towline to my truck and drag 'em home."

"Come on," Randi said impatiently.

"Hurry," said Robin, as if the night and the snow might suddenly end.

Seth and Wendy pulled on their own jackets. Seth wrapped a wool scarf around his throat. Wendy did the same, then added her knit cap. Seth looked her over and tried not to think back to the days when he'd call for her on a winter's night, see her all bundled up like she was now, and try to shake hands with her scowling father and smile politely at her pleasant mother while his wicked brain created images of what it was going to be like to search out Wendy's warm, satiny skin beneath all those layers of clothing.

Her eyes met his. Something flashed in their aqua depths. It was crazy, but just for that instant, he thought she might be remembering the same thing.

He cleared his throat. "Those boots going to be okay?"

"Fine."

"You sure? They look kind of worn, and it's cold out...."

His words trailed away as their eyes met again. This time, he knew they were thinking the same thing. They were sharing a memory from the old days when she'd worn these same boots. They'd get into the cab of his truck and he'd ask if she was sure the boots were okay because it was cold out, and she'd say yes, they were fine, and the whole silly conversation was only a lead-up to what she'd say next, that if her feet got cold, she could always put them in his lap and he could untie her laces, take off her boots, massage her feet with his warm hands....

Hell. This was never going to work. How could he have thought he'd be able to spend evenings so near her and not remember what had once burned between them?

"Uncle Seth?"

Seth looked down at the little face lifted to his.

"Okay," he said briskly, "let's move 'em... Hey! Where'd these teddy bears come from? What happened to Randi and Robin?"

The girls giggled. "Here we are," Randi said.

"Where?" Seth made a point of searching the room. "I hear you, but I don't see you."

"Right here," Robin said. She poked him in the leg. "It's me, Uncle Seth. See?"

"Aha!" Seth snatched up Robin and turned to Randi, but the little girl scampered over to Wendy.

"Can you take me, please?"

Wendy swallowed hard. "I'd love to, baby, but you're such a big girl that I don't think I can—"

"I know you can't carry me," Randi said with a child's honesty. "You hurt your leg, right? I know 'cause you got a limp."

Wendy felt as if someone had dumped cold water over her. Except for her doctors and therapists, nobody had ever been so blunt—and wasn't that ridiculous? She *did* have a limp. It was the visible sign of her failure, her weakness, and she'd hated it for those reasons. Now, stated with such innocence, the word seemed to carry less meaning. Like the story about the emperor's new clothes, it had taken a child to speak the truth.

Seth started to answer but she stopped him. "Yes, honey, you're right. I did hurt my leg. And yes, I limp. So it might not be such a safe thing for me to carry you outside, when it's slippery." She smiled and reached for the child's hand. "But we can hold hands. Would you like that?"

"That's what I meant. We could hold hands." Randi put her mittened fingers in Wendy's. "How'd you hurt your leg, Aunt Wendy? Was it an accident?"

Amazing that such questions could be so easily asked—and even more amazing that they could be so easily answered.

"Yes. I had an accident."

Seth held open the door. She caught a glimpse of his face as she and Randi went by. What was he thinking? She couldn't tell. His eyes were hooded and his expression was noncommittal.

"My mommy had an accident. Lots of wood falled down on her."

"I know. I heard about it."

"But she's almost all better now. Are you all better, too, Aunt Wendy?"

Was she? How did you answer a question like that? Her doctors said she was. So did her mother. And she suspected Seth would say she was, too.

"I—I'm lots better."

"But not all?" Randi looked up at her. "You *look* all better. My mommy didn't, not right away."

"Randi," Seth said from behind her.

"No. No, that's okay." Wendy tightened her hold on the child's hand as they slowly made their way down the stairs and away from the porch. "I hurt my leg skiing," she said matter-of-factly, "and I won't really be better until I can ski again."

"Oh." Randi took a few seconds to digest that. "I like to ski."

Wendy smiled. "Do you?"

"Uh-huh. Uncle Clint and Uncle Seth took us skiin' right back there, behind the house." She looked up at Wendy. "Can't you ski if you have a limp?"

"You can, yes. But I..." But I what? Could she say, I don't want to get on the slopes and have people pity me? I don't want to be just another skier, I want to be Wendy Monroe, champion? Could she explain that she wanted to, *had* to, get that medal her father—well, she and her father— had worked toward for so many years?

How did you explain that to a three-year-old child when it was so hard to explain it to adults? When, more and more, it was hard to explain to yourself?

The sudden realization stole her breath away.

"Aunt Wendy?"

She looked at the innocent face still turned up to hers and found herself tongue-tied. Seth seemed to sense it.

"Hey," he said, coming alongside them, Robin still riding his shoulders, "take a look at the size of those snow-flakes!"

The diversion worked. Randi and Robin both tilted their heads back, oohed and aahed, stuck out their tongues to trap the flakes, and giggled.

"Thank you," Wendy said softly.

Seth shrugged his shoulders. "That's okay. It's bad enough I subjected you to the third degree. No need for you to get it from the kids, too." He cleared his throat and she could almost see him searching for a change of subject. "Quite a night, huh?"

Oh, it was. There was no wind, and though it was cold, it wasn't the piercing cold that could come during a real New England snowfall. For now, the world was beautiful. Leafless oaks lined the driveway, holding their snow-laden branches to the black night in offering to the pagan gods of the storm.

"How are you doing, honey?" Wendy murmured to Randi, trudging along beside her.

"Fine," the little girl said, but she was puffing hard.

Wendy leaned toward Seth, her breath visible in the cold night as she spoke quietly to him.

"It's a lot for her, Seth. Maybe we should go back."

"I have a better idea." He lifted Robin from his shoulders and put her down. "Okay, guys. Everybody wait here."

"Where are you going?" Wendy called as he started toward the house.

"I'll be right back," he yelled, and he waggled his hand over his head. She thought about the night they'd bumped into each other at the Purple Panda and how the gesture then had been one of dismissal. It was so different this time, just a reassuring way of saying he'd be back.

How happy she was that he would.

Drawing the children close, she let them lean against her legs.

"Is it okay?" Robin asked softly.

Wendy knew the child was asking if it was all right to lean on her because of her limp.

"Yes," she said, "it's fine."

And it was. She limped, yes, but years of determined exercise had made the leg strong, or as strong as it could be without Pommier's experimental surgery. What if her mother and Seth were right? What if subjecting herself to a dangerous operation—assuming she could convince the doctor to perform it—was a mistake? What if she could have a life, a good and happy life, without the surgery? Without trying for something as ephemeral as a medal? Without trying to turn back the clock?

What if...

"Here we go."

Seth ran toward them, pulling a children's sled that sailed over the snow behind him like a small red ship. Wendy laughed. So did the twins.

"A sleigh ride," Robin squealed.

"Yup. Let's go, kids. Climb on."

The girls scrambled into the sled. Seth had brought a heavy blanket, too, and he draped it around them until they were bundled up like travelers to the North Pole. Then he and Wendy set off down the driveway, past the old-fashioned street lamps that cast a warm yellow light over the curb. They crossed the empty road and headed for the village green. All around them, the tiny town lay quiet under its soft blanket of white fairy dust.

"You okay?" Seth asked softly.

Wendy nodded. "I'm fine."

"Because if this is too much for you…"

"It isn't." She looked up at him. "I do a couple of hours a day on a stationary bike."

"That old one in the basement?"

"Uh-huh."

He chuckled. "I'd have thought the pedals would have dropped off by now." They fell into a companionable silence, broken only by the faint huffing sound of their breathing. "Your mom says you worked hard, getting back your mobility."

"I guess." Wendy stuck out her tongue the way the twins had, caught a snowflake and let it melt. "But I wasn't about to give up and spend the rest of my life in a wheelchair."

"No," he said, "I didn't think you would." He glanced at her. "You're really something, you know? Your own doctors say you won't walk again, but here you are."

"Here I am," she said with forced lightness.

"I was so proud of you, when Gina told me." His voice was thick with emotion. "But I knew you'd do it."

Wendy gave a little laugh. "You knew more than I did."

"I knew you." He looked at her again. "Wendy Monroe.

The real Wendy, not the one the doctors met that terrible day you fell, or the one your coach saw on the slopes. I knew Wendy. Her strength, her courage, her heart.''

"Seth.'' Wendy could feel tears gathering in her eyes. "I'm sorry. I know I already told you how awful I feel about the way I treated you, but I really, really am sorry. I thought it was the best way to end things.''

"Yeah. So you said. Listen, I don't want to go through this again, okay? I don't need to hear how you lay in that hospital bed and realized we weren't right for each other.''

"That's not what happened.'' Wendy took a deep breath. "I mean…I mean, all I could think was that my whole life had changed, Seth. That I was a different person, that—''

"Oh, look at the snow on the soldier,'' Robin sang out. "Isn't it beautiful? Could we go see him, Uncle Seth? Could we?''

Seth shut his eyes, then opened them again. They'd been so close, so close to talking in a way they hadn't since the night she'd said goodbye to him all those long years ago….

"Uncle Seth? Can we?''

He swallowed hard. "Wendy? You remember the Minuteman? You up to walking over to pay him a visit?''

Wendy didn't answer. He looked at her and saw the glint of dampness in her eyes as she returned his look.

There was so much more he wanted to say to her, but not now, with the twins babbling happily about the soldier.

"I walked them to the green one afternoon,'' he said. "Damned if they didn't feel sorry for the statue, standing there all alone.''

"Nobody should be alone,'' Wendy said quietly.

Seth reached for her hand, his aching heart soaring when she threaded her fingers through his.

"You're right. So I explained that he wasn't alone, that he was surrounded by the hopes and dreams of all the people who'd ever lived in Cooper's Corner. I told them that he was proud to stand here, watching over the town, so many years after he fought for our freedom."

"For our freedom," Robin echoed somberly.

Wendy smiled. "That's nice."

"Yeah." He gave a little laugh. "To tell the truth, I was, what, nineteen when I first saw that statue—"

"Eighteen. You were just eighteen when you came to Cooper's Corner."

"Eighteen. Right." They paused before the Minuteman, so still and resolute, his lean form and stern face gently illuminated by the lights in the pedestal. "Eighteen, and I thought I was so big and tough."

"You were never tough. You were defensive, that was all, because you'd been hurt...." Her voice trembled. "And I hurt you again, Seth. Oh God, I'm so sorry."

He put his gloved fingers lightly against her lips. "That's all in the past."

"No." Her eyes swam with tears. "It isn't. It's still with us. With me. I know you don't understand—"

"You think the old Wendy is gone. That unless you can look in the mirror and see a leg that works like it used to, unless you can make the next Olympic team, unless you can win a goddamned medal, you're not the Wendy you once were."

"Yes—no. It isn't that simple."

He swung toward her. "Then make it simple," he said in a low voice. "Explain it in words of one syllable, if you have to, until I understand why you threw us away."

"Uncle Seth?"

"Because you have to tell me, damn it, or I'm going to be stuck forever in that moment where I opened the note that said you never wanted to see me again."

"Uncle Seth? Look! It's snowin' harder."

Seth took a deep breath. What was he doing, standing in the middle of the village green, pleading with Wendy, while two little kids sat in a sled and the snow turned to a heavy downfall?

"Yeah. So it is. Sorry, guys. You must be freezing."

"Oh, we're not cold," Robin said happily. "We just want to make a snowman."

"Another time."

"Aw, come on. We could do it now. Please?"

"Another time, you two." He forced himself to smile at the children. "As it is, the sled dogs are gonna have a tough go of it, spotting the igloo through the storm."

"What's a sled dog?"

"What's a igloo?"

"I'm the sled dog," Seth said, wrapping the rope around his hand. "And I'll bet Aunt Wendy can explain what an igloo is better than I can."

Explain about igloos? Wendy could hardly think straight. So many bottled emotions, so many tortured admissions were struggling to get out.

But the children were waiting. When she looked at them, she could see the expectation in their faces, so she took a deep breath, invented a Husky named Akela and an igloo that stood at the top of the world.

After a while, she was as lost in the tale as the children.

"Don't stop," they begged.

She didn't. She went on with her story, adding characters, describing the arctic tundra and northern lights and towering castles of ice. She kept talking while they made their way to Twin Oaks, while she and Seth tugged off boots and mittens, undid all those buttons and snaps, and only stopped when they brought the twins upstairs to Maureen, who grinned and took her babies into her arms.

"Finish the story, Aunt Wendy," Robin pleaded. Randi echoed the request, but it was late, much later than Wendy had imagined.

"I'll finish it tomorrow night. How's that?"

"What story?" Maureen asked.

"It's all about Akela," Randi said excitedly. "He lives in a igloo."

Maureen raised her eyebrows. Wendy laughed and explained all about the walk through the snow and how Seth had pretended he was a sled dog. She and Maureen got to talking. By the time they said good-night, long minutes had gone by.

Seth was gone. Would he be waiting for her in the gathering room?

He wasn't. The room was empty except for Clint, who looked up when he saw Wendy.

"Hey. You were terrific. I can see you're going to be a real asset to Twin Oaks."

"Thanks. I had fun."

"Glad to hear it. Well, might as well call it a night. See you tomorrow."

Wendy smiled, said yes, she'd see him the next evening, got all wrapped up again in her parka, scarf, hat and gloves, and went out into the snowy night, telling herself it was dumb to feel disappointed, that there was no reason Seth should have waited for her....

Two hard hands closed gently on her shoulders.

"It's me," Seth said softly, and she turned around, wanting to tell him that she knew his touch, that she'd know it anywhere, that she'd never forgotten it or him...

"Tonight was great."

She nodded. Snow whirled around them, locking them in its white magic.

Seth smiled, lifted one gloved hand to her chin and tilted her face up. "Let's call a truce, okay?"

She smiled, too, a little sadly. "I'd like that, but we already tried, remember? It didn't work."

He looked at her mouth, then into her eyes. "That's because we didn't seal it."

"With a handshake?"

His eyes grew dark. "With a kiss," he murmured, and

when he took her in his arms and covered her mouth with his, Wendy sighed his name and kissed him and kissed him, while the sky and the snow and the planet spun wildly through space.

CHAPTER ELEVEN

AFTER THREE DAYS, peace returned to the Monroe household.

Wendy was very glad it did.

Tiptoeing around your parents when you were ten or eleven and they'd quarreled was uncomfortable. When you were twenty-seven, it was unbearable—especially when they'd quarreled over you. Not that her parents had shouted or snarled or even exchanged harsh words after her mother's outburst.

Wendy pulled on an ivory wool sweater, lifted her hair free of the turtleneck collar and picked up her hairbrush.

Actually, a little shouting might have been better than the formality with which they'd treated each other afterward. Everything was very civilized. 'Please,' 'thank you' and 'you're welcome' were the only words exchanged, hanging in the air like dust motes on a sunny day. Somehow, that had only made the tension more noticeable, perhaps because Wendy couldn't remember her folks arguing over her when she was growing up.

Well, yes. She could. She paused in front of the mirror in her bedroom, the brush in her hand forgotten. She could recall hearing the hum of their voices leaching through the bedroom wall long after she was supposed to be asleep, Gina saying that Wendy should be permitted to spend a few days in Boston with a friend and her parents, and Howard disagreeing because she'd lose vital practice time.

Amazing that she'd forgotten that low-pitched discussion, or others like it. Was it because remembering was too upsetting? Maybe they weren't real memories at all. Children's recollections could be fickle, couldn't they?

No. They were real memories, all right; she could even recall the mornings that came after them, how her father would explain that she could spend time with her friends later, when practice wasn't so important.

Once she reached middle school, she didn't need those pep talks. She didn't want to do anything but ski.

And then, in high school, she met Seth.

Wendy sighed, returned to brushing her hair with even more vigor.

Seth. A smile curved her lips as she thought about him. Their truce was holding. Better than holding. They'd spent the past three evenings together at Twin Oaks, and even when he was with the twins and she was busy with guests, she was always aware of his presence. Sometimes, she'd look up and see him watching her. She'd smile, and he'd smile....

That walk in the snow had changed everything.

They didn't argue anymore or talk about the past. They just enjoyed being together. Seth hung around the B and B after Randi and Robin went to bed. He waited for her to finish up, and they'd drive to a little diner on the road to Lenox or to the Burger Barn, order something to eat and then let the food get cold because all they really wanted to do was look at each other and talk.

"You're not tiring yourself out, are you, baby?" Gina had said just this morning.

It was her subtle way of letting Wendy know she was aware of how late she came home nights, lots later than the job at Twin Oaks necessitated. Wendy had looked up from her oatmeal, considered telling her that she was seeing Seth, and then thought no, she wouldn't. Her mother was too sentimental. Too old-fashioned. She'd leap to conclusions about forever after, and forever after wasn't part of the equation.

There were still too many questions. Not about Wendy's feelings for Seth. She loved him; she knew that. And even though he hadn't said it, she sensed he still loved her. But where did that take them? Where did they go from here? She knew what Seth would want. Marriage. A life in Cooper's Corner. Children. *Children,* she thought again, and felt the old despair creeping up to envelop her.

And then there was the operation. Seth was opposed to it. He thought she wanted the surgery for the wrong reasons, but how could he judge what was right for her? How could he possibly understand how important it was for her to reclaim at least part of herself, when he didn't know how much of herself she'd actually lost?

Wendy put down the hairbrush, took a pair of small gold hoops from the top of the dresser and inserted them in her earlobes.

Pommier had to come back to town soon. He just had to.

She looked at her reflection again.

And she had to get to work. She was due at Twin Oaks in less than ten minutes.

TWO TOWHEADED LITTLE BOYS, a girl with dark-brown braids and a boy about the twins' age all sat cross-legged at Wendy's feet in the gathering room. Randi and Robin were curled against her on the love seat.

All six pairs of eyes were fixed on Wendy's face.

"...and," she said softly, "when Janie heard the wolf's long, lonely howls echoing through the starry night, she wrapped her arms around Akela and planted a kiss on his silky muzzle, just between his sad eyes.

"'Is the wolf your friend?'" Janie asked. "'Do you feel sorry for him? Please, Akela, don't go away. I love you.'

"Akela licked Janie's face. Then he looked up, up, up at

the moon. What should he do? Follow the cry of the wolf or stay with the little girl he loved? It was a terribly difficult choice to make, but he knew he had to make it, and soon.''

Wendy fell silent. The only sounds in the gathering room were the crackle and pop of the logs blazing on the hearth and the soft tinkle of keys as Beth Young, the village librarian, coaxed lush, old-fashioned melodies from the Twin Oaks piano.

At last the children gave long sighs.

''That's a wonderful story,'' Randi said.

''Akela should stay with Janie,'' Robin said gravely. '''Cause he loves her and she loves him.''

''Yeah, but that old wolf out there in the forest is so lonely,'' one of the towheaded little boys said, just as seriously. ''Wendy? What's Akela gonna do?''

''My question, exactly,'' Seth said. He was sitting behind the kids in an old wing chair. ''What's Akela going to do?''

Wendy smiled at him. ''You'll just have to wait until tomorrow night to find out.''

''But we won't be here t'morrow night,'' a small voice said. ''We'll never know what happens to Akela.''

Wendy looked at the little girl with the dark braids. Her bottom lip was trembling.

''Oh, honey.'' Wendy drew the child onto her lap. ''When are you leaving?''

''In the morning,'' a woman said softly. She gave Wendy a quick smile. ''Hi. I'm Amy's mom. I want you to know that she's loved every minute of Storytime.''

Storytime. That was what Clint had taken to calling her nightly sessions with the twins and any other children present at Twin Oaks. He'd even listed it on the chalkboard, after checking with Wendy. She'd been happy to agree to tell stories each evening, though at first she'd thought ''Storytime'' sounded too formal for what she did.

Now she felt a rush of pleasure whenever someone said the word.

"Well, we can't let your daughter go home without knowing what Akela decides, can we, Amy?"

Amy shook her head. "No. We sure can't."

Wendy smiled and tugged gently at one of the child's braids. "Tell you what. Suppose I meet you right here tomorrow morning at..." she looked at the mother "...eight o'clock? Will that work for you?"

"Oh, yes. That would be great."

"Eight o'clock, then." Wendy lowered her voice to a whisper. "And I'll tell you what Akela decides to do."

A happy grin spread across the girl's face. "Thank you!"

"You're very welcome." She hugged her, and the child scrambled off her lap and ran to her mother. "And before anybody asks," Wendy said, her stern tone offset by her smile, "all the rest of you will just have to wait until tomorrow evening."

There were a couple of halfhearted groans, including one from Seth as he came toward her. She grinned as he clasped her outstretched hands.

"You're not gonna make me wait, too," he said, "are you?"

"Yes, she is," Robin declared. "Aren't you, Aunt Wendy?"

Wendy kissed Robin, then Randi, and got to her feet. "Darned right I am. Uncle Seth will have to wait, just like you guys."

"Good!"

"What's good?" Clint asked as he joined them and scooped the twins into his arms. "Surely not the terrors. They're never good."

"We're always good," Randi said decisively. "Right, Uncle Seth?"

"Absolutely! Especially when you go to bed without complaining."

"Brilliant," Clint said with a grin. "Why didn't I think of that?"

Wendy gave each child a hug and a kiss. "Good night, princesses."

"G'night," the girls replied sleepily.

"Hold down the fort, okay, while I deliver these angels to their mother?"

"Sure."

"Be down in five...and Wendy? You're terrific at this."

"Mr. Cooper's right."

Wendy and Seth looked around. A man had come up alongside the little group. He held out his hand as Clint started up the stairs. "Arnold Worshinsky. The pair of tow-headed hellions you held enthralled for the past half hour belong to me."

"Nice to meet you, Mr. Worshinsky."

"Are you a pro?"

"Excuse me?"

"A professional storyteller?"

"I didn't even know there was such a thing."

"Oh, there is. I've heard several, and believe me, you're as good as any of them. Maybe better."

"Well, that's very kind, but—"

"Kind, heck." Seth slid his arm around Wendy's shoulders. "The man's right, sweetheart. You're wonderful."

She smiled up at him. Sweetheart. That was what he'd called her, just like in the old days.

"...any writing, Ms. Monroe?"

Wendy drew her gaze from Seth. "Sorry. What did you say?"

"I asked if you'd ever done any writing."

"Writing? No."

"Sure she has." Seth pointedly ignored the surprised look she gave him. "Wendy took a creative writing course her senior year in high school." He smiled. "And she aced it."

"You remember that?"

"Of course. You showed me that poem you wrote, remember? It was great." His voice lowered. "I remember everything about that year."

Arnold Worshinsky cleared his throat. "Ms. Monroe," he said, handing her a business card, "if you have more stories, I'd be happy to see them."

Wendy looked at the card. "Paper Doll Press?"

"Uh-huh. We publish children's books."

"Oh, but I'm not—"

"Won the Caldecott Medal the last two years."

"I'm sure that's an honor, but—"

She tried to put the card back in Worshinsky's hand, but he shook his head. "Keep it, please. There are thousands of children out there who'd love to be fortunate enough to enjoy your stories."

"But I'm not a writer, I'm a…" She hesitated. What was she? She didn't really know. Slowly, she tucked the card into her pocket. "Well, thank you."

"My pleasure. Ms. Monroe. Mr.…?"

"Castleman. Seth Castleman."

"Mr. Castleman. Nice meeting you both."

Wendy waited until the publisher strolled away. Then she turned toward Seth and gave a little laugh. "Do you believe that?"

"That the guy wants to buy your stories? Sweetheart, I'm telling you, you're terrific. Did you see those kids, hanging on every word?"

"It's just because they don't have anything else to do."

"Oh, right." Seth clasped Wendy's hand. They walked slowly toward the empty office. "Maureen's kids practically have their own FAO Schwarz store upstairs, and the guests' children bring along enough toys to stock a summer camp. Electronic games. Board games. Crayons. Puzzles. Barbie dolls, and whatever you call those weird plastic jobs that look like monsters on steroids."

Wendy laughed. "Yes, but still—"

"But still, they'd rather listen to you tell stories." He

smiled. "Who knows? This could be the start of a whole new life."

A new life. A new start. Wendy saw the flicker of hope in Seth's eyes, felt the answering flicker in her heart. And then she thought of the past years, the grueling regimen, the hours of painful therapy...

And the secret that had almost destroyed her.

"I'm not a storyteller," she said quietly. "I'm not anything right now. I don't know why I didn't tell that to the man."

"Okay." Seth's smile was forced. "Let's not get into this."

"I'm not 'getting into' anything, I'm just stating a fact."

"Sweetheart." He rubbed his hands lightly up and down her arms. "You want to ski again? Hey, you can be skiing tomorrow."

"I can't. Not with this leg."

"You don't have to wear a number on your back and beat somebody else's time down the hill to ski."

"Yes, I do! That's who I am, Seth. Don't you understand?"

The stridency in her voice angered Seth. The last few days, he'd let himself start to hope things were changing. Had he been kidding himself?

He shut the office door. "What I understand," he said, "is that you want to turn back the clock. Well, you can't do it. Nobody can."

"I will. I have to."

She spoke with defiance, but there was a suspicious glint in her eyes. It softened his anger, and he linked his fingers through hers.

"Why can't you see yourself as I do?" he said gently. "You're strong. Determined. Brave. You're Wendy Monroe."

"But I'm not. I'm *not* Wendy Monroe, not the same one you loved."

"Sweetheart, you are."

"I know who I am, Seth. And I don't need you to prac-
ce armchair psychiatry."

"Damn it, can't you see I care?" *Stop it,* he told himself.
op it while you can. But it killed him to see how she
iewed herself. "We're talking about the surgery again,
en't we? How you'd risk everything so you can walk
ithout a limp."

"I don't expect you to understand."

"You can't honestly believe people judge you by that."

Wendy jerked her hands free of his and jammed her
nger against her chest. "*I* judge me. This is my life,
eth, and I need to be whole again. To ski. To compete.
o win."

"Do you?" He could feel his control slipping. There had
 be a way to reach her. "Is that the life you want, Wendy?
r is it the life you think you should want?"

She stiffened. "What's that supposed to mean?"

He didn't answer. What was the point? They both knew
hat he meant, and he'd said too much already. The last
ing he wanted to do was destroy the truce they'd managed
 establish.

"Wendy." He clasped her shoulders. "Come with me
morrow."

"Where?"

"To Jiminy Peak. Let me get you up on skis— No. Don't
rn your face away." Seth cupped her chin and made her
ok at him. "You remember that long, curved run?"

"The Left Bank?"

She spoke with distaste. He decided to ignore it. "Right.
's a nice run."

"It's a run for people who don't know a lot about ski-
g."

"How about it's a run for people who haven't skied in
ears?"

"How about it's a run for cripples?"

She jerked free of his hands, yanked the door open an‹ walked away.

SETH THOUGHT ABOUT going home.

Actually, he thought about saying to hell with it all. Wh‹ good was a dream about love when only one person w‹ dreaming?

He got as far as putting on his jacket and heading for th‹ door. Then he stopped, mumbled some words that fit th‹ occasion and turned back to the reception desk, where Cli‹ was sorting some papers.

Wendy was nowhere in sight, but her parka was sti‹ hanging where she'd left it. She was still around, som‹ where.

"You have anything needs doing around here?"

Clint, clever man that he was, looked at Seth's face b‹ asked no questions. "Well, actually," he said, "we had ‹ couple of deliveries and I haven't had time to organize th‹ boxes. You could move them. You know, office suppli‹ with office supplies, publicity stuff with—"

"Yeah," Seth said, "I get the idea."

He dumped his jacket on a chair in the storeroom. The‹ like Sisyphus endlessly rolling that dumb rock up that eve‹ dumber hill, he shifted boxes from one end of the room t‹ the other.

There was nothing like mindless physical labor for wor‹ ing out frustration. For thinking and coming to some so‹ of a decision.

He was finished letting Wendy push him away. He'd l‹ it happen last time because he was a kid, and what did ‹ kid know about women? Okay. He didn't know much mo‹ about them now—what man did? But at least he wasn‹ nineteen anymore. And maybe, just maybe, the reason she'‹ been able to do it so easily was because, in his heart, he'‹ never really felt worthy of her.

Seth paused, wiped the back of his hand across his forehead.

No. That was the wrong word. What he'd felt was amazed that a guy like him could have touched the heart of a girl like Wendy.

She'd grown up in a picture-postcard town. She had people who loved her, friends who cared about her. And by the time they met, she'd been surrounded by guys who thought skiing was life.

Well, skiing was fun, but Seth skied for sport. For the rush that came of knowing he could control what was actually a dangerous skid down a mountain, making it into an exhilarating ride. Though he'd never say it out loud because it sounded so corny, he skied for the communion he felt with the snow and the mountains.

Wendy skied for those things, too. The trouble was, she also skied for a medal.

There was nothing wrong with that, if a medal was what she really wanted. But after he'd known her a few months, he'd become convinced it was her old man who wanted the medal a lot more than she did.

Seth grunted as he lifted another box. It was marked Fax Paper, but it felt more like bowling balls. He carried it across the storeroom and eased it down on the floor.

Maybe there was nothing wrong with that, either. Her father had turned her on to Alpine racing because he loved it. So what? Lots of parents introduced their kids to sports for the same reason.

The trouble was, somewhere along the way, winning had become all that mattered. Seth would never forget Wendy's exhaustion those last weeks before Lillehammer. Her pallor, her nerves—nerves so bad she'd lost her appetite and even thrown up a couple of times.

"Don't go to Norway," he'd said. "Stay here. Marry me." He'd spoken on impulse. He had no real way to support a wife. He was living in a furnished room, working at

the ski run, taking a handful of college classes he didn't
much enjoy. But if she'd said yes, he'd have taken a second
job, done anything just to make it possible.

But she didn't say yes.

"I have to go to Norway," she'd told him, and he'd
convinced himself to let her go and get this out of her
system.

Except she'd gone to Norway and damn near gotten herself killed. And somehow the fact that she'd lived, that
she'd gotten out of a wheelchair when nobody thought she
would—somehow none of that mattered once she'd heard
there was an operation that might let her get back to chasing
that damn medal.

That they'd found each other again didn't seem to matter
either. Nothing did but that medal.

Seth sat down on a box, reached for a can of Diet Coke
that somebody had left in the storeroom, and popped the
tab. He tilted the can to his lips and took a long, thirsty
swallow.

Wendy had come out with one great truth earlier this
evening. It was her life. If she wanted another shot at the
medal, he had to introduce her to Rod Pommier. He had no
choice.

If the operation was a failure, she'd want no part of him
because of the way she felt about her disability. If it was a
success, she'd have no room in her life for anything but
competitive skiing. She was lost to Seth no matter what he
did. He had to accept that, and forget about the foolish
dreams he'd thought they'd once shared.

The hell he did.

He had one day before Pommier came back, one day to
convince her that she was perfect just the way she was, that
he loved her....

That she loved him.

Seth tossed the empty can aside, grabbed his jacket and hurried into the gathering room. The lights were dimmed and the room was empty except for Beth and Clint, seated on the piano bench.

Wendy was just heading toward the main door. Seth ran after her, caught her by the arm as she reached the porch, and turned her toward him.

"Wendy!"

What he felt must have been in his eyes, because she gasped when she saw him. "Wait," she said, "Seth—"

"The hell I will," he muttered as he pulled her into his arms and kissed her. She made a little sound as his mouth came down on hers, and he felt her raise her hands between them. He was beyond thought, beyond anything but fearing he might have lost her for whatever time they'd have together. He clasped her wrists, figuring she was going to try and shove him away, but she didn't.

God, she didn't.

She burned in his arms, instead.

"Seth," she whispered. "Oh, Seth. I thought you'd left."

"No. Never. I'll never leave you again." He burrowed his fingers into her hair, tilted her head back, traced the elegant arcs of her cheekbones with his thumbs and kissed her again. "I'm sorry, sweetheart."

"Me, too. Please," she said between kisses, "let's not quarrel. Let's not talk about skiing or my leg or what might happen tomorrow. Nobody can read the future. I know that better than anyone."

She was wrong. He could read the future. Part of it, anyway. He knew he'd been wrong to keep his friendship with Rod Pommier from her. The only thing worse than not having told Wendy about Pommier would be if Pommier refused to see her.

Seth wouldn't let that happen.

He'd set things up with Pommier, then tell Wendy. After that, whatever she decided, he'd accept. But the doctor wasn't coming back until tomorrow night. Seth had that much time to make the woman he loved see reason.

For now, all that mattered was holding her in his arms, feeling her heart race against his, hearing the whisper of piano music drifting on the soft, silent winter night. Beth was playing an old standard meant for lovers and it took Seth back in time, to a night he'd never forgotten.

His arms tightened around Wendy.

"Remember that night we parked in our place up on the mountain?"

She gave a soft laugh and slipped her arms around his neck. "I remember a lot of nights on the mountain."

"So do I." Slowly, he began swaying to the music. "But I'm thinking about one night in particular." Gently, he turned them in a little circle; Wendy sighed and laid her head against his shoulder. "It was summer. We drove up the mountain and parked. We had the radio playing and you said we'd never danced together. And I said—"

"And you said that we could." She drew back just a little and tilted her face to his, the memory shining in her eyes. "So we got out of your truck and took off our shoes...."

"And danced in that little clearing, with the moon looking down and the stars lighting your face."

"You kissed me," Wendy murmured, "and we made love for the very first time."

Their mouths met in a kiss as tender as the one they'd shared that night, and just for the moment, instead of dancing on the porch at Twin Oaks, with a slice of winter moon chilling the stars, they were dancing barefoot in the grass on top of Sawtooth Mountain, the night lit by a fat summer moon.

They danced into the darkness, swaying slowly in each other's arms, Seth framing her face with his hands, Wendy clutching his jacket in her fists, and their kisses changed from the sweetness of remembered love to the passion of love long denied.

Wendy began to tremble as Seth's body hardened against hers.

"Seth," she breathed when he swept his hands under her parka, down her spine, cupped her bottom and lifted her into him.

There was only one way for this night to end.

"Wendy." He kissed her, groaned when her mouth opened to his and she drew his tongue between her lips. He pulled back, knowing that he was close to the edge, knowing, too, that he could take her now but that he didn't want to, that he needed to make this perfect. "Wendy. Sweetheart. Come with me."

"Yes. Oh, yes. But where?"

"There's only one place that's right for us, darling."

She looked up into his eyes. "Sawtooth Mountain?" He nodded and she smiled. "It's the middle of winter."

"Uh-huh."

She laughed, and he thought he'd never heard a more wonderful sound.

"We'll freeze."

"I promise," he said huskily, "we won't." He bent his head to hers, kissed her throat, felt the pulse leap beneath his mouth. "I love you, Wendy."

"Oh, Seth." She thrust her hands into his hair and tugged his face up to hers. "How can you? I've been so—"

"I've always loved you, sweetheart. I never stopped."

There were times when lies were simpler and, in the long run, less painful, but this was a night for truth. Wendy drew a deep breath and said the words so long locked within her mind and heart.

"I love you, too, Seth. I always did."

"Will you come with me?"

She smiled. "Yes."

Seth kissed her again, then lifted her in his arms. She buried her face in his throat as he carried her from the porch to his truck, and they drove off into the night.

CHAPTER TWELVE

SETH FELL IN BEHIND a snowplow, its red taillights winking against the darkness. The plow made swift work of the heavy drifts ahead of them, leaving the road to snake like a black ribbon toward the mountain. Behind them, the asphalt quickly disappeared under its new covering of snow.

So did Wendy's euphoria. Were they leaving the past behind and moving toward the future, or were they traveling through a landscape that was more dream than reality? She hoped it wasn't a dream, because dreams never lasted.

Was she making a terrible mistake? Surely there'd be a price to pay for abandoning all these years of steely resolve. She shuddered, and Seth reached across the console and clasped her hand.

"Sweetheart? Are you cold?"

She looked at him and managed a little smile. "I guess I am."

He turned up the heat, then took her hand again. His palm and fingers swallowed hers. Seth was strong in the best possible ways. He'd stood up to all the bad things the years had dealt him. Until this moment, she hadn't let herself admit how much she'd really missed him, not just in her arms but in her life.

"I turned the heat up all the way. That should help."

How could it, when the chill she felt was bone deep? Heart deep. Oh, heart deep. She'd hurt him so much, this man she loved.

"I'm warmer already." She tried to sound happy, but

she failed, miserably. Confirmation came in the look Seth gave her.

"Wendy." She saw his jaw tighten, felt his hand press hard against hers. "Sweetheart, if you're having second thoughts—"

"No."

She was having second and third and fourth thoughts, but she wasn't going to tell him that. They were entitled to this night; whatever came next was beyond her control. That was something she'd learned during the past years. You could try to make plans for your life and think you'd included the smallest detail. In the end, it didn't matter. Life happened. It sort of sneaked up and happened, despite your best plans.

"No," she said again, quietly. She lifted their joined hands and kissed his work-roughened knuckles. "I want to be with you tonight."

The conviction in her voice made his heart swell, but only a fool would have missed that carefully added word, *tonight*. Seth decided to let it go. Once he'd talked to Pommier, taken the first step down the road, tonight might well be all they'd have.

"I've dreamed about bringing you up the mountain again," he said softly.

She sighed and leaned her head back. "You know what I've never forgotten? That first time we drove up Sawtooth. Remember?"

Did he remember? There were times those memories had been all that stood between him and darkness.

"Would a guy forget the first time he made out with the girl of his dreams?" he said, giving it a light touch. "It was our third date."

"It was our fourth," Wendy said in a prim tone. "I'd never have agreed to park on a third date."

"Yeah, but this wasn't just any third date, baby. You were with me. Seth Castleman, the make-out king."

She laughed at his deliberately pompous tone. "Uh-huh."

"The truth is, you couldn't keep your hands off me."

"You wish."

"I *know*."

They smiled at each other and then Wendy let out a long breath. "You know what I really do wish?"

"What?"

"That this was your old truck. It had a bench seat, and I—"

"You used to scoot all the way over and sit right next to me, with your head on my shoulder."

"Remember when that trooper stopped us? He gave us a lecture about seat belts and he said he wouldn't give us a ticket if we promised not to ride like that anymore."

"And then he said he had a daughter just about your age, and that he hoped we'd behave ourselves." Seth grinned. "Would you believe I built a sunroom for him a couple of years back?"

"You're kidding!"

"It was the same guy. I knew he looked familiar, but I didn't actually place him until I'd been working at his house for a few days."

"Did he recognize you?"

"I didn't think so, because he never said a word—right up until the day I finished." Seth chuckled. "He wrote me a check, told me how pleased he was with the work I'd done—and then he gave me a man-to-man grin and said he hoped I'd taken his advice and behaved myself the night he'd stopped me on the road up Sawtooth Mountain."

Wendy laughed. "What did you say?"

"I asked him if he could remember when he was nineteen, and he laughed and said yeah, and that was exactly why he'd given me that warning. We shook hands...."

"And?"

His voice roughened. "And nothing."

"Seth, what is it? What happened after that?"

"He asked me if you and I were still together." Seth let go of Wendy's hand. "And I said no, we weren't, that I hadn't seen you in years. He said he was sorry and I said it was okay—but it wasn't. Until then, I'd done a pretty good job of not thinking about you for days at a time, but afterward—"

"Don't." Impetuously, Wendy undid her seat belt and got as close to Seth as she could. "Don't, please. It was the same for me. I missed you terribly. Every day, every night. You were all I thought about."

Then why did you refuse to see me? Why did you stay away instead of coming back to the life we'd planned?

The questions drove him crazy, which was in itself crazy, because he already knew the answers. Either she'd figured he wouldn't want her unless she was perfect, or a life with him wasn't enough.

No. Damn it, he wasn't going to think about that. Not tonight. He was taking her to his bed, the bed no woman had ever slept in, and to a house he'd always known, in his heart, he'd built for her.

He brought her hand to his lips and kissed it.

"Get back there and buckle up," he said gruffly. "The road's icy."

"Aren't we almost to the top of the…oh, Seth!" Wendy leaned forward and stared out the window. The windshield wipers and the heavy snow made it difficult to see clearly, but surely she'd just spotted…,"There's a house on the top of our mountain!" She swung toward him, her eyes wide with disappointment. "Somebody built on our land."

"Yeah. Somebody did."

"Didn't you know? Why didn't you tell me? Who—"

Wendy's voice broke. Things didn't stay the same. Her life was proof of that, but somehow—somehow she hadn't expected—

"Sweetheart, it's all right." Seth reached for her hand

again. "Forgive me, Wendy. I wanted to surprise you." He kissed her palm. "It's mine."

She stared at him while she absorbed the news. "Yours?" she finally said, and looked at the house again. She could see it more clearly as they headed up the long driveway. The soaring rooflines. The glass. The vertical board siding.

"I bought the land as soon as I could afford it. I began work on the house a couple of years ago." Seth gave a soft laugh. "Actually, I'm still putting it up. A couple of the rooms aren't finished yet, and the back deck needs some work...."

Shut up, he told himself. He was babbling, but damn it, he was nervous. How many times had he imagined bringing Wendy here? He'd planned it so carefully. She'd see the house first by daylight, when the sun poured through the trees and touched the valley and the town with gold. He'd walk her through the rooms and watch her face....

Would she like what he'd built? Would she remember the house they'd planned to the smallest details, and see that they were all here?

"You can't see much at night," he said quickly, "especially with all this snow."

"It's beautiful."

He looked at her. She was sitting forward, eyes fixed on the house, and the way she whispered those words made his throat tighten.

"It's perfect." She looked at him, eyes shining in the muted light from the dashboard. "It's the house we planned together."

The garage door slid open. Seth drove the truck inside and shut off the engine.

"Every inch of it," he said huskily. "I built this house for you."

Wendy turned to Seth. The interior garage lights had come on and she could see his face in their merciless glare.

Tiny lines radiated from the corners of his eyes; his forehead was lightly furrowed. Time had marked him, but he was still the boy she'd fallen in love with. He always had been, always would be, and suddenly she wanted to weep for all the years they'd lost.

"It's the most wonderful gift in the world, Seth. Thank you."

Seth wanted to tell her she didn't have to thank him, that just hearing the love in her voice was more than enough, but he wasn't sure he could get out the words. Instead, he climbed out of the truck and went around to the other side. Wendy slid down into his embrace. For the second time that night he lifted the woman he loved in his arms, and carried her into their house.

The snow had stopped and the pale winter moon they'd danced beneath on the porch at Twin Oaks illuminated the staircase and hall. A sighing wind had blown the snow from the skylight in his room, and the moon cast a soft white light on the bed.

"Here's where I've imagined you," Seth said softly. "In this room, in my arms."

He lowered her to her feet, letting her slide down his body, thrilling to the little sound she made when she felt his hardness against her.

He kissed her and she kissed him back, tenderly, sweetly, little nibbling kisses that grew more hungry as he unzipped her jacket and she unzipped his. Clothing fell to the floor as they stripped away the layers of fabric that separated them, and when they were both naked, more than clothing lay at their feet. All the years they'd been apart, the hurt, the loneliness were discarded, as well.

They waited, looking at each other. Then Seth made a low, rough sound in his throat and gathered Wendy into his arms. Oh, God, the feel of her. She was silk and satin and molten heat. She was all and everything, and how had he ever lived without her?

Wendy caught her breath at the feel of Seth's hot skin against her. The thud of his heart. The definition of muscle and sinew. The exciting feel of his aroused flesh against her belly.

She was dizzy with wanting him, terrified of the depth of that want. What if this wasn't everything she remembered? What if lying in his arms didn't match the memories of those stolen teenage years? She trembled and she knew Seth must have understood, because he caught her wrists, lifted her hands to his lips and kissed them, closed her fingers and sealed the kisses forever.

"Slowly," he whispered. "Slowly, sweetheart." He brushed his mouth over hers. "No curfew, remember?" She felt his lips curve in a smile. "No gearshift knob to get in the way, no cold vinyl seat. We have a soft, warm bed and all the time in the world."

He kissed her again, gently, and she knew he was giving her time to adapt to what was happening. But she didn't want time. She wanted Seth, his hands, his mouth.

His possession.

She moved against him, tilted her pelvis so that her flesh brushed against his erection. The breath hissed from between his teeth.

"Wendy," he said thickly, the word a clear warning.

"Yes," she whispered, "please, yes."

He swung her into his arms and carried her to the bed, laying her down against the pillows while the wind picked up and the blowing snow danced like a gypsy against the windows.

Seth bent his dark head and kissed Wendy's mouth and throat, trailing kisses to her breast. She cried out when his lips closed around her nipple, and rose toward him, her body arching with desire.

"Seth. Oh, Seth. I need—I need…"

He touched her, slid his hand between her thighs. Her head fell back, and when he bent to kiss her, he felt the warmth of her tears on his mouth, the warmth of her body's sweetest moisture on his fingers.

God, he was going to come before he was inside her. All these years. So many, many years—

"Yes," he whispered, "yes, yes…"

Quickly, he took a small foil packet from a drawer in the bedside table. When he was ready, he knelt between her legs and slid inside her. Deep inside her. She was tight and hot, just as she'd been the first time they'd made love. Her sobs and soft cries of pleasure were the same, and when she clutched his biceps and lifted herself toward him, the years fell away. He was nineteen, she was eighteen, and nothing would ever be more important than this.

"Seth. Seth…"

Wendy sobbed his name in ecstasy. Seth saw her face, saw everything he'd ever needed in her wide eyes, and he let go of his loneliness, his denial, his anger, and poured himself into the warm, welcoming body of the only woman he had ever loved.

LONG MOMENTS LATER, Wendy stirred.

"Mmm," she said softly.

Seth smiled as she bit his shoulder lightly. "Mmm is right." He brushed his mouth over hers. "Are you okay?"

"I'm very okay." He started to move and she tightened her arms around him. "Don't go."

"I'm too heavy for you."

"You aren't. I love the feel of you inside me."

He rolled to his side with her in his arms and gathered her close against him. "That's good. That's very, very good, because that's where I intend to spend a lot of my time." He twined his fingers in the hair at the nape of her neck, tilted her head back and kissed her again. "How's that sound?"

He felt her mouth curve against his. "Like a plan I could vote for."

"That's two votes, so it's unanimous." They lay quietly in each other's arms for a few moments. Seth shut his eyes. Was now the time to tell her about his connection to Pommier? Would it be better to wait? No. He'd waited too long as it was. "Sweetheart?"

"Mmm?"

"Sweetheart, we need to talk."

Wendy closed her eyes. He was right, of course, but she didn't want to talk. Not tonight. Not with such new, wonderful joy in her heart.

"Not now."

"Sweetheart—"

"Please. No talking. Not yet."

She rolled over, lay on top of him and kissed him with slow, tender care, sinking her teeth gently into his bottom lip, teasing him with her tongue. She was taking control and, God, she had no mercy.

Just that easily, his brain turned off.

He tumbled her onto her back, clasped her face in his hands, kissed her hungrily. She felt soft as the snow and the night; she tasted like the nectar of a thousand flowers. He bit gently at her throat, her breasts, her belly. The musky female scent of her rose to his nostrils like a drug as he kissed her thigh.

"No!" The word exploded into the silence. "Not my leg. Don't. Oh, don't. It's horrible. Seth, please. It's ugly!"

"Nothing about you could be ugly to me."

She gasped as his lips sought and found the scars, the puckered flesh that would forever mark what had been pieced together with screws and metal plates.

Wendy's head fell back against the pillows. "Why did you do that?" she said in a broken whisper. "I didn't want—I wanted you to remember me the way I was."

She spoke with such deep sorrow that it almost broke his heart.

"You *are* the way you were. You're better. You're

stronger and braver.'' He turned her face to his. ''I love you. Do you really think anything could change that?''

Something could. Oh, yes, something could change that.

Wendy shut her eyes, desperately blocking out the swift rush of memory, that last night when Seth had begged her not to go to Lillehammer, not to leave him. He'd said he was worried because she was so tired, too tired to ski such dangerous runs.

Tears trickled from under her lashes. Seth murmured her name, kissed her closed eyelids, kissed her mouth until he felt it soften.

He bent his head lower, kissed her breasts, lavished attention on the furled apricot buds until he heard her sigh.

''Wendy,'' he whispered. He sheathed himself again, then moved down her body, tongued her navel, nuzzled her thighs apart and kissed her there, where her taste was sweetest.

She cried out and he slid his hands beneath her, raised her to his lips, let her soft, feminine flesh meet his seeking mouth.

She moaned, writhed beneath him, cried out, and when she did, Seth rose over her and entered her, groaning as he felt the muscles in her womb contract around him.

''You're mine,'' he said fiercely. ''Forever.''

''Yes,'' she sobbed, ''yes, yes...''

And then they were beyond speech, beyond anything but love.

SETH AWOKE TO DARKNESS and an empty space in the bed beside him.

''Wendy?''

He sat up. It was late—1:05, according to the illuminated face of the bedside clock—and the wind was still blowing.

Had she left him? She couldn't have. She had no way to get down the mountain, and besides, she wouldn't have left him, not after tonight.

Somewhere along the way, he'd pulled up the blankets. Now he tossed them aside, swung his feet to the floor, felt around for his jeans and pulled them on. Maybe she was in the bathroom. No. The bathroom was dark, but now that he was standing, he could see a soft light seeping under the bedroom door.

He went into the hall, leaned his elbows on the loft railing and saw Wendy in the kitchen, seated at the butcher block counter, her back to him. A thin plume of steam was rising from something in front of her. A mug, probably; there was a kettle on the stove and an open box of tea bags beside it.

He went down the steps quietly. He'd dreamed of seeing her here just like this. Her hair was hanging down her back in the wild tendrils he loved. She was barefoot, dressed only in his flannel shirt; it was long enough to cover most of her scars, but he could see a small area of the puckered skin that he now knew stretched from her knee to her hip, and he wondered, not for the first time, how she'd survived such a brutal injury.

Everything inside him wanted to go to her and press his mouth to the wounded flesh, but he knew it would be a mistake. She still insisted on walling him away from what had happened to her in Norway. It was bad enough she judged herself by the accident, but that she should even imagine he would…

He must have made a sound because she spun around. "Oh," she said, and grabbed for the hem of the shirt. In the process she knocked over the mug.

Seth rushed forward. "Are you okay?"

"I'm fine. See?" She laughed shakily and set the mug upright on the counter. "There were only a few drops left."

He cupped her face, bent to her and brushed his mouth over hers. "Sorry, sweetheart. I didn't mean to scare you."

"And I didn't mean to wake you." She glanced down at

her leg, flushed and tried to tug the hem of the shirt lower. "I just...I couldn't sleep."

He lifted her hair from the back of her neck and pressed his lips to her soft skin. "You should have woken me."

"It's all right. I had to call home, anyway."

His eyebrows rose. "At one in the morning?"

"Uh-huh. I figured my folks might be worried."

"Sure. I understand." He didn't. Yes, the call home made sense, but there was a stillness to her. A removal. What had changed between the time they'd made love and now? He nodded toward the kettle. "The water still hot?"

"I think so."

"Great." He went to the stove, made himself a cup of tea he didn't want. "Shall I make you some more?"

"No. Thank you. This was fine." Her eyes met his, then slid away. "Actually, I should go home."

You are home, he wanted to say, but instinct warned him to keep it light. "Have you looked outside? The drifts are probably four feet deep, and the wind's still blowing."

"I know, Seth, but—"

"Sweetheart." To hell with caution. He went to her and took hold of her hands. They were icy in his. "What's the matter? Did I...did I hurt you? I didn't mean to. I would never—"

Wendy shook her head. "Making love with you was wonderful. It's not you. It's me." Her gaze dropped to the counter. "I shouldn't have let this happen," she said in a small voice.

Seth slipped onto the stool next to her. "Why not?"

"Because it only complicates things."

Her hair had tumbled forward, hiding her face from him. He smoothed it back, put his hand under her chin and tilted her head up, his heart constricting at the sorrow he saw in her eyes.

"How can what we feel for each other complicate things?" he asked softly.

"It just can." She drew in a breath. "Everything changed, the day I took that fall."

"I know."

"You don't. Seth—"

He put his finger across her lips. "You're the one who had the accident, not me. I've been selfish, not fully grasping what that means." His smile was rueful. "Took me a while to figure that out, huh?"

"You've figured out more than I have." Wendy gave a sad laugh. "I woke up in your arms. For a second, I thought I was dreaming—and then I realized it wasn't a dream, that I was really here, with you." She swallowed hard. "Everything seemed so clear in Paris. I would come home, I'd talk to this doctor, he'd agree to operate on me and…and I'd be myself again. But…"

"But?" Seth urged softly.

"But there's more to it than that." Her fingers tightened on his. "How could I have been so foolish, Seth? How could I have thought an operation on my leg could turn back the clock?"

He could almost feel the flutter of hope inside him. "Are you saying you've changed your mind about wanting the surgery?"

She smiled a little at that. "You still think it's a mistake, hmm?"

"What I think doesn't matter," he said truthfully, and wondered how he could not have admitted that all this time.

She put her hand against his cheek. "Thank you," she murmured. "Thank you for saying that." She hesitated. "But I can't answer your question. I don't know what I want. Not now." She drew back and her eyes met his. "The only thing I'm sure of is that we have to talk. About me. About us. About what happened in Lillehammer."

He looked at her, at this woman he had never stopped loving, and knew she was right. They did have to talk. He had to tell her about Pommier, and once he did, things would move quickly.

And he might lose her.

But not now, not at 2:00 a.m. under the cold fluorescent glare of the kitchen lights. Not now, after he'd only just found her again.

"I agree." Seth stood and drew her to her feet. "It's time we talked about everything. And we will, in the morning."

She started to protest, but he kissed her to silence and swung her into his arms.

"Seth," she said with a little sigh, "we can't keep putting this off."

"Okay. We'll talk in bed."

"We can't talk in bed."

"Of course we can."

"Liar," she whispered.

"Yeah," he whispered back, and kissed her. He didn't stop kissing her until they were naked in his bed again.

She reached up to him in the darkness and clasped his face.

"This is a strange way to start a conversation," she said.

"It's the best way to start one."

"Seth? I love you. You need to know that. I love—"

He took her mouth with his, moved between her legs and thrust deep inside her. Wendy cried out, lifted herself to him, and soon they were lost to the world, alone together on a turbulent sea of passion.

CHAPTER THIRTEEN

WENDY CAME AWAKE slowly, drawn from sleep by the kiss of morning sunlight, the scent of coffee and rich spices...and the warm whisper of Seth's mouth against hers.

"Mmm," she murmured, her lips curving against his in a tender smile.

"Mmm, indeed." Seth's voice was early morning rough. So was the stubble on his jaw as she cupped his face. "Good morning."

"G'morning," Wendy muttered, and rolled onto her belly.

"Come on, sleepyhead." Seth planted a kiss between her shoulder blades. "Rise and shine."

"Wha'time izit?"

"Not a morning person, huh?" He sighed dramatically. "Terrible, the stuff a man learns about a woman the first time they spend the night together."

Wendy smiled into the pillow. She rolled onto her back and looked up at him, her eyes filled with warmth. "It was, wasn't it? Our first whole night together."

"And the first time we ever made love in a bed." He grinned and kissed her. "Whatever will they think of next?"

She sniffed the air. "Coffee?" she said hopefully.

"Uh-huh. And fresh orange juice. And a stack of cinnamon French toast with maple syrup. How's that sound?"

"Decadent." She smiled and linked her hands behind his head. "Cinnamon French toast, huh? I'm impressed."

"Don't get too impressed, babe. I should warn you, that's it. Fresh O.J. and French toast is my entire gourmette repertoire."

He said the word with a grin that made it clear the mispronunciation was deliberate. Wendy laughed. It seemed as if she'd done more laughing in the past few days than she had in a very long time.

She touched her fingers to his mouth. "Well, I'm impressed anyway."

"Good." He caught her hand and bit lightly into the pad at the base of her thumb. "It was a toss-up between cinnamon toast or a bowl of cornflakes. The toast won." He leaned down. "How about a kiss for the cook?"

Wendy pondered the question. "If I kiss you, will you tell me the time?"

"Deal."

Their kiss was long and sweet. Seth leaned his forehead against Wendy's and sighed.

"Better than my toast."

"Don't change the subject. It's early, isn't it? Really, really early." She sighed. "You have to go to work."

"Nope," he said, his tongue planted firmly in his cheek. "My boss gave me the day off."

"Your…?" She smiled. "Ah. I forgot the benefits of working for yourself." She drew his head to hers and kissed him again. "Then what are we doing up so early?"

"You have an eight o'clock appointment."

"What eight o'clock appoint—" Wendy gasped. "Amy! I promised to meet her at Twin Oaks."

"The kid's probably awake already, just killing time while she waits for the next installment of Akela the Wolf Dog."

Wendy scrambled up against the pillows. "I can't believe that I almost forgot!"

"I can." His voice dropped to a husky whisper. "And I'm flattered."

"Take that ego of yours and get out of the way, Castleman. I have to shower and dress."

"And have breakfast."

"Is there time? If the roads aren't clear—"

"They are." Seth planted a hand on either side of her. "There's plenty of time. It's just after six, and before you shriek and scream that I shouldn't have awakened you..." He eased her back against the pillows. "...I did it because I thought we'd start the day off slowly." His eyes locked to hers as he drew down the blankets and bared her breasts. "Any ideas how we could manage that?"

Wendy caught her breath as he stroked the tips of his fingers over her skin.

"Lots," she whispered, and drew him into her arms.

THERE WAS NO SOUND but that of Wendy's voice in the gathering room at Twin Oaks as she told more of the wondrous story of Akela the Wolf Dog and his beloved companion, Janie.

She'd said the other children would have to wait until evening to hear it, but they'd all been waiting for her when she and Seth reached the B and B. The children's parents were there, too, and now they were all hanging on every word.

"Akela laid his massive head on Janie's shoulder. 'I promise,' he said softly, 'that I'll always love you.'"

A soft sigh rose from the children seated on the carpet in front of Wendy, their faces turned up to hers. Not one of them had moved in the past twenty minutes. Even Robin and Randi were motionless.

"Janie felt tears sting her eyes. She wanted to cry with happiness for the wolf dog and with sorrow for herself. But she was a brave little girl. Akela had always said she was, so she blinked hard against the tears and wrapped her arms around his neck.''

The man seated beside Seth leaned closer. "She's terrific," he said quietly.

Seth smiled. "Yes. I think so, too."

"'I'll come back to you, Janie,' Akela said. 'Every autumn, when the tundra turns to flame, listen for the whisper of the wind at the first new moon and you'll hear my song as I journey here, to spend winter beside you.'''

Another communal sigh rose from the children. Wendy's soft voice and wonderful story held them enthralled. Seth saw how their faces glowed with excitement. Wendy's eyes held that same bright light. She was happier than he'd ever seen her, except in the days they'd skied together....

And in his arms last night.

For a little while this morning, after they'd made love, he'd held her against him and let himself believe that everything was going to be all right. Then she'd sighed and stirred against him.

"I missed you so much," she'd whispered. "All these years... If you only knew how many times I wanted to fly home and go into your arms..."

"But you didn't."

"I couldn't." She'd lifted her head a little and looked into his eyes. "There's so much you don't know, that I haven't told you about—about my fall and what it did to me."

"You don't have to explain, sweetheart," he'd said softly. "I was too hurt to think things through back then, but I understand now. You must have felt as if you'd lost everything that made you who you were."

She'd nodded, and her hair had feathered like silk against his shoulder.

"Yes. I'd never imagined myself as anybody but Wendy Monroe, champion skier."

The words had hurt his heart. She must have sensed it

because she'd added, in the very next breath, that the only other Wendy Monroe who'd ever existed was the one who loved him.

"And I lay in that hospital bed," she'd said, so softly he'd had to strain to hear her, "and listened to what the doctors told me, and realized that I'd failed *both* Wendy Monroes, the one the whole town had sent off with posters that said, Go for the Gold...and the one who wanted to build a life with you."

Hearing that had baffled him. How could she have thought the town would be disappointed in her? More important, how could she have thought her injuries would make a difference to him? She should have known he'd never stop loving her. All he had ever wanted was to love her and make her happy, to marry her so they could fill their lives with laughter and kids.

He'd told her all of that as he'd held her this morning, but instead of the smile he'd hoped for, Wendy's face had closed up.

"It's getting late," she'd said. "I won't get to Twin Oaks on time if we don't get started."

That was when he'd known that everything wasn't going to have the fairy-tale ending he'd foolishly hoped for. He didn't have her back. He probably never would, but he wouldn't think about that. Last night would have to be enough.

Now, watching her as she spun a magical tale for the children, he knew he was kidding himself. A lifetime of Wendy would never be enough. He had to get through to her, make her see that they belonged together.

The children leaned forward, listening to the last words of the story. Wendy fell silent; the kids were silent, too, and then everyone in the room burst into applause. Seth waited as the children and their parents rushed up to thank Wendy and tell her how much they'd loved the story. When they finally left, he rose and went toward her.

"You were wonderful," he said. He took her face in his hands, lifted it to his and brushed his mouth over hers. "Now I want you all to myself. No B and B, no guests, nothing but you and me and a day full of surprises."

"More surprises?" She laughed. "Will I like them as much as your house?"

He slipped his jacket on, then helped her into hers. "Tonight's, definitely. This afternoon's...well, keep an open mind, okay?"

Her eyebrows rose. "This sounds serious."

Her tone was teasing. His wasn't.

"It *is* serious," he said. "Trust me, okay? No matter what?"

She said she would, but he could see the confusion growing on her face as they drove north. Well, he'd felt just as uncertain when he'd made these plans early this morning. She'd fallen asleep in his arms. When her breathing was slow and even, he'd slipped from the bed and gone down to the den.

First, he'd checked his answering machine. Just as he'd hoped, Pommier had left a message. He was heading back to Cooper's Corner. Could they meet tonight, at Twin Oaks? Seth reached him on his cell phone and cut right to the bottom line.

"Remember what I said about coming straight out if I wanted to ask you to see Wendy Monroe, Doc? Well, I'm asking. I know you've sworn off taking on new patients, and I know I'm presuming on our relationship—"

Pommier interrupted him and said, gently, that he'd been waiting for Seth's call.

"You were?"

"Aunt Agatha's always right," Rod said.

Seth had hung up, chuckling. Then he'd made a call to Larry Cohen, who was in the volunteer program with him at Ski Wee. Would it be okay to stop by later and bring someone with him? Someone who might find the program interesting?

"Absolutely," Larry had said, sounding pleased.

At least somebody was looking forward to this, Seth had thought, and decided not to consider the possible consequences of either phone call. Instead, he'd busied himself by making breakfast.

He looked at Wendy, sitting beside him in the cab of his truck. One thing was certain. When he introduced her to Pommier, she'd be delirious with joy.

But when she saw where he was taking her now...

He was running one hell of a risk. For all he knew, what he was doing might ruin any chance they had at a permanent relationship, assuming they had a chance at all. But he didn't have any choice. He loved Wendy. He had to do this.

Seth tightened his hands on the steering wheel.

Gina had been reduced to wringing her hands about her daughter. Howard was still trying to relive his life through her. Who was there to open her eyes to the truth, to who she really was, except him?

Wendy thought she knew all her options but he was willing to bet that she didn't. Not deep inside, where it counted.

He had to make her see that there were many ways to be a winner in life.

A sign flashed by. Seth's stomach did a slow roll. *Just another few minutes,* he thought, and put on his turn signal.

"Almost there," he said lightly.

"Almost where?" Suspicion put an edge on the words. "Seth? I want to know where we're going."

He'd taken a back route, counting on the fact that the crossover road that would lead them to their destination was new enough that she wouldn't figure things out until the last minute. Now he had to tell her the truth.

"To Jiminy," he said, and braced himself for the explosion.

Wendy didn't disappoint him. She swung toward him, her face white with shock.

"Are you crazy? We are not going to Jiminy!"

"We're expected."

"*Expected?* By whom?"

"I'm a volunteer at Ski Wee. I spoke to a friend this morning and told him we'd be dropping by."

"Why would you tell him that? Ski Wee hasn't a thing to do with me!"

"It has to do with kids," Seth said calmly, "and with skiing. And it seems to me that you like both."

"I *hate* skiing."

Her voice was low and trembling. He wasn't sure if it was with anger or pain. He suspected it was both, and he was almost afraid to look at her, because if there were tears in her eyes, it would be the end of him. Was he doing the right thing? He had to believe he was. Someone had to make her see that she was as whole as she'd ever been, that her life had not ended the day she fell in Norway, but had only gone in a different direction.

"Is that why you want to go through an experimental operation that's risky as hell? So you can do something you hate?"

"So I can compete. There's a difference, Seth. Don't twist my words!"

"If the only reason you want to ski is to chase after medals, you might as well give up before you start."

"And what's that supposed to mean, Dr. Freud?"

"When we met, you didn't only ski to compete. You skied because you loved it, because it was part of you."

"Past tense. *Was* part of me."

"It still is, even if you're determined to deny it."

Wendy glared at him. How could he know what she felt? Her doctors had thought they did, too. One of her therapists had even brought a man who ran a program for handicapped skiers to meet her. Handicapped skiers? The phrase, she'd told him coldly, was an oxymoron.

"Perhaps you haven't noticed," the man answered calmly, "but I'm an amputee."

Wendy had barely glanced at the empty sleeve that hung from his jacket.

"What I noticed," she'd replied with brutal candor, "is that you're a cripple, the same as me."

She'd instructed the therapist to work with her body and forget about playing games with her head. After that, no one had tried to talk to her about skiing.

Seth knew even less about how she felt than the therapist. He was convinced she'd devoted her life to winning and that she thought less of herself now that she couldn't compete.

But that wasn't all of it. What would he say once he knew the truth?

Wendy turned her face toward the side window and stared blindly at the forest flashing by. What a mistake she'd made, letting herself fall in love with Seth all over again. She hadn't intended for it to happen, but when he'd kissed her outside the Purple Panda, he'd made her remember what love could be like. She'd wanted to taste it again, if only for a little while.

What she'd told him about there being two Wendys was true. One had competed for medals; one had planned a future as a wife and mother. Neither had survived the accident. Now Dr. Pommier's new technique offered hope that she might bring one of them to life again.

She had to take the chance or die trying.

Tears blinded her. She looked away from the trees and out the windshield...

And saw Jiminy Peak straight ahead, rising from the trees.

For a moment, she felt nothing. It was only a mountain and not a terribly high one at that. Jiminy was nothing but a steep hill compared with some of the places she'd skied in the West and in Europe, but it was where she'd learned to fly down a mountainside, feeling as if she could take wing and soar.

Something seemed to tear free deep inside her. Seth was right. She belonged in a place like this, where mountain peaks pierced the sky, where the snow was deep and all you heard was the sound of the wind and the whoosh of your skis.

Seth pulled into a parking space and shut off the engine. She felt his eyes on her, but she was riveted to the sight of the slopes and lifts ahead, and to a time when she'd felt truly alive.

He got out of the truck and came around to her side. He opened her door and looked at her, his face pale beneath its year-round tan. Tension narrowed his eyes.

He didn't speak. He didn't have to. She knew that the next move had to be hers. Slowly, she stepped from the truck. Tears welled in her eyes. She bowed her head and tried to blink them away before Seth noticed, but she wasn't quick enough.

"Oh, sweetheart." His voice was rough with misery. "Baby, I'm sorry. I was wrong. I should never have—"

Wendy lifted her head. He could hardly believe what he saw. Yes, tears were streaming down her cheeks, but her eyes were glowing. Her smile was radiant.

"Wendy?"

She laughed. Or maybe she cried. All that mattered was that she flung her arms around his neck and kissed him, and he was sure that his Wendy had come home.

LARRY COHEN WAS a great guy. He had a nice sense of humor and an easy way with the kids, who gathered around him on their skis, some of them so wrapped in parkas and pants that Wendy figured they'd never be able to get up if—*when*—they fell.

But they did get up, and laughed, and tried all the harder. At first, there were six kids and Larry. By noon, there were a dozen tyro skiers having fun with Seth and Larry.

Wendy stood around and watched. Then she offered a little help. By the time Seth suggested she put on skis and really get into things, she didn't even hesitate. How else could she encourage the kids to try to do a snowplow, or sometimes just try and stand up?

How else could she really remember how much she loved this sport?

And when Ski Wee classes ended, what could she do but ride the lift with Seth, stand at the top of the Left Bank run, flash him a thumbs-up when he grinned at her, and then fly down the mountain?

In late afternoon, Seth said he was exhausted. Wendy doubted it. He looked wonderful, his cheeks ruddy from the cold, his eyes bright, his smile stretching across his face. She knew the truth—that he was concerned about her. Her leg did ache, yes, but it was a wonderful ache, the kind she hadn't had and couldn't get from therapy workouts, no matter how strenuous. She felt alive in a way she'd all but forgotten. Last night, making love with Seth; today, skiing with him...

Could life actually be like this? So filled with joy that you felt as if you might burst?

"Me, too," she said. "Let's call it a day."

She sat as close to Seth as the bucket seats would permit all during the ride back to Cooper's Corner. When he started to apologize for taking her to Jiminy without asking, she stopped him.

"You're right," she said. "You did a terrible thing...but I'm happy you did. I guess I'd blanked out how it feels to ski and how much I love it." She lifted his hand from the wheel and pressed it to her cheek. "Thank you."

"We can try a tougher trail next time, if you like."

"If I like?" She grinned at him. "Is tomorrow too soon?"

Seth smiled back at her. It was wonderful, seeing her like this.

"You're happy," he said softly, "aren't you?"

She nodded. "Yes. Very." She took a deep breath. "Seth? I've been a coward."

"No, babe, you haven't. I understand why you didn't want to ski. Anybody would have felt—"

"I'm not talking about skiing. I'm talking about...about how I turned away from you. How I sent you away when you came to Norway to be with me after the accident."

"You don't have to explain it to me, sweetheart."

"Yes. Yes, I do. You're entitled to know the reasons."

"I already do." Seth wound his fingers through hers and placed their linked hands on the gearshift. "The accident devastated you. If I hadn't been so self-centered, I'd have figured that out right away."

"It did, but that isn't—"

"Babe." They'd reached the town. Seth pulled into the driveway at Twin Oaks and parked next to the car Wendy had left there the night before. He shut off the engine and turned to her. "You want to talk about things? Fine. But let me go first, okay? I have something to tell you."

Wendy smiled. "Not another surprise?"

"Yeah. Another surprise." Seth cleared his throat. He took her other hand and held both tightly. "Why did you come back to Cooper's Corner?"

"What do you mean?"

"What did you come back for, Wendy? What do you want that I—hell, let's be blunt—that I tried to convince you not to want?"

"The operation?"

"Yes, sweetheart. The operation. Specifically, a chance to meet Rod Pommier and convince him to accept you as a patient."

Wendy sighed. "I'm close to giving up hope. My father thought he'd be able to get me a few minutes of Dr. Pommier's time, but—"

"I can do it for you."

She stared at him. It wasn't a joke; Seth's expression was completely serious.

"You? I don't understand. How could you connect me with Dr. Pommier?"

Seth hesitated. His news was going to make her happy. He just wished it was doing the same thing for him.

"I know him," he said, after a minute.

"You know..." Wendy looked puzzled. "You mean, you've seen him on the slopes?"

"I mean we're friends. Well, more or less. We're not pals or—"

"What are you talking about?"

"Rod is—"

"Rod?" Wendy blinked. *"Rod?"*

There was a note in her voice he didn't quite understand. An edge. A hint of anger.

"Uh-huh. See, he bought a cabin. An old ski chalet up on—"

"Rod did," she said coldly.

Seth frowned. Things weren't going exactly as he'd anticipated. There was definitely an edge to her words and a look in her eyes he didn't like.

"Yeah. And I'm doing the renovations for him."

"Since when?"

"Since he bought it. I don't know, maybe ten days, two weeks ago."

Wendy jerked her hands from his. "Let me get this straight. I've been going crazy waiting for a chance to meet this man, and all the time you've been working on his cabin?"

"Well, yes."

"I suppose you have coffee with him, too, and discuss the work as it progresses."

The edge to her voice took on the sharpness of a paper cut. Oh, yeah. Something was definitely wrong here. Seth reached for her hands again but she pulled away and sat rigid, her spine tight against the door.

"He's been out of town, babe. Your father must have told you that."

"My father isn't on a first-name basis with the doctor, Seth."

Let that go, he told himself. *Just let it go.*

"What I'm trying to tell you is that I talked to him this morning." She didn't answer and he plunged on to fill the silence. "I called him on his cell phone."

"You called him on his cell phone," she repeated, so coldly that he almost shuddered. Slowly, the light began to dawn. She was upset because he hadn't told her sooner.

"Babe," he said gently, "you're ticked off because I didn't tell you about Pommier before now. But I had my reasons."

"Which were?"

"Well, I thought you were making a mistake. You want the truth? I still think that, but I finally realized you have to make your own decisions." He was quiet for a few seconds. "Okay. I guess I can see how this looks, but—"

"How it looks," she said softly, far too softly for his comfort, "is that you could have helped me but you didn't."

"Babe, you've got it all wrong. I thought about this a lot. I even talked to Pommier about you."

"How generous of you."

"Damn it, will you try and see this from my viewpoint? I've already admitted that I didn't think you should have the surgery." Her eyes flashed with condemnation and he winced, suddenly realizing that this wasn't coming out as the gift he meant it to be. "Try to understand, Wendy.

was afraid for you, and afraid you wanted the surgery for all the wrong reasons.''

''So you decided to eliminate that possibility by thinking for me.''

''Yes. No!'' Seth slapped the heel of his hand against the steering wheel. ''It's not that simple.'' She was still looking at him as if she'd never seen him before. ''Okay. I blew it. I made a mistake, but I did it out of love. Doesn't that count for something?''

''Love isn't an excuse for trying to run someone's life. Isn't that what you once said when you were trying to convince me that my father was running mine?''

''It's not the same thing,'' he said, making an effort to sound patient when what he felt was that he was sinking deeper and deeper into a pit of his own making. ''Howard's willing to let you risk everything for a medal.''

''And you're not willing to let me risk anything. Either way, I don't seem to have much to say about what happens to me.''

''Sweetheart, I wanted to protect you, that's all.''

''But you can't. Don't you understand that? The accident changed my life. Nobody can protect me, not unless they can find a way to turn back the clock.'' Wendy wrenched open the door and stepped from the truck. She looked back at Seth, her eyes hot with anger. ''The fall took everything from me. I've spent all these years trying to live with the realization that the Wendy Monroe who left Cooper's Corner doesn't exist anymore. Now I have this one slim chance of regaining at least part of who I once was, and you took it upon yourself to deny it to me!''

''That's not the way it was, damn it!'' Seth jumped down from the truck and strode toward her. ''And it's exactly why I think you're making a mistake. The surgery's not just experimental and risky, it's wrong.''

Wendy slapped her hands on her hips. ''I see. *You* know what's right, not me.''

Seth grabbed her by the shoulders. "Listen to yourself! The fall took everything from you? Huh? Is that what you really think?"

"Let go of me!"

He didn't. If anything, his hands tightened on her. She was angry? Well, so was he. And, damn it, maybe he had more to be angry about. He could feel it rushing through his blood, vibrating along his nerve endings, something live and palpable that he knew he'd kept bottled inside him from the minute he'd opened the note that told him the woman he loved didn't want him anymore.

"You almost died," he said roughly, "but you didn't." She tried to twist away but he wouldn't let her. "They said you wouldn't walk, but you did. The truth is that you came through that accident better than anybody could have imagined."

"You have no right to say these things to me!"

"I have every right, damn it!" He lifted her to her toes, his face dark with anger. "When did you get so selfish? When did you forget the people who love you?"

"Damn you, Seth—"

"No. This time, you're going to listen. Your mother still cries for you. Do you know that? Do you even care? Gina misses you, but you'd rather nurse your wounded pride, your ego, whatever you want to call it, than think about what it's like for her to spend every day thinking about you, four thousand miles from home, and wondering if you're okay."

"That's between my mother and me. It has nothing to do with you."

"The hell it doesn't!" Seth bent toward her until he was all she could see. "It has everything to do with me. You were the best part of my life. You *were* my life, my dreams, my future—and then you had that accident and suddenly nobody else mattered except you."

Wendy shook her head. When she spoke, her voice trembled. "That's not true."

"It damn well is! *You* didn't lose everything. It was the rest of us, the people who loved you, who came out the losers."

"You don't know what you're saying."

"Oh, I know, all right." Seth dropped his hands to his sides, the anger gone and nothing but emptiness in its place. "Well, I'm done trying to figure it out. Pommier's meeting me at Twin Oaks tonight at seven. Figure on showing up at seven-fifteen or so. That'll give me enough time to talk to him and get out of there before you show up, because you know what, babe?" The corners of his mouth curved down. "I don't want to see you anymore. Hell, I don't want to see you ever again."

Wendy recoiled as if he'd struck her. A sob broke from her throat as he got into his truck and started the engine.

"Seth," she whispered, "Seth..."

He drove away, the truck picking up speed as it went down the driveway toward the road. After a while, all she could see were the bright red dots of its taillights growing ever dimmer in the encroaching dark of the midwinter afternoon.

And then, finally, even those tiny beacons blinked out, and were gone.

CHAPTER FOURTEEN

GINA MONROE SIGHED as she tied her apron strings and then turned on the kitchen lights.

The days were so short this time of year. Darkness crept in before you expected it.

She glanced at the clock. It was after six. Time to get dinner on the table. She'd spent the afternoon baking, something she'd done a lot more of now that Wendy was home.

She didn't know how long her daughter would be here. The operation, assuming the doctor agreed... The risks...

No. She wouldn't think about it. Not now. She'd think about how glorious it was to have her here—and what the protocol was for facing your adult daughter after she hadn't come home all night.

"Isn't Wendy here yet?"

Gina looked over her shoulder. Howard had been napping on the sofa. His hair was standing on end and his eyes were puffy. She knew he was upset, but she had no idea whether it was because Wendy hadn't come home all night or because she'd been with Seth. Both, probably, she thought with a little sigh. Knowing that your daughter had spent the night with a man was a delicate issue for a mother, but it had to be twice as difficult for a father.

"Not yet, no."

"You told me she called and said she'd be here for dinner."

"I'm sure she'll be here soon, Howard."

"I don't know how you can be so calm about this. Don't

you care that our daughter didn't come home last night? Aren't you concerned?''

"No," Gina said, although that wasn't entirely true. She was concerned about Wendy, but not about her safety. There was no reason to be. Howard wasn't worried about their daughter's safety, either, but it was easier to pretend that was what they were talking about. "Why should I be? Wendy's fine. She called to say she wouldn't be home, and then she phoned a second time to let us know she'd be back by early evening."

"She stayed out the entire night!"

"Yes, she did," Gina said mildly. "Sit down, Howard. How about peeling some potatoes?"

She put six small potatoes, a bowl and a paring knife on the counter. Howard shook his head as he sat down.

"It's not right that she stayed out all night. What will people think?"

"They'll think Wendy is old enough to live her life as she pleases."

He took a potato from the counter. "That boy is taking advantage of her."

"Seth isn't a boy," Gina said mildly.

"Our daughter is emotionally vulnerable right now." A long paring dropped on the counter. Gina pulled some paper towels from the roll, put them on the counter and dumped the potato skin on them. "Being home for the first time in years, waiting for the chance to talk to Pommier... It's the wrong time for her to get involved with that boy all over again."

"He's a man," Gina said, "and our daughter is a woman, and if they want, as you put it, 'to get involved' all over again, that's their business."

"They're wrong for each other."

"Cut those potatoes in quarters, please."

"Did you hear me, Gina? That boy—that man—and our daughter don't belong together."

"We had this same discussion years ago, Howard. I didn't agree with you then and I don't agree with you now."

Howard dumped chunks of peeled potato into the bowl. "She shouldn't be starting this nonsense with him all over again."

"It isn't nonsense."

"Of course it is."

"Are you done with those potatoes yet?"

"Is that all you can think about? Potatoes? I'm talking about something serious, for God's sake!"

"I know you are, Howard. I just don't see the sense in arguing."

"Our daughter came home for a reason. An important reason, and that's what she should be concentrating on."

"The operation you want her to have."

"The operation *she* wants to have!"

Gina opened the refrigerator and took out a pan of marinating chicken. "Please, let's not argue. You know how I feel about this."

"Gina, don't you see? We're talking about Wendy's future!"

"We certainly are." She turned to him. "This surgery terrifies me, Howard."

"I know it does." His voice softened. "It frightens me, too, but Wendy wants to get her life on track. Surely we should stand by her."

"We have. We always will. But this operation…"

"The operation, the technique Dr. Pommier's developed, is a miracle. Don't you see that?"

"Our daughter almost died," Gina said in a trembling voice. "Then her doctors thought she might not walk again. Well, she lived. And she can walk. Most people would say those things were miracles enough for one lifetime." Her eyes beseeched him. "But Wendy is embittered and filled with anger. She lives for a past that isn't half as important

as the future she could build if she learned to accept herself
as she is.''

''That our little girl lived and walked again is certainly
a miracle, but if she wants to compete again—''

''Does she really? Or is it just that she doesn't want to
face something else?''

Howard put down the knife. ''What something else are
you talking about?''

''I don't know.'' Gina sighed and folded her arms. ''I
just get the feeling that Wendy's hiding something.''

''From us?''

''From everybody, including herself. Oh, I know. I'm not
making sense, but, well, sometimes I think she's using this
surgery as an excuse to run away from herself.''

Howard picked up the knife and attacked another potato.
''You're right,'' he said coolly, ''you're not making sense.
You just don't understand the importance of having a goal
you worked toward all your life.''

''Listen to yourself! Who are you talking about, Wendy
or you?''

''That's not fair. You know how much I love our daughter.''

''Of course you love her. But you're so busy projecting
your own wishes on Wendy that you haven't taken a good,
hard look at her. Howard. I'm telling you, she's in denial.
She can't accept what happened to her and she thinks if she
has this surgery—''

''There's no 'if' about it,'' Wendy said calmly.

Her parents, startled, swung toward the door.

''I *am* having the surgery, Mother—assuming I can talk
Dr. Pommier into it.''

Wendy saw her mother's eyes widen. Well, why
wouldn't they? She'd seen herself in the car mirror; she
knew she looked as awful as she felt. She'd been driving
around for over an hour, unwilling to go home until she got
herself under control. She'd tried not to think about any-

thing but Rod Pommier and what she'd say to him, because thinking about anything else, like Seth's arrogance in assuming he knew what was best for her, or her own foolishness in almost telling him the truth, was the stuff of defeat.

"The doctor's agreed to talk with me at Twin Oaks in half an hour."

She could see the excitement flash across her father's face. "That's wonderful news, honey! I didn't even know he was back in town. Did you meet him last night?"

"I haven't met him at all." Wendy hesitated. "Seth set it up. He's remodeling a cabin the doctor bought."

"Well," Howard said coldly, "I suppose I'll have to thank him for arranging this meeting." He stood up. "Shall I go with you?"

Wendy nodded. "Mom? Will you come, too?"

No, Gina wanted to say. *I don't want any part of this.* But her adult daughter was watching her with a child's hope in her eyes.

"Of course, if that's what you want." Gina took off her apron while Howard went to his den to get Wendy's medical files. "Baby? Are you okay?"

"I'm nervous," Wendy admitted with a quick smile. "That's all."

There was more to it than nerves, Gina suspected. When Wendy had called to say she was with Seth and wouldn't be home until evening, her joy had radiated through the telephone. Now her eyes were red and swollen.

"How fortunate Seth knows Dr. Pommier," Gina said.

"Yes. Yes, it is."

"Has he changed his mind about things? He wasn't very happy about you wanting surgery."

Wendy's eyes grew veiled. "What Seth wants isn't an issue here."

"I only meant—" Gina started again. "Well, then, are you sure this is what you want?"

"It's what I came home for, Mother."

It wasn't an answer, but from the resolute expression on her daughter's face, Gina knew it was the only answer she was going to get.

ROD POMMIER LOOKED at Seth over the rim of his brandy snifter.

The gathering room was empty tonight, except for the two of them. They were in front of the fireplace, Rod seated and Seth pacing the room like a caged bear. Rod figured that if Wendy Monroe didn't show up in the next five minutes, Seth might wear a hole in the floor.

"I told her seven-fifteen," Seth muttered, glancing at his watch.

"Uh-huh." Pommier took a sip of brandy. "And here it is, seven-seventeen. The lady's definitely late."

"Yes, she is. And..." Seth narrowed his eyes. "I suppose I sound like an idiot."

The doctor smiled. "You want an answer from Rod Pommier, M.D., or from Aunt Agatha?"

"Do me a favor, Doc. Can the Aunt Agatha thing, okay?" Seth jammed his hands deep into the pockets of his cords. "You might be one hell of a surgeon, but you're a dud when it comes to advice for the lovelorn."

"The only thing I told you was that you still had a thing for Wendy Monroe."

"That's what I mean. You were wrong."

Pommier lifted his eyebrows. "The whole town's buzzing about the two of you being back together as a couple."

Seth gave a derisive snort. "You mean you stopped by at Philo's to buy a candy bar and he filled your ear with gossip."

The doctor grinned. "It was a bag of potato chips, and if you ever tell that to the blond nutritionist I met in Vermont, I'll certify you as mentally incompetent."

Seth laughed. "A blond nutritionist, huh?"

Rod smiled. "Yeah. Good-looking, and good for you, too."

The easy remark lightened things, but only for a minute. Then Seth started pacing again.

"Not that it has any bearing on this, but Wendy and I aren't together again. We had a major disagreement this afternoon."

"And you still want me to see her?"

Seth nodded. "It's what she wants, Doc." His smile was tight. "This is a farewell gift, you might say."

"I just hope Miss Monroe understands that all I'm doing is agreeing to talk to her. I'm not making any commitments."

"She knows that. I just wish you'd see her without me around. She and I agreed that I'd leave before she arrived."

"Well, you agreed without consulting me first." Rod's smile took the edge off the rebuke. "Look, I'm not trying to be a hard-ass about this, Seth, but I don't know the lady. You do, and you've made a couple of interesting observations about why you think she shouldn't have surgery."

Seth looked puzzled. "Yeah, and you pointed out—and rightly so—that decisions about Wendy's life were hers to make, not mine."

Pommier shrugged. "True. But deciding whether or not a patient's suitable for what I do isn't strictly dependent on reading X rays and taking case histories. The dynamics of a situation are often as vital as the physical aspects."

"Meaning," Seth said wryly, "you think you can learn something about Wendy by watching us play off each other."

"Yes," Pommier said bluntly. "I find myself wondering if Miss Monroe's feelings for you and her feelings about this operation aren't somehow connected."

"Only if you mean she'd rather have surgery than have—"

"Here she is," Rod said quietly, looking past Seth. He

put down his glass and stood up. "At least, I'm assuming that's her coming toward us."

Seth turned around and saw Wendy and her parents. Wendy was smiling, but her smile disappeared when she looked at him.

"What are you doing here, Seth?"

"I asked him to stay," Rod said smoothly. He held out his hand. "How do you do, Miss Monroe? I'm Rodney Pommier."

IT WAS AS IF they'd all been cast in a play.

After introductions, Pommier led them upstairs. His room was one of the larger guest rooms and had a small sitting area in front of a marble fireplace.

Everyone but Seth took a seat. He stood to the side, a reluctant observer wishing he could fade into the wallpaper as Rod Pommier, easygoing Rod Pommier with a good sense of humor, turned into Dr. Rodney Pommier, world-renowned surgeon.

Wendy seemed to know her part, too. She made a point of turning her back to Seth as soon as the doctor began asking her questions. She referred to the accident with a detachment Seth first admired and then found troubling, referring to "the" injuries, "the" operations, "the" treatments she'd undergone as if they'd happened to someone else.

He tried not to listen. He didn't feel detached at all. The terrible litany of what Wendy had endured took him back to the first weeks after the accident, when he'd almost gone crazy, imagining her suffering.

Pommier asked Howard for the medical files. They were all quiet as he scanned them. At last he looked up.

"Miss Monroe," he said slowly, "surely you know that I've decided not to take on any new patients."

Wendy nodded. "Yes, but I'm hoping I can change your

mind. I can't believe you'd turn away someone who's a perfect candidate for your technique, Doctor.''

Pommier smiled. "Why do you want this surgery? At best, there's a long and arduous recovery period.''

"I know that. But—''

"My daughter was a champion skier, Dr. Pommier,'' Howard said. "She wants to ski again.''

"She *has* skied again,'' Seth said. All heads turned toward him. Wendy looked angry. Her parents looked surprised. Pommier's expression was resolutely neutral. Seth could feel his cheeks coloring. He'd promised himself he wouldn't say a word. "Today, at Jiminy Peak.''

Howard's brows lifted. "Wendy?''

"I skied a beginner's slope,'' she said impatiently, "that's all.''

"It was a low intermediate slope,'' Seth said coolly, "and she skied. That's all I'm pointing out—that she *can* ski if she wants to.''

"Skiing an easy slope isn't skiing,'' Howard said, turning his back to Seth. "Wendy wants to compete again. Will she be able to do that if she has this surgery, Doctor?''

"There's an excellent chance she might, if the surgery goes well.'' Pommier hesitated. "There's also a chance she might spend the rest of her life in a wheelchair.''

Howard blanched. "What?''

"Surely you're aware that this procedure is risky, Mr. Monroe.''

"Well, yes, but I didn't think—''

Pommier turned to Wendy. "That's what you must consider,'' he said quietly. "I admit you're a prime candidate for surgery.''

"You mean you'll do it?'' Howard said excitedly.

"You're a good candidate,'' Pommier continued, speaking only to Wendy, "but I want you to consider the ramifications. Most of the people who come to me are in terrible pain. Others can't walk and have been told they never will.

The risk for such people is worth taking, but you're in neither group. You're pain free at this point, are you not?''

Wendy nodded. ''Yes.''

''And you can walk.''

''I limp,'' she said in a barely audible whisper.

''Did you say…'' Howard leaned forward. ''Did you say she might end up in a wheelchair if you fail?''

''I did.''

''But you won't fail. Why would you?''

''If I never failed, Mr. Monroe, I'd be God, and I make no pretense at being a deity.''

''Can you give us an idea of the odds, Doctor? I mean, can you break it down to percentages?''

''I'm not a fortune-teller, either, sir. Fifty-fifty is the best I can do.''

Howard took Wendy's hand. ''And…and she might end up in a wheelchair?'' he said again.

''I'm afraid so.''

''But she might be able to ski competitively—''

''And aliens might have designed the pyramids,'' Seth said furiously.

Wendy flashed him a warning look. ''Stay out of this, Seth.''

Seth took a breath. ''Yeah.'' He folded his arms. ''You're right. I've got no part in this discussion.''

Howard squeezed Wendy's hand. ''Honey? You want to ask the doctor any other questions?'' She shook her head. ''You think we have enough information to go home, talk this through and come up with a decision?''

''Howard!'' Gina's voice shook. ''Are you crazy? Didn't you hear what the doctor said? People who come to him are desperate to walk, or to be free of pain. What is there to talk about?''

''How to convince Wendy to go through with this operation,'' Seth snarled. ''*That's* what you have to go home and talk about.''

Everyone looked at him. He knew he was out of line, that whatever the Monroes decided had nothing to do with him anymore because he was out of Wendy's life. But, damn it, he still loved her. He would always love her, and he wasn't going to keep quiet. Not this time.

"Seth." Wendy stood up. "You have nothing to say about this."

"I had nothing to say the last time, too, when your old man pushed you so hard you couldn't see straight."

Howard looked shocked. "I never—"

"The hell you didn't." Seth swung to face him, his expression taut with pent-up fury. "You worked her night and day. She was always on the slopes or on a treadmill, and when the roads were clear that winter, she was out on her bike, pedaling up the mountains."

"Seth." Wendy's voice was hoarse with emotion. "Stop it!"

"No. I won't stop. I was a kid, too young and too afraid of losing you to speak out, but I don't have anything to lose now." He strode toward Howard, stopped only inches away. "You know why Wendy fell on that mountain in Norway?"

"Seth. Seth, please—" Wendy clasped his arm.

He shook her loose. It was time, it was past time, and nothing would silence him now.

"She was tired. She was sick. Did you take a good look at her those weeks you were busy training her to win that damn medal for you, Monroe? Did you see the circles under her eyes?"

Howard's face was white. "Wendy? I didn't... I was only trying to help."

"I know, Daddy. Believe me, my accident had nothing to do with—"

"The hell it didn't!" Seth's mouth twisted. "He was so wrapped up in that miserable medal that he forgot you can only push somebody so far before they break."

"Stop it," Wendy said. She stepped between Seth and her father. "You have no right. You don't know anything about why I wasn't in top shape for Lillehammer."

"I was there, remember? You were so tired you were like a sleepwalker. You were sick to your stomach, too, or don't you remember throwing up the night before you left Cooper's Corner?" Seth clasped her shoulders. "You were exhausted!"

"I was pregnant!"

Wendy's shrill cry seemed to echo in the room. She heard her mother gasp, heard her father's equally sharp intake of breath, but most of all, she saw what she'd been afraid to see for nine long years, the shock and then the dawning look of pain in Seth's face.

"I was pregnant," she said in a voice so low it was almost a whisper. "That's why I was tired and sick, Seth. I didn't know it but I was carrying our baby. I lost it. I lost our child. Seth, I'm so sorry. I'm so—"

Her voice broke. She buried her face in her hands. Her sobs were deep and wrenching. Seth wanted to take her in his arms and comfort her, but all he could think was that she had lost their baby. His baby. Her ambition had taken away the only things he'd ever wanted: her love and the family he'd dreamed of having.

Gina was the first to recover. "Oh, my sweet girl," she said, and reached for her daughter. But Wendy shot past her and rushed from the room.

CHAPTER FIFTEEN

For what seemed an eternity, the little group standing by the fireplace seemed frozen in place. Then Howard and Gina ran after their daughter.

Seth didn't. He had the feeling his legs would give way if he tried.

Rod grabbed a ladder-back chair and turned it around. "Seth? Sit down."

Seth shook his head. "I'm fine."

Rod put a hand on Seth's shoulder. "Sit," he said firmly. "Doctor's orders," he added with a trace of a smile.

Seth lowered himself into the chair. He stared blindly at the wall, looking up only when Rod pressed a glass into his hands.

"Brandy." Rod pulled up a footstool. "I always keep some on hand for medicinal purposes. Go on, man. Drink it."

Seth tried. The brandy was rich and aromatic. Any other time, he'd probably have enjoyed it, but now, one sip and he handed the glass back.

"Thanks, but I don't..." He blinked, felt the hot bite of tears behind his eyelids and took a ragged breath. "God," he said thickly, "oh God..."

"Yeah." Rod sighed. "Sometimes life is really a bitch."

"I never knew. I never even dreamed... We'd talked about having children someday, but I had no idea—"

"No. Of course not."

"Jesus." Seth looked at the floor, then got to his feet.

He walked to the window, looked out on a perfectly normal January evening in Cooper's Corner. Down the hill, on the village green, the Minuteman gazed solemnly over the darkened town. Life was going on as if things were normal, but nothing would ever be normal again. How could it be, after what he'd just learned?

Wendy was pregnant when she left him nine years before. She'd lost their child on a snow-covered mountain in Norway.

"Why didn't she tell me? I flew to Europe to be with her. She wouldn't even see me. She…she sent me a note, said she didn't love me.…''

Rod joined him at the window. "Trauma does funny things to people," he said. "Wendy expressed it best. She lost everything in one devastating moment."

"But why didn't she tell me?"

"You'll have to ask her, Seth. I can only speculate. Perhaps she was afraid of how you'd react. You'd been opposed to her going to Norway, right? Well, maybe she figured you'd blame her for losing the baby."

"I'd never have done that." Seth's mouth twisted. "It was her father's fault."

"Seth." Rod hesitated. "This is really none of my business, but don't you think you're going overboard? I admit, I don't know all the details, but from what I heard and saw a little while ago, Wendy's father just wanted her to succeed at something she loved."

"Succeed?" Seth laughed. "He pushed her. I'm telling you, he set down the rules, dragged her from competition to competition—"

"Wendy didn't enjoy skiing?"

"I didn't say that."

"She didn't like entering those competitions?"

"I didn't say that, either. She loved to ski. She lived for it. And she loved to win. And…" Seth shut his eyes, then blinked them open. "Are you saying he didn't push her?"

"I'm saying that there are two sides to every story. Whatever problems may exist between Wendy and her father, they didn't have anything to do with the fall she took."

Seth looked out the window again. "You're right," he said after a minute. "That was strictly my fault. She was carrying my baby, and she was feeling sick and tired and—"

"It wasn't anybody's fault. Don't you see? She didn't know she was pregnant. Neither did you or Howard Monroe. The bottom line is that Wendy was an experienced skier who suffered a bad accident. That's it. End of story."

"You're wrong, Doc. The end of the story is that she needed me and I let her push me away. I let us lose each other. I was angry at her father for taking her from me, and at myself for not being the only thing she needed. Hell, I was angry at Wendy for going to Lillehammer!" Seth thrust his hand through his hair and looked back at Pommier, his expression anguished. "I know it sounds crazy but that's the way I felt."

The doctor shook his head. "Don't be too hard on yourself. You were only, what, eighteen? Nineteen?"

"I was a fool, and I'm not going to make the same mistake twice." He moved past Rod, stopped at the door and looked back. "You may have missed your calling, after all," he said quietly. "You're a fine surgeon, but you'd have been one hell of an Aunt Agatha."

Rod smiled and raised a hand in salute. Seth returned it, then went out the door and down the stairs.

Nine years wasted, him nursing a dented ego and Wendy blaming herself for what had been nobody's fault. They should have been together, helping each other understand that nothing mattered but that they faced the darkness together.

"Seth?"

It was Clint, calling out to him, but Seth kept moving.

"Later," he said. Whatever Clint wanted could wait. The only thing that mattered was Wendy.

He went out the door with his keys already in his hand, and dashed to his truck. The tires kicked up rooster tails of snow and the transmission protested as he floored the gas pedal and sped down the drive. Moments later, he came to a skidding stop at the Monroes.

Howard and Gina came to the door before he reached it.

"Oh, Seth," Gina said shakily, "we didn't know! She kept it from all of us. She must have told her doctors not to say anything about her being pregnant and losing the baby."

"Where is she?"

"Gone." Howard said, putting his arm around his wife. His face was chalk-white. "Wendy took Gina's car keys and drove away."

"Did she say anything?"

"Only that she wanted to be alone someplace where she could think."

Sawtooth Mountain. Seth knew it instinctively. "I'll find her." He started to turn away, then looked at Wendy's father. "Sir." This was hard but it needed doing. "I owe you an apology."

"No." Howard shook his head. "You were right, Seth. I never saw it that way, but maybe…maybe I was trying to live my dreams through my daughter." He blinked hard. "But she loved skiing. She loved competing. At least I thought—"

"She did. She loved all of it." Seth hesitated. "We both love Wendy, and we both wanted what we thought was best for her her. I guess we should have stopped and tried to find out what Wendy wanted for herself." He took a deep breath. "I'm only sure of two things, Mr. Monroe. Her fall was nobody's fault. And if I'd known she was pregnant, I'd have come to you, told you I loved her and that we were getting married."

Howard nodded. "Find her, Seth. Tell her that we have a lot to talk about, and that I was wrong about a lot of things—especially about you."

The men's eyes met in understanding. Howard stuck out his hand. Seth smiled and shook it. He gave Gina a quick hug and went to find Wendy.

FINDING HER WAS EASY.

He'd figured right. He spotted Gina's car pulled onto a wide spot on the shoulder of the road that led up the mountain. Footprints in the snow disappeared into a grove of oaks that marked the start of an old hiking trail.

Seth pulled his truck alongside Wendy's car, got out and started up the path.

Ten long minutes later, he saw her standing in a little clearing that overlooked the valley, her back to him. She had to have heard him coming; the sound of the snow crunching under his workboots was loud in the mountain silence. But she didn't turn around. She stood with her hands tucked into the pockets of her anorak, her head tilted down, and he thought how lonely she looked, how lonely she'd been all these years.

It broke his heart.

He wanted to go to her and take her in his arms, hold her and comfort her and tell her how much he loved her, but there was such fragility in her posture that he was afraid. Instead, he called her name, softly. Then he waited, while time seemed to stand still. At last she turned and faced him. Her eyes were wet and dark, her face pale against the red hood of her coat.

"Seth. Seth, I'm so sorry...."

"No," he said quickly, "no, sweetheart, I'm the one who's sorry. I should have been with you. You never should have carried this burden alone."

"I didn't know about the baby." Tears streamed down

her face. "If I had, I'd never... No medal in the world was that important, Seth. You have to believe that."

"Sweetheart." He moved toward her, his eyes locked to hers. "You don't have to explain. I'd never think—"

"I hadn't had my period in a month, but that wasn't unusual. Sometimes, when women athletes train really hard..." She inhaled deeply, then let out a breath that turned to frost on the frigid air. "The nausea didn't mean anything, either. I'd had that happen before, when I was stressed out. Sometimes...sometimes I couldn't keep anything down a couple of days before a race, so I didn't once imagine..."

A sob burst from her throat. Seth covered the few feet that separated them and took her in his arms.

"Wendy." She felt stiff and cold; her face was tear-stained and bleak. "Sweetheart, please. Listen to me." He put one hand under her chin, applied gentle pressure until she yielded and lifted her face to his. "If only you'd told me, once you knew. If only I'd had brains enough to see through that brush-off."

Wendy closed her eyes. "Oh, God," she whispered, "that horrible note..." She looked up at him. "I couldn't face you. I thought you'd hate me."

"Hate you?" Seth gave a broken laugh. "I could never hate you, babe. You're my life. My heart. My only love. But when you wouldn't see me, it was like—it was kind of what I'd always expected. That one day you'd say to yourself 'What did I ever want with a guy like Seth Castleman?'"

Wendy framed his face with her hands. "I wanted a life with Seth Castleman," she whispered. "That was all I wanted, from the minute we met."

Seth bent and kissed her mouth, salty with tears. When the kiss ended, he sighed and drew her head to his chest.

"After the first operation, I asked when I'd be able to

ski again. They told me I wouldn't,'' Wendy said into his jacket. ''I lay there thinking what that would mean.''

"No chance for an Olympic medal. It's all right. I understand what that meant to you.'' He held her shoulders, stepped back just far enough so he could see her face. ''I always wanted you to win, honey, but maybe…maybe I was a little jealous, worried that once you had that medal, you'd want to leave Cooper's Corner and the life we'd planned.''

Wendy shook her head. ''You didn't let me finish,'' she said. ''I thought, okay, I won't be able to ski. But I'm alive…and then they said I'd never walk again. I couldn't believe it. Me, never walk again? 'But you're alive,' my mother kept telling me, and I tried and tried to think that was enough—'' Her voice broke. ''And then, the next day, they told me the rest, that I'd been pregnant and I'd lost the baby. That was when I knew how meaningless everything else was, that all that had ever mattered was you.'' She began to weep. ''Oh God, Seth! I wanted to die.''

Seth held her closer. He remembered his flight to Norway, the suffocating fear that he'd have lost Wendy by the time he reached Oslo.

"Don't,'' he said. ''Sweetheart, don't.''

"Everyone said it was a miracle that I'd lived, but when I looked in the mirror, all I saw was a woman who'd lost everything.'' Her throat worked as she swallowed. ''You. Our baby. And me, the me that I knew. And of all those things, the only one I could recover was the last. I could get *me* back.'' She gave a sad laugh. ''So I made up my mind that I'd walk again, but once I could, I still woke up each morning feeling as empty as the day before.''

"Wendy, please. You don't have to explain.''

"I have to, Seth. I should have done it long ago.''

He sighed, then stroked her hair as he brought her head to his chest again.

"One day,'' she said, her voice low, ''I looked in that

mirror and thought maybe the real me never existed any-where but on a ski slope. Maybe that was all that I'd ever been, not a woman, not a girl who loved you, but a skier. Maybe if I could ski again, race again, I'd have a reason to get out of bed in the morning. And then, just as if fate had touched me, I stumbled across an article about Dr. Pommier.''

Seth cupped Wendy's face. "I love you," he said clearly. "And I'm with you, all the way. You want this surgery? I'll be there for you." His voice softened. "I'll be there, no matter how it works out." He smiled into her eyes. "Just say you still love me."

"You're my heart, Seth. My soul. I'll always love you."

"Wendy. Will you marry me?"

She laughed, even though tears sparkled like diamonds on her lashes. "I thought you'd never ask."

They kissed and held each other while time slipped by. Then, hand in hand, they walked back to where they'd parked.

"I want to tell your folks," Seth said.

Wendy nodded. "Yes."

"But we should stop at Twin Oaks first." He lifted her gloved hand to his lips and smiled. It was a stiff smile, because he couldn't pretend he wasn't afraid of what could happen to this woman he loved with all his heart when Pommier operated on her, but it was her life and her choice to make. "The doc's probably still trying to figure out what happened."

"Well, we'll just have to tell him." Wendy put her hands on Seth's chest. "I've decided against the surgery."

"Sweetheart, you don't have to do that for my sake. Whatever you have to do—"

"Exactly." She smiled. "And I don't have to race to be happy. All I need is you and the life we'll make together."

"The children we'll have," Seth said, smiling back.

"The stories I'll tell them." She laughed. "Heck, the

stories I'll *write*.'' She caught her bottom lip between her teeth. ''You really think I can do that?''

''I *know* you can.''

Wendy grabbed Seth's collar and dragged his mouth down to hers. ''Then there's only one thing left to ask you.''

''Ask me anything. You want the moon? The stars?'' He grinned. ''A house on the top of Sawtooth Mountain? You can have 'em all.''

''I have the moon and the stars.'' She kissed him. ''And, thanks to a very fine carpenter, I have that house on Sawtooth Mountain, too. I need only one more thing from you, Seth Castleman.'' Her lips curved against his. ''Will you take me skiing tomorrow?''

Seth tried to answer but he couldn't. There was a lump in his throat. Instead, he gathered Wendy close and kissed her.

The sky had cleared and the moon and stars shone down brightly on the town by the time they reached Twin Oaks. Arms around each other, they went into the B and B. A fire blazed cheerfully in the massive fireplace. Rod Pommier was sitting in front of the hearth. When he saw Seth and Wendy, he rose to his feet.

''Doctor,'' Wendy said, ''I'm sorry I ran off.''

''No need to apologize, Miss Monroe.''

''Please, call me Wendy.'' She took a deep breath. ''I want to thank you for your time, Doctor.''

''Rod.''

''Rod. Thank you—but I've decided not to have that operation.''

The doctor looked from Wendy's smiling face to Seth's. ''Why do I get the feeling congratulations are in order?''

Seth's smile became a grin. ''Must be those Aunt Agatha genes kicking in.''

Wendy furrowed her brow. ''Who's Aunt Agatha?''

Both men laughed. ''A mutual friend we'll have to be

sure to invite to the wedding,'' Seth said, and hugged her close.

"Who's a mutual friend?" Clint asked as he joined the group.

"You are." Seth held out his hand. "If it weren't for you and the twin terrors, Wendy and I might not be announcing our engagement."

A slow grin spread across Clint's face. "Hey. That's great." He shook Seth's hand, kissed Wendy's cheek. "That's terrific, you guys. Congratulations." He looked up, spotted Maureen coming into the gathering room from the door that led to the back of the house. "Sis? Want to hear some good news?"

Maureen hesitated. She had some news herself, but she wasn't sure it was good. She'd gone out to the woodshed a few minutes ago. Clint had asked her not to do that anymore, but a guest wanted firewood in a hurry and Maureen couldn't see hunting up her brother for something so simple.

Except it had turned out not to be simple at all.

She'd loaded a canvas carrier with some logs and started back to the house. Then, for no reason, she'd stopped. This was her first time in the shed since the accident. She wanted to take a better look.

Slowly, she'd retraced her footsteps and poked at the fallen roof. A couple of logs shifted and tumbled into the snow, exposing one of the braces that had snapped when the roof came down.

Maureen had bent down and peered at the brace. What were those marks on the end of it? Gnaw marks? Could be, if someone had left the door open. There were lots of porcupines in the woods and they loved to chew.

That explanation was logical…unless, like Maureen, you were a former New York City police detective who'd put a man named Carl Nevil in jail. Carl's brother, Owen, had vowed revenge.

Had a man, not a porcupine, made those marks? Had Owen Nevil found her? Had he, or someone sent by him, deliberately weakened the woodshed so it would collapse and kill her?

Maureen had half run back to the house, her heart pounding, but she'd stopped before she entered the gathering room. The last thing she wanted to do was alarm the guests at Twin Oaks.

And now Dr. Pommier, her brother, Seth Castleman and Wendy Monroe were waving at her and grinning. Good news didn't deserve to be answered by bad news, Maureen thought, and she managed a cheerful smile as she headed for the little group. What she'd discovered could wait until later.

"Hi," she said. "What's up?"

Seth's smile, and Wendy's answering one, were enough to light the room.

"We're getting married," Seth said, and even Maureen forgot her worries as she watched him take Wendy in his arms and kiss her.

*   *   *   *   *

Welcome to Twin Oaks—
the new B and B in Cooper's Corner.
Some come for pleasure, others for passion—
And one to set things straight....
COOPER'S CORNER
a new Harlequin continuity series
continues in January 2003 with
ACCIDENTAL FAMILY
By Kristin Gabriel

Ex-TV soap star Rowena Dahl wanted to be a mom, but her biological clock was ticking too fast to wait for some slowpoke Mr. Right. So she opted for the fertility clinic—and was thrilled to be pregnant. There was only one problem. She got the wrong sperm!

Here's a preview!

CHAPTER ONE

A SURGE OF JOY shot through her and her eyes blurred with tears. "I can't believe it. This is so..." But she couldn't put her feelings into words. After so many years of living on her own, she was finally going to have a family again.

"Here," Dr. Milburn said, reaching over to hand her a tissue.

"I've never been happier," she said at last, wiping her wet cheeks with the tissue. "Thank you."

He sighed. "I hope you'll still feel that way when you hear what I have to tell you."

Apprehension fluttered through her. "What?"

"I was hoping we wouldn't need to have this discussion," he began, then took off his bifocals and folded them in his hand. "But I'm afraid it's unavoidable now."

Her fingers gripped the armrests as she prepared herself for another roller-coaster ride. "Please just tell me, Dr. Milburn. Is something wrong?"

"There was a problem with the insemination procedure. A mistake, actually."

"A mistake?" she echoed.

"Nothing to be too alarmed about," he assured her. "My office discovered it when the clinic sent a copy of your records here."

"I still don't understand."

He hesitated for a long moment. "It turns out that you were not inseminated with the donor sperm you selected, Rowena."

She stared at him, trying to make sense of his words. "How can that be possible?"

"I wish I knew." He closed her file. "In my experience with the Orr Fertility Clinic, they have stringent verification procedures. That's one of the reasons I recommended them to you. Unfortunately, a fluke occurred in your case, due either to human error or some kind of computer malfunction. I've contacted the clinic and they're naturally very concerned and trying to discover the source of the mix-up."

She didn't care about the Orr Clinic. She cared about her baby. "So who is the donor?"

He lifted his narrow shoulders. "That's something that may remain a mystery. Apparently, there is no profile available on the man. At least, not one that has been discovered yet."

She looked at him in disbelief. "You don't know *anything* about him?"

"I'm afraid not."

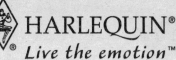

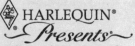

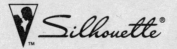

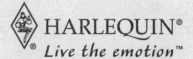

HARLEQUIN®
INTRIGUE®

BREATHTAKING ROMANTIC SUSPENSE

Shared dangers and passions lead to electrifying
romance and heart-stopping suspense!

Every month, you'll meet six new heroes
who are guaranteed to make your spine tingle
and your pulse pound. With them you'll enter
into the exciting world of Harlequin Intrigue—
where your life is on the line
and so is your heart!

THAT'S INTRIGUE—
ROMANTIC SUSPENSE
AT ITS BEST!

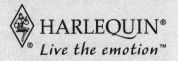
HARLEQUIN®
Live the emotion™